ONCE UPON A WICKED WAGER

Spies Like Us, Book 1

Cassandra Samuels

ARE YOU SIGNED UP FOR DRAGONBLADE'S BLOG?

You'll get the latest news and information on exclusive giveaways, exclusive excerpts, coming releases, sales, free books, cover reveals and more.

Check out our complete list of authors, too!

No spam, no junk. That's a promise!

Sign Up Here

www.dragonbladepublishing.com

Dearest Reader;

Thank you for your support of a small press. At Dragonblade Publishing, we strive to bring you the highest quality Historical Romance from some of the best authors in the business. Without your support, there is no 'us', so we sincerely hope you adore these stories and find some new favorite authors along the way.

Happy Reading!

CEO, Dragonblade Publishing

CHAPTER ONE

London
May 5th, 1816

From the diary of Lisbeth Carslake, Countess of Blackhurst.

I refuse to give in to the curse of the Black Raven.
I will change my destiny, my future.
I will re-enter society.
I will find my husband's killer.
I will prove my innocence.
I will reclaim my life.

"This is my solemn vow," Lisbeth bit out between clenched teeth, snapping the nib of her delicate quill. She slapped her diary shut, disregarding the inky mess it would leave and for a moment rested her head on its cool leather cover. Every day her anger grew but she *could* not let it rule her. She *would* not let it rule her.

She breathed in and out slowly until her composure returned. Only then could she unfurl her fingers one at a time. She had lived long enough under the shadow of the Black Raven; it was time to put her plan into action and use her reputation to her advantage. It was time to fight back.

Lisbeth knew her plan to re-enter society would take all her strength and determination, all her courage and conviction. Every smidgen of self-worth she had left which told her she deserved more than this life as a social pariah.

The clock on the mantel chimed the quarter hour. She

glanced up and frowned. No longer shackled to her abusive husband, she still found herself a slave to the relentless tick of time, of which he had made her so dependent. She felt in her pocket, pulled out a shiny silver pocket watch, and flicked it open. Ascertaining the two timepieces were in accord, she closed the lid, pausing to finger the Blackhurst crest that adorned the cover. She closed her fingers around her husband's watch until her knuckles were white.

"I will never forgive you for what you have done to me, Nathaniel."

Lisbeth let out a loud sigh. Hating someone who had been dead for two years was useless. She needed to put her energy to better use. As she placed the watch and diary on the desk, her schedule caught her attention. It was only ink on a page, a list of things to do in a logical time limit, to fill her days from dawn 'til dusk. It showed all her daily activities in a precise and orderly fashion—even the length of time it should take to complete. She always completed her tasks in the allotted time.

Oh, how she both loved and loathed it. She longed to pick it up, scrunch it in her fist and hurl it into the fire, but she dared not. It gave her purpose and direction when there was little in her life but misery and uncertainty. Now it protected her from the melancholy that threatened her every day since her husband had met his demise.

A murder for which she had been blamed. She closed her eyes as the injustice of her situation flowed through her, like a rapid of bitter, vile poison.

A soft knock startled her. She opened her eyes.

"My lady?" Rollands, her butler, stuck his head of gray hair through the doorway. "Sorry to disturb," he said as he entered the room. His tall, lanky frame always moved at an unhurried, even pace.

She smiled and felt a little of the tension leave her shoulders. Rollands was always a comfort to her. "What is it, Rollands?"

"It is Lord Bellamy."

"He's refusing to leave, I suppose? How typical," she said. Lord Bellamy had first pounded on her door and demanded entrance to win the Black Raven Wager over two hours ago.

Her butler came forward until he stood in front of her desk, hands clasped in front of him like an apologetic child. "I'm sorry, my lady, but he says he will camp out on your steps until he is let in. I know you are heartily sick of his sort trying to win that wager. Would you like me to call the Watch on him now?"

She was momentarily distracted by a noise coming from outside, but then turned back to Rollands. "It is freezing outside. He picked a bleak night to carry out his attempt to win that ridiculous bet... Whatever is he doing down there?" she asked.

"Whistling," he replied in a tone that showed he cared little that Lord Bellamy may catch his death of cold.

Was that the sound she had heard outside? Lisbeth raised a brow. "Whistling? Well, at least he isn't singing. Remember that one?"

"With horrifying clarity, my lady."

Lisbeth looked down at her diary, remembering the words she had only just written within its pages, then up at Rollands and asked, "Do you think Lord Bellamy will do? For my plan, I mean."

Rollands considered her question for a moment then rubbed his chin with his thumb and forefinger. "He is an earl. He is well connected. He does have the look of a hell cub and he seems... determined." Rollands took a step closer to the desk. "Are you sure you want to go through with this?"

I must reclaim my life, she said to herself. "No," she answered. Her heart beat fast all at once at the task she had set herself. "But I have to. I can't keep living like this. Using someone like him is the only way back into society. And getting back into society is the only way I will be able to find Nathaniel's killer and prove my innocence once and for all."

Rollands nodded. "I understand. The staff is ready to help, my lady. You need only tell us what you want us to do."

She glanced at her pocket watch on the desk, her focus blurry.

She would not get emotional in front of Rollands, even though he was her only confidant. Instead, she gathered a breath, and her courage. "I will do this, and Lord Bellamy is going to help me. He just doesn't know it yet."

Rollands bowed. "Very good, my lady. I'll fetch him up, then?"

Lisbeth nodded.

Her butler's weathered features softened. "Is there anything else you require?"

She gave him a weak smile. "No, that will be all, thank you."

Rollands bowed and left the room.

She rose from her chair to search out the warm comfort of the fire. The flames leapt and danced in the grate, but the warmth never quite penetrated her outstretched hands. The coals seemed to glow with such life, but she knew it was all an illusion. The embers were nothing but the last warm breath of death.

I am like this fire, she thought. *I look alive but inside I feel dead.*

She took a deep, painful breath. Still, tears burned behind her eyelids. Is this what she had become? A wisp of smoke, a hazy vapor, a ghost of someone who used to be? She longed to be someone again. To feel wanted. Loved. To prove to them all how wrong they were about her.

The only way to do that was to go through with her plan. A plan that would put her right in the middle of the viper's pit called the *ton* and on the arm of a man she did not know, nor want to. But there was no choice. Fate had decreed that man to be Lord Bellamy.

She could hear him whistling, the faint joyful tune so at odds with how she felt. The sound rose up through the incoming fog that slithered like a snake in search of prey, winding its way in and out of laneways and around lampposts as it consumed everything in its path, smothering it in a scaly, smoky blanket of silence.

She had not always felt lost in the fog. There was a time when she had thought life to be full of music and candlelight and dancing. That was before. Before she had married Nathaniel, before she had been accused of his murder. And before everything had turned from light to dark. The *ton* had branded her the Black Raven—the bringer of bad luck and death. And so it had begun: the wagers, the taunts outside her window, and the horrified stares in the street. Was it any wonder she stayed indoors by herself, hardly leaving the house unless necessary?

"Enough!" Her voice quivered with emotions she had spent years binding tight within her.

It was time.

THIS IS BOLLOCKS! He'd lost all patience, and feeling in his arse, an hour ago and now the entire bottom half of him was numb. Oliver wiggled his toes in his shoes and was happy to see they were still under his control. Although, were he to shoot himself in the foot five times he would surely not feel it. A comforting thought when one was *freezing to death!* He'd faced worse weather as a soldier on the Peninsula, of course, but that was a different place and a lifetime ago.

Oliver took a swig from his flask and saluted the Bow Street Runner who watched him from across the shiny, cobbled street. The runner, hired specifically to report on Oliver's success or failure, was no doubt cursing him as much as Oliver cursed himself.

What had possessed him to take on this wager? Temporary insanity caused by too much claret at his club, surely. Oh, and a fair amount of bravado as well. A slight fascination with the story of the Black Raven probably had something to do with it, and money, of course. Hours later, he could care less if the Countess of Blackhurst had two heads and a tail, let alone whether she had killed her husband or not. His sole motivation now was to get in and get out of her house and win said wager.

Back in London for only a few weeks after cashing in his

commission, Oliver had spent the time ignoring his late brother's debts and drowning his misery by any means possible. London, he'd found, had *many* means. It wasn't his usual strategy to try to avoid difficulties of any sort, but this was not the physical battle he was familiar with. He'd found himself unable to fathom his grief and the fact he was well and truly in dun territory.

The night had turned chilly indeed and although the runner seemed quite comfortable in his shabbily tailored coat, Oliver was not quite so prepared, dressed as he was in his evening clothes. Even now an ungodly fog rolled in from the Thames.

He hated fog!

Taking out his pocket watch he squinted at it in the dimness of the countess's front steps. She'd made him wait for two interminably cold hours. If not for his pride, and the emptiness of his pockets, he would have abandoned this ridiculous wager long ago. Had he known his only reward would likely be nothing more than a loss of sensation in his lower limbs, he would have stayed at his club and taken his chances at the gaming tables.

Unfortunately, he'd allowed himself to be coerced into this damnable situation by his brother's friend Dalmere, amongst others.

He took another swig from the flask and groaned. That was the last of the brandy. Now what was he to do? A sensible man would have gone home, where it was warm. It became more apparent by the minute that he was *not* a sensible man. For lack of any other alternative, he started whistling again.

He'd just built up a really good tune when the door behind him suddenly opened. Thank God!

The Black Raven's butler stood in the doorway. "The countess will see you now, *Lord* Bellamy." The butler's sneer was enough to make Oliver think his camping out on her steps was perhaps unwelcome.

Oliver tried to stand up. His legs were mostly drunk, it seemed, and disinclined to participate. It wasn't until he finally stood he realized how drunk the rest of him actually was. It was like the brandy had abandoned his lower limbs and now rushed to his head to play havoc with his equilibrium. The butler swayed sickeningly from side to side. This was not a good start.

Get in and get out, Oliver told himself.

He gave a quick glance over his shoulder at the runner, who now stood up with his mouth agape, and realized that he, Oliver Whitely, Earl of Bellamy, was about to enter the Black Raven's house. It was a place where no gentleman had entered before, or at least not in the last two years. It was quite the achievement, really.

Bravado was a marvelous thing when one was desperate and drunk.

It was to be short-lived.

Legs like lead made Oliver stumble over the threshold. The warmth of the entryway seared his chilled flesh. Another discomfort soon followed—pins and needles racked his lower extremities with merciless fervor. He whirled to leave, wager completed, but the butler closed the door behind him so he was forced to turn back to face the entryway.

Capital! Trapped, by his own cleverness.

The butler seemed as eager as Oliver to have this business over with. He demonstrated such by snatching the hat from Oliver's head then waiting impatiently for Oliver to peel off his gloves. If the man only knew how difficult standing was at the moment he may have shown some mercy. The butler's eyes narrowed to slits. *Perhaps not, then.*

They began down the hall. Every step shot agony up Oliver's legs, but he carried on stomping loudly to regain some blood flow to his legs. The butler stopped and looked over his shoulder at him with a raised brow.

"Pins and needles," Oliver offered.

It was obvious the spindly fellow was unconcerned by Oliver's predicament and simply carried on down the hall. Oliver looked around him as he followed. He wasn't sure what he expected to see as they continued. Cobwebs, maybe, or ghoulish statues at least, but the house was remarkably unremarkable. This could be his Aunt Petunia's place for all its apparent dullness. No, Aunt Petunia's house smelled like her foul tonics and, besides, there was no snoring coming from the parlor.

He now stood at a door. Another one! How long would he have to wait outside this one? He realized the butler had left him. He followed the grain of the wood on the door with his forefinger.

Without warning, the door opened, and Oliver was confronted with the two faces of the butler, both frowning. "This way, my lord."

Oliver nodded and fell in step behind the butler and soon found himself in the library. But this was not Henry's library; it was somebody else's. He took a few seconds to steady his stance and cleared his throat as discreetly as was humanly possible, blinking rapidly to get his eyes to focus appropriately.

"The Earl of Bellamy, my lady," the butler announced.

"Where?" Oliver said, expecting to see his brother. Then remembered *he* was the Earl of Bellamy now. An ache erupted in his chest, but weeks of practice had enabled him to keep from choking on his grief. The butler gave him one last ferocious frown, then backed into the hall and closed the door.

He was going to be alone with the Black Raven. All of a sudden, he didn't feel quite so clever and realized he was more than a little foxed. His lack of intelligence was directly related to his state of intoxication, but even in this lowered mental state he knew it was a bad combination. He was in no state to stand, let alone converse with this woman.

What had he been thinking? Not much at all apparently. His brain seemed to be swimming in porridge and no small amount of brandy. Belatedly, he recalled the Black Raven was a suspected murderess. *Not at all convenient timing.*

From what he could recall of Dalmere's hasty tête-à-tête on the hack ride over, which was precious little now, she had never been convicted. Not enough evidence or some such thing. Still, one could not be too careful. Never underestimate the enemy and all that.

He could make his apologies now and leave before this turned embarrassing. He had accomplished what he set out to do, which was simply to gain entrance to the Black Raven's lair. He was sure ravens didn't have lairs, but entry to the Black Raven's *nest* didn't have quite the same ring to it.

He could have left, but he didn't.

Before he could quite make up his mind what to do next, a swishing sound came from behind him and a fragrance he knew could only belong to a woman drifted across his nostrils. Fresh, sweet, with a hint of something else he couldn't quite put his finger on. His heart sped up considerably. A tingle of awareness settled uncomfortably between his shoulder blades. He tried to shrug the discomfort away.

A soft, slightly husky voice emanated from some place behind him. "Stay still. I want to have a look at you."

He straightened, tensed. Ready for what, he wasn't sure.

She came around from his left side, disarming him instantly. He could do naught but stare at her. Lord, she had the most incredible blue eyes. They were dark and rimmed around the edge with an even darker blue. They were intense, unnerving, remarkable—and studying him.

"Lord Bellamy?"

He had to shake himself mentally. Dalmere had left out some important information, it seemed. He had expected an old crone not this... goddess before him.

"Lady Blackhurst." He bowed, though it was risky and not nearly as elegant as it should have been. Had she noted the slight wobble?

He really shouldn't have kept looking at her. He didn't expect to turn into stone or anything as dramatic as that, but because what he saw stunned him more than if he'd been bitten by a cobra. The reality of her made him regret every drop he'd taken tonight. It was a sobering effect indeed, yet made him feel lightheaded in a whole different way.

Surreal in the shadowy light of the library, her features were small and elegant. Oliver couldn't look away, hypnotized, lured into the dark sapphire depths of her eyes where he would surely have drowned, and gladly.

He was damned for sure now! Well, he'd be damned if he would be damned alone. So, damn Dalmere, damn brandy, and damn the French for makin' it. Damn Henry, too, for dying and leaving him in this damned position. If not for his brother, he wouldn't have taken on this damned ridiculous wager or any of the other damn wagers he'd taken on in the last couple of days.

Damn, but she was beautiful!

Her eyes widened slightly for a moment before long dark lashes lowered and broke the contact between them. She walked a few paces and turned back to him. "I don't believe we have met before, Lord Bellamy. I must say, I am intrigued to hear why you are so anxious to see me."

Her voice was calm and extremely alluring. He could have listened to her all night. He tried not to sway in her direction.

A finely arched brow rose in unimpressed expectation.

He cleared his throat. "Well, yes, I imagine you are. Intrigued that is. I came here because…" Bloody hell, why was he here again? He couldn't think of a damn thing, except he was hungry and felt like eating toast smothered in marmalade. Citrus! That's what she smelled like.

"Come, Bellamy, surely you know what it was that had you camped out on my stairs?" she urged.

Oh, yes, the wager. Well, he could hardly tell her that, could he? He gave her his best half-smile to cover the fact he could only come up with the most pathetic of excuses, none of which he could use. "Of course, I know why I am here."

"Then pray continue, my lord. You have ten minutes left." She made a cursory glance at the mantel clock.

"Ten minutes?" *Ten minutes 'til what?* He looked at the clock too, but it did little to help him with his current dilemma. It was a nice enough clock to be sure and he supposed it kept good time—

"Yes. I would hate to see you out on my steps again tomorrow when you finally remember why you wanted to see me."

"Ah, yes, that…" Oliver looked around him as if the shelves would somehow whisper some sort of logical answer, but to no avail.

She sat now in an olive-green, overstuffed chair situated in the middle of the room with its mate opposite, a small inlaid table set between and occupied by a silver coffee service. Hastily he glanced around him. Nothing unusual here. A large desk over towards one corner was the only other piece of furniture. All else seeming safe to ignore, he returned his gaze to the woman who had her eyes directed solely at him.

The intensity with which her eyes bored holes in him was a little off-putting, to say the least. They were like the ocean before a storm, dark and broody. He felt a storm brewing in this very room and then a little voice inside his head yelled, *"Retreat now!"*

At least on the steps below he hadn't felt like a lummox, having trouble putting two words together. *Reality was such a cruel mistress.*

The Countess of Blackhurst was in black, of course. What else would she be in? She was a widow, after all, and they didn't call her *The Black Raven* for nothing. She wore a delicate black shawl over her shoulders, which made her look oddly small and fragile. This conflicted exceedingly with the other image he had of her—the one where she stood over her husband's dead body with a smoking pistol in her hand.

"Perhaps some coffee will help your memory, Lord Bellamy?"

Her emotionless yet husky tone made him start to sweat but for what reason he wasn't quite sure. His breeches seemed tighter too. Perhaps he did know the reason after all. "That would be lovely, thank you." Coffee would sober him up enough to get out some sort of decent excuse and get this doomed interview over with. But how to explain a lie when one had not yet thought of the lie? *Think, Oliver, think.*

She handed him a cup, and he sniffed at it suspiciously. "What is this strange smell?" he asked as he eyed his cup.

"It could be a touch of cinnamon," she informed him. She sipped delicately at the edge of her cup, watching him all the while.

"Oh," he replied, and happily stirred in an extra lump of sugar.

Wait a minute! Could be?

He put his cup down on the table so fast it clattered and spun on its saucer. He wanted to say, *"Now see here, just because you are beautiful and I am full to the brim does not give you the right to toy with me in this manner,"* but of course he didn't. It was simply too many words all in one go.

The Black Raven's lips twitched slightly. "Are you all right, Lord Bellamy?"

"Ah, yes, fine. I just remembered I have to be… somewhere." *Yes, definitely somewhere else.*

"But you have yet to tell me the reason for your visit."

"I believe…" He gave her a sheepish look meant to charm. "I wanted to make your acquaintance."

"Oh?" Her tone turned cold. "For what reason, Lord Bellamy? You wanted to advise me on a financial matter?" she suggested, sipping her coffee and watching him intently. "Perhaps you thought I needed a protector? Were you about to volunteer your services to the poor little widow?" she enquired.

This is going very badly, Oliver thought. He was usually so good with women, charm being one of his more rewarding traits. Somehow he knew his usual tactics would not work here, nor unfortunately his brain.

"Did you say you required a protector?" he said, nearly picking up his coffee cup again.

"No," she replied. Her hands held her cup with long graceful fingers which were slightly ink-stained. "Not exactly."

Confusion set in like a rotten tooth. He must get out of here. He looked up from his study of her delightful digits to be confronted with eyes that blazed with an impatient intensity. It set his pulse racing in a way he hadn't experienced in quite a while—not since he had been back in England at any rate.

Her eyes still bored holes in him. He must look like Swiss cheese by now.

"Perhaps you wanted to see the *Black Raven* for yourself?" Her voice remained even and calm though she probably wanted nothing better than to put those ink-stained fingers around his neck. This barely concealed dislike was novel, and because of who she was he couldn't dismiss it. It made him itch with anticipation.

"Let me put you out of your misery," the countess said. She stood up and walked over to the fireplace, where she promptly picked up a fire poker, weighing it in her hands.

Oliver looked at the poker and nearly laughed out loud. Surely not! He had been threatened by much worse and survived.

"How much are you getting?" she asked.

"Pardon?" His eyes were riveted to her hands, studying the way her fingers curled around the shaft of the wrought-iron poker. *Damn me.*

"How much are you getting from your little bet?" she asked; the fire poker tapped against her black skirt in a steady rhythm.

"Wager," he corrected, before he mentally smacked himself. *Oh, yes, that was very well done, you foxed fool.*

She inclined her head. "I stand corrected."

He watched as the fire poker changed hands. He could take her if he needed to, he decided. She was only a slip of a woman, after all. He'd feint to the right, catch her wrist and kiss her witless. *Oh, yes, good plan.*

"Lady Blackhurst, this is not necessary. I really should go. I am disgracefully intoxicated and shall remove myself immediately."

He was up in a wobbly flash, but his legs refused to move any further. His eyes never left the fire poker, which she now raised and poked at the coals in the grate with exaggerated stabbing motions. He could not see her face but imagined she was scowling fit to make spring birds drop stone-cold-dead from their branches. He smiled at the thought. It was an involuntary reaction, surely, to the ludicrousness of this situation.

She spun to face him, fire poker drawn level with his heart. "Do sit down, Bellamy."

This time he did laugh. He was in no doubt he could over-power her before she did much harm with that mere stick in her hand—as pointy and well-crafted as it seemed.

"I believe you owe me an answer, Lord Bellamy." She moved towards him brandishing the poker like a rapier. He couldn't believe his bloodshot eyes. He laughed louder. He nearly told her to keep the tip up, until he saw where her target was and it was no longer his heart. He stopped laughing.

"Two hundred pounds," he confessed with a slow smile, for there was no longer any reason to conceal his true mission here. Confounded woman had him at a disadvantage though. If only Henry had not been such a blasted fool, leaving him with more debt than he knew how to handle, a doddery old aunt, and two entailed estates full of dependents. *Oh, and no money.*

He saw her glance at the mantel and realized his time was up. Should he start praying now or...? He wanted to laugh again. If only the Frenchies could see him now. Undone by a handsome widow and a fire poker.

Her gaze left the clock and seemed to focus on his cravat. "I fail to see what is so amusing to you, Lord Bellamy. I can only assume you know of my reputation. Why else would you be here? Ah, yes, the money. Two hundred pounds, was it? How would you like to earn a lot more?"

This was a twist he had not expected. "Excuse me?"

She glided over to him and pointed the poker at his vitals. "Let me explain it for you. These *little wagers* have been happening for quite some time, Lord Bellamy. You see, you are not the first man to sit on my steps and demand entrance. Some have even tried to break in. I find this whole business *very* childish and most annoying. Can you understand my frustration, Lord Bellamy?" The poker came very close to his pride.

"Yes, most annoying," he replied, his eyes riveted on the poker. She had no idea how easily he could turn this scenario on its, or in this case, her derrière. He was too intrigued, however, by her suggestion to bother demonstrating just now.

"However, if you will assist me, Bellamy, I think you will be more than happy with the arrangement I am proposing." She stared at him coolly.

"Arrangement?" The fire poker remained hovering above his most important asset.

"Yes. I find I require an escort. You see, I presume there are a number of… outstanding wagers concerning my reputation as the Black Raven, and I will allow you to collect them on the condition you but play the *gentlemanly* escort." She took the poker away from his crotch. "Are we in agreement?"

He took a deep breath. He hadn't realized he'd been holding it. This annoyed him more than her gall to try and threaten him. "And where would I be escorting you, madam?"

"To the theater, the opera, some balls, soirees, and the like." She turned as if dismissing him as a danger to her.

"And for how long would I need to be your escort?"

"Until the end of the London season," she announced.

This was certainly not what he had expected, but then he had anticipated some old hag with a black bird on her shoulder.

"And I get to collect *all* the wagers?" he asked, contemplating the vast amount of money that could become available to him, with little or no effort. It would give him the perfect cover. So far, he had been able to hide his desperate financial situation from not only the *ton* but the creditors as well and he wanted to keep it that way.

The occasional wager and gambling win had kept him from having to fight off creditors at his door, but every day his situation became more desperate.

"Within reason, of course," she replied placing the fire poker softly back in its stand.

"Of course." He couldn't help the slight lift of his lips. "That is very generous of you, Countess," he said.

He watched her put a long finger to her chin in a thoughtful pose. "Is it? I suppose there are a great many wagers." she remarked in a dismissive gesture.

It was all too evident to Oliver the countess was indeed deeply bothered by these wagers. There was something about her eyes, but in his state his perception could hardly be relied upon.

"There may be a few," he lied. In actual fact he had no idea how many there were. There could be hundreds for all he knew, but the prospect of being able to claim them was immense.

"Can I depend on you, Lord Bellamy?" Her voice was strained, and she kept looking at the clock on the mantel as though if it were to chime midnight she would turn back into a pumpkin or perhaps… a black raven?

"Yes, of course," he answered. If there was one thing he knew it was duty. Duty to his family name, his inheritance, his King and his country, and now, it seemed, to the Black Raven for whatever it may be worth.

"Then we are agreed? Good. You may go." She dismissed him with a wave of her hand. "I shall send a messenger in the morning with our first appointments. Good night, Lord Bellamy."

She looked once more at the mantel clock, collected a little book off the desk, and left him.

Oliver looked around him. Not feeling at all well.

Out in the hall her butler was waiting for him with his hat and his gloves. Oliver blinked. The old man was nearly smiling.

"Did that just happen?" he asked the butler as they made their way back to the front door.

"Yes, I believe it did, my lord," was the butler's only reply.

CHAPTER TWO

THE SCANDAL SHEETS were full of lies, half-truths, salacious rumors, and slander. For the first time in over two years Lisbeth was glad to see her name in print. Though the subject matter was distasteful to her, it had done what she had intended—brought her back to the lips of every member of the *ton*.

Her plan was in motion.

"I expected much worse," she said to Rollands as he hovered by her elbow in the breakfast room. "Lord Bellamy must have been very kind in his recitation of our meeting."

Her butler's tone was dry as he replied, "I expect he had half-forgotten it by the time he reached his cronies, my lady."

"Oh," she said. "I hadn't thought of that. He wouldn't have forgotten our agreement, do you think? In any case, I dare say he is feeling very unfavorable this morning. It is little more than he deserves, of course, but I admit I was a little harsh on him."

"No harsher than necessary, I'm sure, madam."

Lisbeth nodded at her butler and folded the paper. He immediately poured her some tea.

"Thank you, Rollands."

He bowed and left the room. He had been here from the very start and had stood behind her throughout all the days, months, and years after. No thanks would ever be enough. She knew his loyalty was beyond reproach and she trusted him implicitly.

Lisbeth sighed and sipped her tea.

Alone again.

Even when Nathaniel had been alive she had been alone. His dedication to their courtship had been nothing but a dedication to her dowry. What a naïve, silly little fool she'd been then, believing in the fairy tale. A fairy tale which had so quickly turned into a nightmare.

She sipped her tea and closed her eyes a moment. Yet, even in these few moments memories assailed her. Flashing images passed behind her eyelids in quick painful succession, each frame of memory causing her to jolt and shudder in her seat. She felt every fist, every boot as they connected; his angry tirades hardly heard through ringing ears. Every cruel word he'd uttered was a scar upon her very soul.

She gasped, her lungs struggling for air, and opened her eyes as she looked around frantically.

Sun poured in from the windows. A cheerful flower arrangement displayed vibrant reds, yellows, and green. Her mother's china graced her table, and in the distance she could hear the sound of the servants going about their business.

Safe.

She released a breath slowly, then another, until her heart had slowed to a more temperate rate.

She picked up her schedule sitting neatly on the table and fanned herself with it. Lisbeth usually took comfort in knowing she had something else to think about besides her horrid, pathetic past but her schedule's purpose had morphed overnight into something more than a direction for her day. The origins of this simple sheet of vellum lay in her desperate attempt to do everything in exactly the manner and timing Nathaniel had demanded. It had become her sole means of self-preservation.

And it had worked… most of the time. No plan was ever foolproof. Which brought her thinking right back to the present.

She sipped her tea and pondered the possible kinks in her plan, the main one being Lord Bellamy. Last night she'd had trouble dealing with him, despite his obvious inebriation. She had not expected him to be young, nor handsome, nor have a smile that made one's heart falter.

It had taken considerable effort not to admire his fine physical attributes at first. She had stared at him like he was an ice from Gunter's, for heaven's sake. His eyes had been a warm brown, almost like melted chocolate, and she'd always been partial to men with a cleft in their chin, though his cleft was not so deep as to be the focus of his face. This honor belonged to his mouth and the charming brackets which led her focus there again and again.

She'd had to remind herself why he had been standing in the middle of her library in the first place. It did not matter what he looked like, she told herself now. Only what he would allow her to do in terms of her plan.

Lisbeth retired to the library where she sat behind her father's huge desk and began her house accounts. She loved this beautiful desk and skimmed her fingers over its highly polished surface. She felt her father was with her when she sat at this desk. He would not have abandoned her, she was sure, but he was gone, as was her mother. Anyone who had cared or loved her was gone or had abandoned her. She only had herself to depend on now. There was no use feeling sorry for herself and she banished the maudlin thoughts away.

However, it wasn't long before her thoughts wandered towards further pitfalls of her previously perfect plan. Was she doing the right thing? Could she handle this man? What about tonight? Lord help her, he might be sober and then what? She knew what men were capable of and if he got even an inkling she wasn't in control he would take over and destroy her. She couldn't afford for him to think he could do what he wished. She would have to put him in his place right from the start. She had no choice.

It all had to be perfect. She wanted no one to misunderstand her position and everyone to wonder what the devil her intentions were. Confusion would keep them guessing and inviting her to their gatherings.

Her greatest pleasure would be to see the *ton's* stunned faces when she revealed the identity of the real killer and they realized how wrong they had been about her.

OLIVER SAT IN his brother Henry's breakfast room and looked at the sealed envelope. He rubbed his eyes. He was in no shape to be dealing with last night's consequences. Was it too much to hope the Countess of Blackhurst was informing him she had changed her mind about their agreement? No amount of money could be worth it, surely... and yet... He rubbed at his forehead with increasing pressure which, of course, didn't help at all.

As a self-imposed punishment he seriously considered taking one of his aunt's tonics. After sending her his apologies this morning, claiming a headache, a bottle of some dubious concoction had arrived. *As if he did not feel bad enough already.*

Dear Aunt Petunia. It was just the two of them now. An elderly woman of uncertain mental faculties and he of uncertain financial security. What a pair they made. She depended on him now. He could not let her down.

His temples contracted in pain, a staccato of pounding fists against his skull. He had to face facts. Until Henry's investments came in, if they came in, he needed money—a lot of money. The kind of money the countess's plan could ensure.

He glanced at the note.

It still sat patiently to his left.

He needed a new strategy, a new campaign, but the territory was unfamiliar to him.

When Henry had inherited the title at the grand old age of fifteen, he'd had Aunt Petunia's husband, Uncle George to advise him, teach him. Uncle George was gone now too, in the family crypt that held all the Whitely family including the whisper of his parents' memories.

Henry had loved him, there had never been a doubt about that, but he had never been a parent to him. The brother who had always seemed so steadfast had left him, abandoned him. He needed him now, and he wasn't here.

Why, Henry?

Now Oliver was alone with a huge debt-ridden inheritance he didn't know what the hell to do with and the bank was breathing down his neck.

And the note.

A footman politely coughed behind him before announcing the arrival of "Lord Anthony Ashton."

Tony? Here? This was a surprise.

Oliver shoved the note away and turned to greet his friend.

Tony walked in, paused, his eyes taking in the room in a single glance before settling his summer eyes on Oliver.

"This is worse than I expected," he commented as he moved farther into the room, inspecting Oliver.

"I don't remember you being so dedicated to interior design. What are you doing here, Ashton?"

"Well, it is an interesting story, actually. You see I've been back in the country for two days and all I seem to hear about is you. Why is that, Bellamy?"

Oliver closed his eyes for a moment. He could really do without the interrogation right now.

Tony laughed. "What, no smart remark? You must be suffering." He picked up the morning post and unfolded it. "Now, where was it? Blah blah, Napoleon is rumored to be ill, blah, blah. Can you believe it? Bonaparte has been near death every other week and still the Prince Regent nearly vomits at the mere mention of his name." Tony shook his head.

Oliver raised a brow. "You came here to tell me about Bonaparte?"

Tony sighed and flipped through a few more pages. "Only if his missives suddenly began to be written in code. Fortunately for you, he still prefers French. Vile soppy stuff too. Sentimental old fool."

A pained expression passed over Oliver. "Ashton, what do you want?"

Tony looked up and smiled. *"Lord B,"* he read in a clear voice. "That would be you, *single-handedly won the long-standing Black Raven Wager last night. Witnesses confirmed he spent over twenty minutes in the infamous countess's townhouse and came out unscathed. Whatever did he do there, dear readers? Do tell, Lord B. We are all anxious to know."* Tony raised a brow. "Yes, Lord B, do tell."

Oliver watched as his friend abandoned the paper to prowl around the room, and it was not an exaggeration. It was the way he moved.

"I'm not telling anybody anything," Oliver replied, pretending to look interested in his breakfast.

"Oh dear, you really did do it then. I thought perhaps my source had had one too many ales."

"Are things so slow in the Home Office you must spend your time spying on me? How dull, but if you are asking me if I won the wager the answer is, yes."

Tony looked out the window. "I suppose, I shouldn't ask you why you did it?"

"No." He poked at the cold beefsteak in time with the throbbing in his head.

"You should have told me about Henry." Tony appeared at his elbow.

Oliver wasn't surprised. "Why? What could you have done? Brought him back from the dead? Stopped him from riding that day?" Oliver looked away.

Good lord, his chest hurt.

"He was my friend."

"He was my brother!" Oliver spat out standing up and knocking his chair over. He walked over to the windows which overlooked the busy street beyond. "Your mother sent flowers," he said, his voice flat. "Your brother, Warrington, wrote a lovely eulogy for the papers."

Tony nodded. "Yes, he's good at those. I am sorry, damnable way to go."

Oliver looked back at him. "No, hardly a glorious ending, was it? Breaking your neck is dramatic, but not glorious."

"It could have happened to anyone," his friend said.

Oliver didn't reply. Why was he so angry at Tony?

Tony was a man you would never guess as being anything other than what he was—a younger son of an aristocratic family. He was so much more. Of average height, with sandy blond hair he was able to blend into a crowd easily. However, if he wanted to have his presence known there was no way of escaping his gaze.

Oliver had met him during the war where Oliver was a code breaker under Scovell. Oliver had been quick-witted and handy with a pistol and so he had found himself often picked to go on special missions. He missed those times. At least then he'd had direction in his life, a purpose. The danger for some reason had never bothered him.

"Oliver, there is something else…"

"Please. There is no need of any pity. You can go away now."

"Oliver," Tony began.

"It is done." And it was. There was nothing anyone could do for him or say to him, which could make this right. It was all wrong. It was supposed to have been him. He was the soldier, after all. He was the one who should have died on the battle-field—not Henry—with his neck broken and his face in the mud. Oliver rubbed at his chest again. Will this ache ever leave him?

"The *ton* is going to want to know what happened last night," Tony explained.

"The *ton* can go to hell!" he said, and he meant it.

Tony's lips quirked. "Right, well, that would make the queues at Covent Garden less tiresome, but it won't make this go away. You need a plan."

"I know." Oliver glanced at the note again. The precise handwriting mocked him.

Open me!

"I'm thinking on it."

Tony smiled then. "Good, because I need you."

"You need me?"

"I assume you know the story. The Black Raven, her dead husband, and a certain financial speculation?"

"What of it?"

"It's the reason you are in this… situation."

Tony knew? Well, of course he knew. "Oh, that situation." He narrowed his eyes then. "How exactly is she the reason?"

"Henry invested in the speculation with Blackhurst, along with others. When Blackhurst died, the scheme was found to be fake."

Oliver sat down in the nearest chair. "Henry invested in a fake speculation? He gambled the family fortune on a *speculation?* It doesn't sit right. Henry never did risky things." *Except jump fences.*

"Blackhurst was known to be very convincing; he managed to persuade many high-profile men into this farce. They all lost out, but Henry…"

Oliver nodded but still it didn't make sense. He tried to picture Henry but it was getting harder. Perhaps he didn't know his brother as well as he thought. Perhaps, he let himself become distant from him. How had his life fallen apart so quickly?

"I suppose I should have known you would find out. I suppose everyone knows. Should I start packing for the Continent?"

"Don't be ridiculous. Nobody knows and nobody will if you do the sensible thing."

Sensible thing? Easier said than done it seems.

"We need you to continue whatever it is you started with the Black Raven. You're the first, Bellamy. No one else has been able to penetrate her inner sanctum."

Oliver coughed. "What makes you think I *penetrated her inner sanctum?*"

Tony rolled his eyes. "I mean you were the first to be let in."

Oliver looked away. "Oh, right."

Tony watched him. He hated when he did that. Like he knew what he was thinking simply by where he put his hand or moved his eyes. Could he tell he had been very attracted to the Countess of Blackhurst? Under better circumstances, Oliver would not have been opposed to being near her inner sanctum at all.

"This wager has been in place for two years. Two years we have been trying to get someone in with no success… until you."

Oliver turned back to Tony, his eyes narrowed in anger. "We? Are you saying the Home Office is behind this?"

Tony laughed at the apparent stupidity of his accusation. "No."

Oliver was beginning to dislike the turn in this conversation. "Then who?"

"A very influential person lost a lot of money in the speculation." Tony shrugged. "He wants answers. I'm doing it as a personal favor."

Oliver shook his head but the knocking on his skull was still there and getting louder. "What has it to do with the countess?"

"She was Blackhurst's beneficiary. Everything that wasn't entailed went to her. An obscene amount of money. There are persons who think she killed him or had him killed. She refused to repay the investors their capital. It made her very unpopular."

"I thought she was acquitted of his murder?"

"She was, but still there is reason to believe she knows more about her husband's dealings than she is willing to tell. We need you to find out what that more is."

Now it was Oliver's turn to laugh. "And you think she is going blurt it all out to me?"

"Given time and certain incentives, I am sure she will slip up and give herself away." Tony pushed the countess's note towards him with a forefinger. "Read it," he said, taking a seat back at the table.

Devil take him, Tony was right. If she was the cause of Henry's misery, if she was the cause of his current despair he must find out.

Oliver looked at the note again. How bad could it possibly be? The fact last night was more blur-ish nightmare than actual memory was contributing to his lack of muster, but it wasn't as though she could kill him with ink, unless of course, it was poisoned. He shook his head to shake away the cobwebs.

He picked it up, weighed it in his palm, and frowned for the forty-fourth time this morning. It was a little heavy for a note. What was in there, her whole life story, a confession, his requiem mass? *Open it*, his brain buzzed.

He broke out in a sweat as he broke the wax seal and unfolded it. He read it briefly and stifled a laugh, read it again and then roared with laughter, ignoring the pain in his head. He was quite sure now she *hadn't* killed her husband. "The daft bugger must have dashed his own brains out if this is the kind of thing she forced upon him on a daily basis," Oliver said, passing the note to Tony.

He gave it a cursory glance but not more. His face still serious. "Glad to find you are so amused by it."

"It hardly matters what's in it. I'm not going to do it anyway."

Tony's eyes turned cold. "I think you are. You have to."

"Ashton, I can hardly conceive how you know about any of this, let alone what this note might say."

"I don't really care what the note says, but I knew who it was from. I saw it being delivered this morning from the lady's house. I had to ensure you read it."

"So, you are spying on me?" Oliver put his hands on his hips.

Tony smiled. "Not you, Bellamy. Her."

"Why should I do this for someone I don't even know?"

"You're not. You're doing it for me. And, if you do, I will make sure you are handsomely rewarded. Is that incentive enough?"

"Do I have much choice?"

"Not really," Tony replied before patting him on the shoulder.

"Well, hell, now you've taken all the fun out of it."

"I am sure you will find the countess more than entertaining. I'll be gone for a few weeks. When I return, I'll come to see you. Or, if you find out something interesting, you know how to contact me, discreetly." Tony turned and left the room.

Oliver looked around the now quiet room. This certainly changed things. He picked up the note again. Could she have had anything to do with Henry and the loss of the family fortune?

AN HOUR LATER and feeling much more the thing, Oliver took a hackney to his tailor in Piccadilly. He needed decent clothes if he was going to be escorting a certain female around London. He pulled out the note and just for fun read it again.

Bellamy, he read. *Here is your schedule for tonight. You will notice I have allowed fifteen extra minutes' time between appointments for traffic and fog.* "How thoughtful, Countess." *Do not be late.* "As if I would dare," he said to the interior of the hackney. *I will expect you to be properly attired and sober.* "Cheeky chit!" *I will expect you at exactly nine o'clock tonight. Tardiness will not be tolerated, as we must keep to the schedule at all costs.*

"No, Countess, at your cost."

Only it wasn't at her cost at all, was it? She had quite cleverly arranged for the *ton* to pay her debt to him. He could only tip his hat to her. Combined with what Tony had said would come to him for information on the countess, he could find himself retiring to the country and raising hunting dogs before he knew it.

Surprisingly, the Black Raven never strayed far from his thoughts all day. Not because of the natural interest of all who had met him, but because her schedule had outlined exactly what she was doing practically every minute of the day.

While his tailor was being astonishingly gymnastic in his bending and scraping and general groveling, trying to extract details of his famous client's night with the Black Raven, she was having a dress fitting. While Oliver was enjoying an excellent glass or two of claret with his slightly overdone spatchcock in orange sauce, she was tending her garden. Despite the toughness of his lunch the thought of the Countess of Blackhurst bending over was a more than appealing picture.

By the time he reached his brother's townhouse on Cavendish Square in the late afternoon, he was quite familiar with the lie he had made up for the masses.

He and the Black Raven had become quite cozy on her Egyptian-styled chaise lounge, while she had lured him with good French cognac and seduced him with her crystalline eyes and husky dulcet tones until he gave in to her considerable charms. It was so far from the truth as to be almost believable. If there were a few who didn't trust his story they would no doubt be choking on their disbelief when he strolled into Wainwright's ball tonight, with the delightfully beautiful and terrifying Countess of Blackhurst on his arm. The thought alone made him smile. Men were making more wagers by the moment, intent on catching him out, when really all they were doing were aiding him on cashing in.

He had been at a distinct disadvantage last night, but tonight he would be in full control of all his mental and bodily faculties. She would not be holding the trump card this time for he had one or two aces up his considerably well-turned-out sleeve. The Black Raven was to find Oliver Whitely, Earl of Bellamy, could easily handle one fussy black-clad female.

CHAPTER THREE

Nathaniel Carslake, the infamous Earl of Blackhurst, was an imposing-looking figure. At least his portrait was. The countess's very dead, apparently murdered, husband was scowling from his impressive position above the parlor fireplace. He looked like a rabid dog had bit him on the arse. All dark bushy brows and inky menace oozing from two equally matched pits of hell.

Oliver scowled back. It wasn't as though he was happy about this situation either. Subconsciously he straightened to his full six feet and raised a brow. After a moment he shook his head and laughed. The situation was ludicrous enough without him trying to out-glare a painting.

"I'm going to expose your lady as a fraud and a thief. Hope you don't mind," Bellamy said to the portrait. "Then again you were a right bastard yourself, so I doubt you care much what happens to your wife."

Blackhurst looked like he kept his sense of humor in his little toe. With a demeanor like that, was it really so surprising the sapskull had gotten himself killed by persons unknown, or most likely upstairs?

Oliver ignored the portrait as he inspected the stark parlor for oddities. There was nothing particularly special about this room, although it might once have been quite cozy.

It was spotlessly clean, like the rest of the house, but it lacked the warmth and inviting touches females usually brought. Where were the flowers, the hundred or so attempts at water coloring, or the army of tiny miniature dogs along the windowsill? Then again, his Aunt Petunia's house was full of miniature dogs, of the living variety. Oliver was not a fan of small crotch sniffing abominations. The worst was that Aunt Petunia in all her frail eccentricity would not let him push them away, saying, "Oh, leave them be, Bellamy. They do so enjoy it, and we get so few visitors these days." He had taken to carrying a book with him when he visited. Both as a defense against the crotch snufflers, and to read when Aunt Petunia drifted off, as she often did—usually in the middle of a sentence.

Oh, how he loved that old woman.

He sighed as he looked around him. The room felt familiar in its emptiness. He had the same problems with the townhouse he lived in. It wasn't his home, never had been. It was Henry's house even if it now belonged to Oliver. He didn't want his dead brother's house or anything in it, but for now it was necessary to keep up appearances. For some reason people became somewhat suspicious when one started selling off the family heirlooms. Instead, he'd packed them away, leaving the house a little desolate. He preferred desolate to depressing, which is exactly how he had felt before he had—cleaned house. Perhaps the countess had felt the same. In this at least he could understand her Spartan theme.

He picked up a small book from a table. His eyebrows rose in surprise. Well, well, well.

LISBETH WATCHED FROM the doorway as Bellamy paced around the room, touching things. Her things. In profile she admired his lean, athletic form. A Corinthian, her sister would have said. Her eyes drank him in. She watched his muscles flex under his jacket as he picked up a book, opened it, and fanned through the pages. Her mind easily imagined rippling muscles carved from years of hard living in the army.

She touched her cheeks. *Was it hot in here?*

Lisbeth's hand went to her breast. Her heart was pounding quite fast. Surely it was just nerves. She was *not* attracted to Bellamy. She disliked everything about him and his kind. Men like him had tortured her with their incessant attempts to win that loathsome wager for years.

Although, she had to admit as she watched him, he was the perfect compromise between masculinity and elegance. He had a tightly bound energy about him. It surprised and frightened her. On top of that he was physically strong. She must always keep that in mind. As if she could forget. However, she must be prepared. If he sensed a weakness, some vulnerability in her, he would swoop in and trample her into dust. She would never again allow a man to control her like Nathaniel had.

"Never," she vowed in a whisper as she turned away and back towards the stairs to her room. She knew just how she was going to ensure he knew his place. She just hoped he was a quick learner.

OLIVER PICKED UP another book off the small table. It was a horrid novel, the likes of which his Aunt Petunia had such a fancy for. He would not have taken the Black Raven as one who would have the temperament for such a wickedly popular obsession. To laugh seemed beyond her, though he supposed these kinds of books might have helped her research her disapproving scowl.

He wouldn't have been surprised, however, to find several treatises on *How to live an extraordinarily dull life without leaving one's house* or *How to plot your husband's demise before high tea*. It was better he think of something other than the Black Raven's reported reputation for… well… bad luck and death.

The wager of choice tonight was sure to be simple considering he was escorting her to a ball. All he'd had to do was lure her out of her house. As it was her choice to go to this ball in the first place there was no luring necessary. It felt a bit like cheating.

Secretly, he hoped to waltz with her. That was bound to put a bit of puff into the fan-fluttering matrons and yet a few more coins in his purse. Oliver felt strange taking it on, although it would make a fine dent in his brother's loan repayments. The bank loan Henry had taken out to go into the doomed speculation in the first place.

It still didn't make sense; Henry had never been a foolish man, but Oliver had to remember what Ashton had told him. The Countess of Blackhurst wasn't to be trusted. If she had made sure she had profited from this whole miserable affair, she deserved whatever punishment she got.

He would personally see to it.

"Bellamy," the Countess of Blackhurst announced as she glided back into the room.

He closed his eyes for a moment before he turned to her and offered her a courtly bow and a cheeky smile.

"I'm glad to see you are on time." Her voice held that crisp, husky tone that had kept him up last night as he debated his foolish agreement to her plan.

She was as beautiful as he remembered. No, more so.

"I am at your service, madam." Despite what she may or may not have done in the past, he could not deny his body's reaction to her. It was intense, instantaneous and, surprisingly, inconvenient. When he straightened, however, he saw she was looking at a gentleman's pocket watch and wasn't giving him the least attention. She probably hadn't heard a word he'd said. So, he added, "You look like you need ravishing, my dear."

She frowned. "Pardon? What did you say?"

"I said you look ravishing, my dear."

She looked at him, shocked for a moment before turning

away. "Oh, well, you look passable, I suppose," she replied.

It was too late. He had already seen the blush on her cheeks. Perhaps she was not so immune to his charms after all. He smiled to himself. Was she nervous or just indifferent? He quite liked the idea that he might make her nervous.

When she turned back, all traces of maidenly embarrassment were gone, replaced by a fierce look of displeasure. Had he mistaken her blush? She took the few steps it required to stand before him.

He raised a brow and let one side of his lips lift. "Pray, don't strain yourself with such compliments, Countess; they will only go to my... head," he said as he looked down at hers. She was staring at his jacket, her fingers hovering just above the superfine of his jacket. He could not help but admire the elegant slant of her neck and shoulder, the glorious consistency of her pale skin, the pulse at her throat, and the fine dark curls at her nape. His gaze traveled lower. The soft rise and fall of her breasts as they strained at her low neckline was hypnotizing.

She remained silent, her long and graceful fingers on the gold buttons of his dark-blue jacket. He watched her, fascinated. His heart thumped madly. His throat constricted and his hands flexed. What was she doing to him? Did she *know* what she was doing to him?

Slowly and with determination, one button, then another, then another slipped through their moorings. She was undressing him? A request for his permission would have been nice. Not that he would have said no.

This little exercise is going to seriously dent her carefully crafted schedule, he thought, as he watched her beautiful hands at their work. Thankfully she had allowed fifteen minutes for fog in her schedule. Perhaps fog had been a code all along. Even in his dreams, where such thoughts had free reign, he would not have expected her to be so... bold. It was thrilling, uplifting—in more ways than one.

She reached in under his jacket and... what was she doing

with his pocket watch? She'd pulled it out and flicked it open as if it weren't still attached to him.

"I believe that belongs to me," he said to break the tension between them.

She looked up at him. "As I suspected," she announced. "You're slow."

His mouth fell open. She didn't seem to notice for she was too busy re-adjusting his... slowness. Was she trying to issue an insult or was she really talking about his watch?

ALL HE DID know was she was close, very close, and that mysterious scent of hers had filled his nostrils like an oriental drug. He wanted more, much more.

He stepped closer, his own hands itching to span her waist, lift her off the ground, haul her Viking-style over his shoulder, and take the stairs two at a time. He would definitely need more than fifteen minutes!

Her gown was much more to his liking than the black sack she'd worn last night. He wondered how long it would take to get it off her. It showed a lovely amount of décolletage, and the style was much more flattering to her curvaceous figure. Yes. He would enjoy taking it off, indeed he would. It took him a moment to digest the color. It was so dark only the shimmer of the lamplight showed it to be a glorious midnight blue and not black at all.

Oliver's hands were nearly touching the tiny beads at her waist when she stepped back and away from him.

"Have you quite finished with your inspection, Bellamy?" Her voice laced with a threat.

He grinned. "Not really, Countess, but the night is young." He gave her a wink and went to reach for her again. The unfamiliar yet unmistakable feel of the cold muzzle of a small pistol jabbed his stomach. His hands came up instantly.

"Good God, woman! What the devil are you playing at?"

"Surely, you are not surprised?" She pointed the gun away

from him and put it back in her reticule.

"Is this a joke? What can you be thinking, pulling a cheeky stunt like that?"

Her look was all innocence, and for a moment he could picture her at any given night on a Drury Lane stage posing poetic about betrayal and love lost.

"I thought you ought to know I will be keeping this in my possession at all times." She turned then, picking up her gloves in one hand. "Oh, and Bellamy? I don't take kindly to manhandling or being called, *Countess*. Perhaps you ought to remember that also." She put on one glove before adding, "Now hurry, we must keep to the schedule."

He crossed his arms over his chest and scowled at her retreating form. "Well, this is a grand start!" he muttered to the now empty room. "I don't take kindly to female-handling either." *Well, at least, not much.*

He spared a glance at Blackhurst. Unbelievably, Oliver was actually beginning to feel sorry for him, not to mention himself. As if having to escort a suspected murderess around town wasn't bad enough, now he had to contend with her being an armed bedlamite as well. Luckily, he was not a man to run from danger. A serious character flaw he was sure. It was not as though she would really shoot him with that tiny thing, would she?

He shook his head at the ridiculous thought. What did she plan to do, shoot him if he ruined her schedule? He took his time getting into the carriage. He didn't want her to think her little pistol ploy had scared him into a state of obedience. Although he was very aware she had a firearm at the ready, probably aimed at his heart, or lower.

"YOU KNOW," HE stated when the carriage was underway. "It isn't very ladylike to carry around loaded pistols. What if it were to go off in your reticule? You could shoot your foot off, or worse, shoot mine off."

Lisbeth raised an eyebrow. "Your foot is safe, Bellamy," she assured from the shadows, "for the moment."

"Do you really think it is necessary to have it on you at a ball?" he asked, shifting a little on the seat opposite her.

"Especially, at a ball."

"All right, but maybe you should give it to me… for safekeeping," he suggested. "Carrying around a loaded pistol is extremely dangerous, not to mention… dangerous."

"Which is precisely why I am keeping it safe myself."

The carriage swayed from side to side as they stared at each other in the dimness of the interior. They were two strangers sitting uncomfortably across from each other in silence. He knew that to take her at face value would mean death on a battlefield. He wouldn't be so naive as to think her a safe companion to travel with. He would keep her in front of him where he could keep an eye on her, and her reticule.

The occasional sliver of light from the street lamps illuminated them for only seconds at a time and he tried to study her while he could get away with it. She was something of an enigma, this woman called the Black Raven—shrouded in scandal and mystery but inherently interesting to him nonetheless, despite the fact she quite obviously had bats in the belfry.

"I really think you should give it to me, Countess."

"I really think I shouldn't, Bellamy."

"I see." He didn't. "Why is that, exactly?" He would feel a lot better with that thing in his possession instead of hers. A woman and a firearm was a volatile mix. Considering her reputation, he thought it strange she would have shown it to him at all. If she wanted to cast shadow over her innocence, he could see no better way of doing it.

"Because, my dear sir, you are a man," she was saying now. All said in a tone which gave the impression it was not something he should be proud of.

He crossed his arms over his chest. "While I am glad you noticed, *Countess*, I hardly see what it has to do with a rather perilous object sitting in your reticule."

A fierce look of disapproval crossed her features for a moment. Was it his use of the word "Countess" which had rewarded him with such a look?

"It is my opinion that men should never be allowed to have possession of a firearm. You are notoriously clumsy with them."

"We are? Now hold on a minute…" he began, "… clumsy with them?"

Was the exaggerated sigh meant to imply he should already know this and she was simply repeating a well-known fact? He knew he had been out of the country for a long time but surely he would not have missed such a reform. His pistol had been his best friend for ten years. Evidently, this would be hard for her to comprehend, determined as she seemed to be to put down all men as idiots. Even now she was talking. He listened only because he was intrigued with what other complete twaddle she would come up with.

"Yes, and you shouldn't be allowed to have sharp objects, either," she stated with as much conviction as she had about the pistol.

He smiled in the darkness. "I presume you mean a sword, or are we now talking of cutlery?"

"You were right the first time, although now that you mention it—"

"Would you care to explain your theory, Countess?"

This ought to be good, he thought, sitting back. She was very negative towards his gender and really, he shouldn't find it at all amusing. He was, after all, a man, but he did nevertheless.

"Of course," she said before taking a breath. "It is well known that men use weapons like toys, like they are meant for your enjoyment, but I assure you they are not. They end up killing people."

Like your husband, Countess? "I think you are being a little unfair. We don't *all* use them like toys."

"The majority of you do, so I'm afraid my statement stands. Do you not patronize *Manton's*? Do you not have all manner of killing apparatus strapped to your walls as trophies of some dead ancestor or in cabinets and boxes tucked away waiting for the next time you want to play with them? If you want to go off and kill each other in duels and other such pathetic methods, by all means go ahead, you are only proving my point," she said, her tone altogether too smug. "Is there ever a hunting party where one of the guests isn't shot, maimed, or otherwise disfigured?"

He'd never been on a hunt in his life, not a civilized one at any rate, and they had certainly not been parties. "You don't like us very much, do you, Countess?" Oliver hoped she could hear the frown in his voice even if she couldn't see it.

He could hardly believe he was having this conversation with her. Duels, although outlawed, still occurred among gentlemen. It was a matter of honor. He couldn't deny the fact, but it wasn't as though they did it as a form of recreation, an activity to do for fun before breakfast.

As for the hunting party, Henry had written to him about such things, usually conveying them in a humorous light. So, yes, there were sometimes unfortunate accidents, but it usually involved a jealous husband who took advantage of shooting at his wife's lover and being able to pass it off as a wayward shot. Hmm, still…

"I like you well enough," she was saying now. "You do have your uses, after all." Her tone was bored, like she might let out a loud yawn.

"We do? I'm surprised. One would think you thought we were good for naught but hacking each other up on a whim, or blowing the stuffing out of one another for target practice," he stated in disgust. "Might I remind you that men with these particular objects have been at war for a decade and more to keep you from having to eat frog's legs, Lady Blackhurst? You should be damn grateful." She should be damn grateful he didn't shake her till her teeth rattled.

"I heard they taste like chicken," she said, looking directly at him with those eyes.

"They do, a little… but that is beside the point," he grumbled. Oh, she was a dirty player.

She looked at him then for a long moment. "While I stand by my theory, in terms of certain types of gentlemen of the *ton*, I would never undermine the military's importance to the safety of England. Though, through history, it is a repeated scenario that it is a lust for the spoils of war which often necessitates the need for one."

"You don't know the first thing about war, *Countess*. I do not think you should presume to have any opinion on the matter." Oh, he loved it when he made her twitch. She obviously did not like his pet name for her. He decided he would continue to call her Countess, just for the pleasure of seeing her twitch.

"I know the taxes I pay go to fund them," she parried.

"And I know the soldiers who fight them die," he deflected.

"That is very true, and sad, don't you think?"

Touché, Countess. "I think we should talk of something else."

"Of course," she replied, but said nothing further and neither did he.

He had just realized what she was doing. She had neatly distracted him from his purpose, to get the pistol from her. He would let her assume for now it had worked. She leaned closer to the window to try and catch the lamplight on her pocket watch. He knew how she felt; he was thinking the same thing. Was this carriage ride ever going to end?

"I wish you would put that thing away," Oliver said, folding his arms across his chest. It must have been the fifth time she'd done it since getting in the carriage. If she was going to do it all night it was going to drive him to drink—heavily.

"I must know what the time is," she stated, her voice as cool as ever.

"Does it really matter if we are a few minutes late?" He was baiting her on purpose, and he knew it was dangerous considering what was in her reticule, but it was dark so he did have an advantage.

"Yes, it does."

He waited. Nothing. "Is this another one of your theories, Countess? I suppose we men can't be trusted with timepieces either? God forbid we may tell each other the wrong time."

Frowning, she set the watch back in her bag and looked at him. "You are like a child, aren't you? Must you know *every* little thing? I think I liked you better when you were a witless drunk." She folded her hands in her lap and waited.

Nice. What was she expecting, his blood to start boiling, or his face to take on the look of chopped liver? Prove he was a child and throw a tantrum? *Not bleedin' likely!* Instead, he laughed, for what he really wanted to do was take her over his knee and give her a good spanking on her conceited derriere.

Whatever she may think of him, which was obviously not much, he was a man of his word, a man who was intimate with the word duty.

"Are you ever serious, Bellamy?"

He could see by the severe set of her mouth she wasn't the least impressed. "Occasionally, but I am usually ill at the time," he replied flippantly as the carriage came to a stop. They both sighed in relief.

He sprang out of the coach and handed her down. "Your audience awaits, my lady." Her hands were cold, so he tucked them in the crook of his arm and glanced down at her for a moment. "Ready?"

"Yes, of course." Her face, in profile, was serious and intense. He almost felt sorry for her. It was no mean feat to walk into a room full of people. People who thought you were a murderess.

"You're allowed to smile. People are going to think I dragged you here by your hair if you don't," he said, trying to lighten the mood.

"Don't be ludicrous, Bellamy. The last thing they will expect is for me to smile."

CHAPTER FOUR

OLIVER WAS SURPRISED the Countess of Blackhurst wasn't combusting right here, in the entrance of the Wainwright's ballroom, so intense was the focus of the assembled crowd around them.

This is what it must be like to stand in front of a firing squad, he thought.

Heads turned in ripples across the room as the word spread of their arrival. It reminded him of the quiet before the battlecry. The nervous energy that would surround you until you could not stand still. Every muscle would contract, tense, ears straining to hear the command that would send you riding down the hill and into the mêlée.

Despite his own resolve to feel nothing for the Black Raven, a small dose of respect stole over him, until he recalled their encounter in the carriage. He felt her fingers tense on his arm and then release.

The hosts scurried over, their expressions wary. Lady Wainwright looked a little pale and in need of some smelling salts, but was rallying. Wainwright bowed and babbled like a fool.

Beside him the Black Raven kept her chin high, her gaze regally down her nose, and stared at the assembled crowd with a chill that made him shiver.

Released at last from the formalities, the Countess of Blackhurst inclined her head and sailed off in the manner of a war ship heading straight for the enemy, all cannons primed and ready to go. What exactly her mission was still needed to be determined because he didn't believe for a moment that she just wanted to have an excuse to wear a pretty gown.

A few in the crowd gave her the cut direct, turning their backs to her, but most were too caught up by their curiosity to act so hastily. The infamous Black Raven was in their midst, and they were all no doubt wondering why. A lesser woman would have swooned from the lack of air in the room and the amount of eyes watching her every breath, but not the Black Raven.

Their whispers billowed up behind her like the dust of a racing coach but she remained stoic and her step never faltered. The music resumed and everyone scurried to take up their places on the dance floor or resume the best vantage points in which to view the goings on.

She sat then in the style of a queen taking her throne and looked around the room.

Oh, bravo, Countess.

He stood then at her shoulder for a few minutes, counting familiar faces and their varying expressions. They were all watching intently on what might happen next. He had to admit, he was too.

Later, they took a few turns around the room in which she asked him general questions regarding those who were new to her. She seemed intently interested in the standing of several gentlemen but paid surprisingly little attention to the women.

"What, no snippy comments about the dampness of the debutantes' gowns, Countess? What about the latest hair styles or the ridiculous amount of feathers protruding from their heads?"

She gave him an annoyed look but said nothing.

"I agree," he went on. "There must be bald ostriches all over Africa. What a sight that must be." He could have sworn he'd seen her lips twitch slightly at the edges.

When he returned her to her seat, she took out a small notebook from her reticule and began scribbling down a list.

"Taking notes, I see," Oliver said, handing her a glass of champagne.

"Yes."

"Notes on?"

"None of your business." She closed the notebook, returned it to her reticule, and resumed her study of the ballroom and its occupants.

"You cannot write a list in front of me and then not tell me the nature of the list. You are a cruel tease."

"You expect me simply to hand over my private thoughts?"

Well, no, he supposed. Still… it was damn annoying. Now he was going to have to steal it from her, read it, and decide whether it was worth worrying about. He just hoped it wasn't a list of, *ways to kill Bellamy, slowly and painfully.*

The strains of a waltz started. This would be the perfect time to take care of his wager. He'd snag her little notebook later. He hadn't spent nearly a decade as a soldier and code breaker and learnt nothing useful. "The pleasure of a dance, Countess?"

"No, thank you." She turned her eyes back to the dancers, her hands folded in her lap.

"Perhaps later then. Let me put it on your card." He went to take up her dance card.

"I do not enjoy dancing, Bellamy."

"Never say such a thing," he joked. "Next you will be admitting you don't like kittens."

She turned towards him then and regarded him with thinly veiled irritation. "Would you like me to confess to such a crime, Bellamy? Would you like me to embellish further by adding that I detest flowers, spring rain, and chubby-cheeked children?"

He chuckled. "It is just a dance, Countess. It is not like I am asking you to hitch up your skirt and do a jig while balancing two mugs of ale."

She rolled her eyes. "Your imagination is immeasurable. One would think you had actually witnessed such a scene."

He took the seat next to her. "Yes, once, in Germany. They

are very skilled and well balanced dancers in Germany, you know."

"So it seems," she said flatly. She looked around and then took a sip of her drink he had fetched off the refreshment table for her earlier.

He figured he'd lost her somewhere between skilled and Germany. It was actually a most amusing story but certainly not one for ladies' ears, even the Black Raven's, so it was probably just as well.

He realized she had neatly ended the subject of dancing, with her, at least. Still, he could wait. He imagined dancing with the infamous Black Raven was going to be a most interesting and entertaining business—eventually.

LISBETH DECIDED SHE disliked him immensely. It mattered not that Bellamy was as handsome as any man in the room. He was acting like a love-smitten pup. A hand on her waist here, a brush of his fingers on her shoulder there, a faint breath near her ear. What game did he think he was playing? It was… ridiculous. She wanted to smack him with her fan. Hard.

She did not like the way he was making her aware of every breath he took, of every move he made, and every annoying flash of his warm chocolate eyes. It was hard enough to breathe as it was. She told herself she was not the least bit jealous of his ability to converse with such an ease of manner she looked like a walking stick he just happened to be holding on to—She had better things to do than be any man's accessory.

A half hour later and Bellamy was now happily bantering on about some horse at Ascot to an elderly gentleman and she looked around for an escape. She saw an opening in the crowd and excused herself.

She made as if to the withdrawing room but then made a

quick right turn and found herself in the servant's hall. Squaring her shoulders she took the first step.

"SO, BELLAMY, HOW did we manage to get the devil's daughter to leave her crypt?" Dalmere asked in a jovial tone.

Oliver turned to find his brother's friend at his elbow. Dalmere had the look of an angel about him. His halo of golden curls had made him the subject of much female admiration. He was a thin man, with a sharp eye and a vicious wit when provoked. He had also been the first to offer his condolences after Oliver had returned from the Continent. He didn't know how he would have survived the first few days in London without Dalmere.

"I would take offense to that if you had not described her so aptly." Oliver took a sip of his drink, the stress like a boulder between his shoulder blades.

"Lord Fitzsimons and the others are going to be ill when they hand over their pounds to you on the morrow. I don't think anyone quite believed you."

"Considering the wagers put on in the last day, I would say a great many didn't believe me."

"Do you blame them? The woman has hardly left her house in years."

"There is a first time for everything. This is your fault anyway. If not for you I would never have taken up that wager in the first place."

"Don't put the blame on me. I tried to talk you out of it."

"That is not how I remember it."

"I was surprised you remembered your own name that night."

"You handed me the flask."

"You didn't have to drink it."

Dalmere inspected Oliver with concern in his pale-green eyes.

Oliver raised both brows. "What are you doing?"

"Looking for bite marks and bruises," Dalmere replied.

Oliver laughed. "Believe me there are wounds aplenty. Verbal ones. The woman has a tongue like a horse whip."

"Ouch!"

"Indeed."

Dalmere's gaze turned serious. "Then what are you doing with her? You won the wager; surely you are under no obligation to adopt the chit."

Good question. I'm selling my soul to a she-devil in return for money I make on wagers. It sounded ludicrous and desperate, even to him. As it was, Oliver wasn't even sure about this arrangement with the Countess of Blackhurst himself, so how could he explain it?

Oliver looked at Dalmere. "Besides the obvious, you mean? Have you looked at her? Really looked at her?"

"I have eyes, Bellamy, same as you, so yes, besides the obvious."

"I don't really know, but she is an interesting woman. I am determined to figure her out," Oliver explained.

Dalmere laughed. "Give up now then, my friend. The female species is a puzzle not even the brightest male minds have been able to comprehend."

"Oh, I don't think she will be so hard to understand, once I crack that shell of hers."

"Is that bravado talking, or do you really believe your own balderdash?"

Oliver winked at him, took a sip of his champagne, and glanced around, looking for Lisbeth. Beside him Dalmere huffed, but Oliver ignored him. The truth was he wasn't sure at all, bravado or not, whether he would live long enough to make even a small dent in her shell the way things were going so far. First things first; he had to get her pistol and notebook.

Where the devil was she, anyway? Why he felt the need to keep her within arm's reach was beyond him. She was as likely to try and break that arm as not. Still, he felt he should protect her from those who might like to make mischief, and there were plenty.

"Well, old boy, you had better think of some novel ways to say nothing because the hordes are about to descend." Dalmere motioned towards a group of young men coming towards them. They were already smirking and jeering within their little group before they had reason to do so.

Oliver groaned. He knew he would have to deal with this kind of situation but had foolishly hoped to avoid it.

"I say, Bellamy, just the man we wanted to see," said one fellow who was bleary-eyed and sweating profusely. "How are you and the Black Raven getting on? At this rate you'll be leg-shackled and spending her inheritance by the end of the month."

"Really? Why on earth would I want to do that, Bently?" Oliver said in reply.

"Why, for her fortune, of course. It's why she did it, don't you know, for the money?"

Oliver decided he didn't like Bently.

"Leg-shackled to her? I'd rather think he doesn't want to wind up dead, like the last one," said Dalmere in mock horror.

"Dalmere, that accusation was never proven."

"If it was proven, Bellamy, she would have swung from the *Tyburn Tree*. Doesn't mean she didn't do it," said Lord Chalmers.

"Mind you," said a young man who Oliver had seen last night at his club, but whose name had escaped him. "I'd risk it for one night with her. I've never seen anything like those eyes before, makes me so hot I could fry eggs."

The men all laughed, all except Bellamy. For some reason he didn't find their banter at all funny.

"I have nothing to fear from the Countess of Blackhurst I assure you, gentlemen, though your concern is touching."

The others all snorted, coughed, and laughed in their amusement. He, on the other hand, had had enough of amusing them. "Excuse me, gentlemen, but I believe I need to see if the

Black Raven is sharpening her dagger correctly."

Their laughter followed him through the crowded room. *They are all simpletons,* he thought to himself and then stopped. Yesterday, he would have been laughing along with them. This thought did not sit well at all considering his dislike for the woman. He looked around the ballroom again. *Now, where is she?*

"WELL, ISN'T THIS is a *very* pretty picture of a *very* naughty little countess?"

Lisbeth's heart froze at the sound of Bellamy's voice behind her. How had he found her? She turned slightly from her position on her hands and knees, where she had been searching for a key or a hidden panel to Wainwright's desk. Didn't they all have hidden panels? The quick glance over her shoulder confirmed his presence, and the arrogant look on his handsome face as he leaned against the doorframe with his arms crossed over his chest and one brow raised nearly to his hairline made her groan. She closed her eyes. This could not be happening to her. The man was a veritable homing pigeon.

"What are you doing here?" she asked.

"Looking for my mistress, actually," he replied casually. He stepped farther into Wainwright's study, looked around, and tested the top of the nearest table for dust, before turning his attention back to her.

"Well, she isn't here, is she?" Lisbeth hotly retorted, sitting up and absently checking her hair. She tried to convey she wasn't the least bit flustered by his having found her. By the look on his face she hadn't succeeded. She would like to wipe the grin right off his face but there were no fire pokers on hand.

"*Au contraire,* my dear, she is right where she ought *not* to be."

It took a few seconds for her to realize to whom he was referring. "What? Me? No!" She put her hands on her hips. "What have you been saying, Bellamy?"

"*I* haven't had to say anything," he said as he pushed away from the doorframe and walked into the room. "They all presume it. You're a widow, I'm an unattached man, and I am bandying you around town on my arm. What did you imagine they would think? We are whist partners?"

Lisbeth hadn't thought about it. She was astonished she even cared what those people downstairs thought of her or her arrangement with Bellamy. If anything it made things more believable, but it also made her feel distinctly at his mercy, a feeling that was definitely uncomfortable. Of course he hadn't expected her to answer his last question. He was now hooking one hip on Wainwright's desk and looking down at her.

"What exactly are you doing in here? Do you have a rendez-vous with Wainwright?" He frowned. "No, that would be inconceivable. If not, why are you sniffing about in his... drawers?"

"I am not sniffing his dra... anything!" she retorted. "And, why would it be inconceivable? If I did have a rendezvous with him or any other man, it would be none of your business." She turned away so he would not see her blush and pretended to be looking for something on the floor. This was humiliating. Of all the positions he had to find her in this one. More ridiculous was she was still pretending to have some dignity left. She sat back on her heels, which was the most she could do with her skirts restricting her movements.

"Oh, I see," he said, picking up a paperweight from Wain-wright's desk and examining it. "Who is it, then?"

"Who is who, Bellamy?"

"The man you are meeting."

"I'm not meeting anyone, you idiot!"

"Have you hurt your ankle then?" he asked in a casual tone, dismissing her nasty comment.

"No, I have not hurt my ankle, though I hardly see what that has to do with anything."

"Then I can only assume you make a habit of getting about on your hands and knees. You know you really should have warned me, Countess. One could get the wrong idea when one is presented with such a view."

"Oh! For Heaven's sake! I am simply stuck by my skirt."

He smiled, stood, and held out his hand. "Then let me lend you assistance. I would hate to have you tear such a lovely gown."

She shook off his hand. "You really are intolerable, do you know that?"

He looked at his hand to see what had been so distasteful to her then let it fall back onto his thigh. His very impressive thigh. Thighs. Right at her eye level.

He looked down at her. "I thought you found me irresistibly charming?"

She lifted her gaze back up to his face, glad to be focusing on something other than his thighs. "Not in the least."

"Then I will simply have to try harder," he said with a chuckle as he hauled her up by the shoulders and against his massive chest which Lisbeth imagined would be what it would be like to slam into a warm, and not bad-smelling, cliff face.

Damn the man. She immediately tried to put space between them by turning her back on him and crossing her arms over her chest. "Go away, Bellamy."

He ignored her as usual.

"Do you realize you have the most beautiful neck? These little curls back here are very fetching, indeed. They are like little gates guarding the treasure beneath."

"Oh, please!" Lisbeth rolled her eyes but his whispered words and hot breath had sent sparks down her spine. Confused, she went to turn towards him to give him a good push in the chest, so she could storm out, but the warm cliff was in her way.

"Shh!" he said, stopping her. "Why don't you try being quiet for a change." He turned her back around towards the desk and for some unfathomable reason she let him.

He leaned in close behind her and spoke into her ear again. "You put both of us in a devilish position when you scamper off to play treasure hunt." His voice was deep and seemed to vibrate through her whole body in quite an unexpectedly pleasant way. "Especially, in the middle of a ball containing over a hundred people. All of whom are waiting for you to do something... Raven-ish. Disappearing was not wise."

She closed her eyes for a moment as sensation tingled from her toes right to the top of her head. She wanted to tell him to go to the devil, to leave her be, that she had changed her mind and would find some other way to find her husband's killer. Although she knew there was no other way. All her nerves were singing, trying to tell her danger was near but her traitorous legs were frozen to the spot as his fingers caressed her bare neck and shoulders and her voice caught in her throat.

"Perhaps we should return then," she finally choked out, her voice just above a whisper.

"Perhaps you should just tell me what it is you are looking for?"

Lisbeth, still facing away from him, placed her hands on the large mahogany desk, as her legs wobbled. She could not tell him. He wasn't a man who could be trusted, yet she would have to tell him something.

"I thought I had lost my ear bob." Willing her legs not to desert her, she focused on the ghastly deer head mounted on the wall.

"On the floor, in Wainwright's study?"

She looked sharply over her shoulder at him. "No, Bellamy, in the Tower of London. Of course, here, you lack-wit."

He smiled as one of his fingers tugged on one of her curls. She was seriously starting to think he actually liked her to call him names. She looked helplessly at her reticule on the far end of the large desk.

"All right, Countess, why were you in here in the first place?" He was tracing the edge of the back of her gown where it dipped low.

She shivered again and hoped to God he did not notice. "I was looking for the withdrawing room and I got... lost. I was about to return when I realized my earring was gone."

"How unfortunate. Let me help you find it. My eyesight is exceptional."

Tiny sparks of awareness erupted all over her body. She panicked, felt hemmed in by the desk, her lie, and his body. "No, it really doesn't matter. Let's return to the ball."

"Countess." His voice was even but charged with anger now. "I can plainly see you are in possession of both your ears *and* their accessories." Just for good measure he flicked both of her earrings with his fingers. He turned her now so they were facing one another, their lips mere inches away, his eyes intense and searching. "I do not like being lied to and yet I get the distinct impression you have not told me a single truth since I met you."

She went to speak but he put his finger to her lips. She froze, not sure what he would do next or why her lips were tingling. Would he hit her or kiss her? She closed her eyes, waiting, expecting. All she could hear was the beating of her heart and the rushing of her blood in her ears, but nothing happened. She slowly opened her eyes to find him frowning.

"We will discuss it in the carriage and it had better be good... and the truth."

She wanted to tell him hell would freeze over before she would give in to his demands. She looked up at him, her best scowl between her brows. His frown was far more effective. His eyes were more like dark bitter chocolate now and she knew then and there with a sinking heart she would have to tell him the truth or at least some of it and another lie would simply not do. Unless... it was a really, really good one! She nodded her acquiescence and he studied her features.

"Good. There is just one thing I must do before we leave—"

His lips descended so quickly on hers there was no time for her to react rationally.

He did not crush her in his arms but held her softly with one arm while the backs of his fingers on the other hand skimmed her cheek. She just stood there, letting him kiss her. What was wrong with her?

His lips danced lightly over hers, causing all sorts of chaos to invade her body. Shock was the least of her worries. She had not been kissed in such a long time and certainly not like this. She had forgotten how potent a kiss could be, how the simple act of pressing lips together could result in such a dangerous force of feeling. Her heart lurched and plunged inside her chest, causing her blood to thrum so violently through her veins it was almost painful.

Oh, how she wanted to kiss him back and that was the real shock. After her husband, she had thought she could live without the touch of a man for the rest of her life and happily so. Her body did not completely agree, it seemed.

She fisted her hands in her skirts, trying desperately to cling to something stable, something real. She failed and her legs sagged, but wedged between Wainwright's desk and Bellamy's chest meant she remained standing despite the desertion of her lower limbs.

Unexpectedly, his kiss became more ardent, persistent, as his hands brought her forward and fully against him before caressing her back, his large palms heating her flesh in their wake. She had to resist him, but it was getting harder by the second.

She tried to remember how annoying he was, how arrogant and male he was, but it didn't help at all. Now all she could think about was how male he was, how hard and strong his body was against hers and how much she… liked it.

She was surprised her body was responding at all. It had always closed off whenever her husband had forced his way into her bed. Numbing herself was the only way she had known how to endure. Numb was not how she was feeling now. Every nerve ending was fully functioning and shooting pleasure in all directions.

It wasn't fair. She could picture clearly how his face changed to boyish when he smiled. Her hands unclenched, itched. Her fingers stretched and fisted spasmodically in her skirt as she fought to keep control of her traitorous body. She could not let him know how he was affecting her. She could not lose control; it would destroy her and her plans for any kind of future.

Finally he lifted his head and gave her a devastating grin. It was obvious he was immensely pleased with himself and his handy work.

Lisbeth touched her lips which were now throbbing and longing to be kissed again. She gathered her anger and pushed him in the chest. "Damn you, Bellamy! How dare you… kiss me!"

His smile never altered. "'Twas a chore but, I had little choice; it had to be done."

"Was it another one of your wagers, Bellamy?" She pushed him aside, fighting for some air.

"What use would it have been with no witnesses?" He examined the fingernails of his hand while replying with, "The thing is, if we returned downstairs looking like we had spent our time looking for fictitious ear bobs there would be hell to pay and questions asked, I assure you. This way, with you looking like you have been thoroughly kissed, everyone will understand precisely what they think we have been doing. Do you see?"

No, she did not see! She was so angry she could see nothing but a haze of red before her. "Don't. Ever. Do. That. Again," she warned, poking him in the chest with her forefinger with every word. She grabbed her reticule and stormed from the room.

Bellamy laughed and brought his other hand from behind his back. He looked at her notebook in his palm. Just a little longer and he would have had her pistol too. He wasn't too worried; he'd have it before the night was through. He flipped open the notebook and read the names on the list.

CHAPTER FIVE

"I THINK YOU had better tell me everything," Oliver said. He had just consumed three long eye-watering swallows of brandy from a flask he had hidden under the seat of his carriage. He took another swallow and looked at the woman who sat so stiffly in the seat opposite him.

He was still reeling from the kiss and her reaction to him. He had expected her to slap him silly, shoot him, skewer him with one of her hairpins, or all three. The fact she'd just stood there and let him kiss her was not what he had expected, but then he found she did nothing he expected.

Her expression when he had lifted his head from their kiss had shocked him. For the sheerest of moments something in her eyes had given him pause. Had he upset her? Certainly. He hadn't been lying when he said they needed a reason to be away from the ballroom for so long, but the look she had given him had been something else entirely. Her lovely, bejeweled eyes had held what he thought to be bewildered wonderment and damn if he had imagined a touch of desire there too. Unfortunately, it had been so fleeting he could not be sure. Looking at her now, he must have been mistaken. She looked as calm and cool as she always did.

He raised a brow. "Well, Countess?"

Folding her hands in her lap, she pinned him with those burning sapphire eyes. "What would you like to know?"

"How about the truth?"

"Ah, the truth. About what?"

"Come, let us not keep playing these games. What were you doing in Wainwright's private chambers?"

"Looking for something, obviously." Lady Blackhurst smoothed her skirts and then clasped her hands lightly on her reticule and returned his assessing look.

Oliver smiled. "Obviously," he drawled. "What was it you were looking for, exactly?" He sat slightly forward so he had a better view of her face in the dim light of the carriage.

This would be a lot easier if she were not so beguiling. The seriousness of her features, which he found charming but at the same time irritating, made him want to laugh at the perverse nature of his very thoughts as they were surprisingly gentleman-like. He most certainly did not want to get involved with this fallen angel even as his lips were desperate to find hers again.

He couldn't trust her, that much was clear, but for some insane reason he wanted her to trust him. There was definitely something going on in her pretty little head and he was determined to get some answers.

Sighing dramatically, she said, "Oh, Bellamy, can a lady have no secrets?"

He laughed and shook his head. "Lady Blackhurst, you cannot expect me to play the doting beau while you disappear to rifle through our host's—"

"Things?"

"Exactly! Now, if you please, what are your purposes for wanting to return to the *ton* in such a fashion?"

Lisbeth pondered her answer. There was little to excuse her rifling, as he had put it, but she could hardly tell him she was on the hunt for her husband's killer. He was, after all, a man who would probably do just about anything for money. A man like Bellamy could not be trusted with a cup of tea let alone her whole plan for finding out what had truly happened to Nathaniel that fateful morning.

"The truth, Bellamy, is it has been two years since my husband's death and, well, it was time I rejoined life. I have been a virtual prisoner in my home for nearly the whole time. I do not really have any friends or... or... family who are willing to receive me and..."

She had not meant to choke up and she swallowed hard to contain the lump in her throat before it formed into tears. She had not realized that to place her cards, even if only a few strategic ones, on the table would be quite so hard.

Lisbeth could feel him looking at her, his eyes upon her. What did he think he would see? There was so little left of her that if he looked too hard he may see right through her altogether. Like a ghost shimmering but of no substance. If only she *could* turn to smoke and disappear.

His body was suddenly next to hers. She shuffled back in her seat in shock and gasped as he took her hand. She snatched it back and stared hard at him, warning him to keep his distance.

She couldn't bear it. "No! Don't you dare pity me," she said with a resolve which took more out of her than he would ever know. "I may be a friendless wretch but I am determined, you see, to hold my head up high no matter what they say, or how often they whisper behind their fans. I will no longer have them decide on my guilt or innocence based purely on gossip."

"But have they not already condemned you... despite a trial which found you not guilty?" He was searching her face, and she wished he would see the bleak emptiness within and leave her be.

A silence fell over them, whereupon Lisbeth tried to keep her tears at bay and Bellamy seemed determined to see them. It made her feel sick. She wanted nothing more than to go home, curl up in a ball of misery, and forget everything and everyone. She'd done it once before. It hadn't helped her then and she doubted it would help now, but it was tempting. So tempting.

Keep it together, Lisbeth, she said to herself.

"The *ton* can be cruel," he said, looking at her hands as they lay on her lap. "However, it doesn't explain Wainwright's study," he went on.

She took her chance. "Oh, I quite agree."

He looked up and frowned. Suspicious. "You agree?"

"Oh yes, Wainwright's study is terribly stuffy. What can he have been thinking? There are simply not enough windows and his desk is awkwardly situated."

"Countess." Oliver raked his fingers through his hair.

"Yes, I know. Some people just have no understanding on the proper placement of furniture and the importance of light in proportion to… what are you doing? Give me that!"

She was trying to snatch the flask away from his lips but he'd be buggered if he was going to give it up. He needed fortification and lots of it if he was going to get through *this* night. Could the woman be any more infuriating?

She pursed her lips and placed her hands on her hips. "I won't have it, Bellamy."

He chuckled. "Of course you won't, because *I'm* having it."

"Give it to me," she said, holding her hand out like he was some errant child caught with a sweet stolen from the kitchen.

"I'd be happy to, Countess." He put his hand out in a similar gesture. "In exchange for the pistol."

She snatched her hand back. "No!"

"What will make you hand it over?"

"Death!"

He laughed. "Hmm. This conveyance may be bleeding me dry, but I am loath to bloody it for real."

"Then you shall have to learn to live without it."

"The carriage? Oh, good, because frankly—"

She rolled her eyes and replied, "The pistol, you dolt."

He sighed. "It seems we are at an impasse then. Although, I reluctantly confess you'll be getting the better deal." *She wanted to play games? Well, he could play them too.*

She looked perplexed for a moment. "Oh? How so?"

"If you give me the pistol and I give you the brandy, then both of us would be spared the embarrassment of you being

accused a *second time* of shooting someone. As for my brandy…"
He thought of the small notebook in his jacket pocket. The list of
names. Men's names. Influential men of the *ton*, all. "It would
perhaps loosen you up enough to act in a more rational manner
and once and for all tell me the truth about your little plan for
revenge against the *ton*."

"Don't be ridiculous," she said, waving her hand in a dismissive gesture.

"What were you planning? Blackmail? Or were you just going
to play with their minds?" For the first time tonight he had the
upper hand, and he was not going to give it back to her.

"You're delusional," she scoffed. "The pistol will remain in
my possession as will the brandy, thank you." She put her hand
out again. "To be drunk will only make you look like a fool."

He lifted the flask again.

"Let me warn you now, Bellamy, just so we know where we
both stand, if you think to betray me, in any way, at any time, I
will make sure everyone knows of your financial… position."

His smile fell from his face so rapidly Lisbeth clutched the
seat for safety. Her hand went quickly to the shape of her pistol in
her reticule and firmed around it.

What did she truly think he would do, laugh? Well, yes, she
thought he might, but of course, he didn't. The fact she knew of
his financial difficulties had certainly hit a raw nerve. A raw nerve
indeed.

"Ah, it is to be blackmail then. Are you really trying to threat-
en me, Countess? If you are, you had better do better than that."
His voice was fierce and dark and his features matched, making
her regret having played such a dangerous card.

She lifted her chin high. "Of course not. Unless… you leave
me no other choice."

He sat back then and studied her for a moment. "What do
you want from me, Lady Blackhurst?"

"I told you last night."

"Last night I was drunk, madam. You took advantage of my

inebriation then, but now I am in full control of my mind, and I want there to be no confusion between us as to what we expect of each other." He took hold of her elbow to guarantee her attention, and she gasped. "You need me," he went on. "Otherwise you would have simply hired some fool to go digging in Wainwright's study and stayed at home in your library reading *Lady Radcliff's* works."

He hauled her closer so there was no way she could ignore him. "How you found out about my financial *difficulties* when even my closest friends have no idea also intrigues me."

Lisbeth bit down on her lip to stop from crying out. He was angry. It was to be expected; she had provoked him, after all.

She waited for it, but no fist connected nor was she slammed against the side of the carriage. No hand clamped around her throat or slapped her so hard her neck would feel like it had snapped off its moorings. What was he waiting for?

She felt a scream building but knew it would do her no good. No good at all. It was her fault, all her fault! She had brought herself to this end. She waited, her eyes shut tight, for her punishment for surely it was coming. She kept her eyes closed and despite her resolve to stay silent through what was to come, a whimper escaped.

Oliver watched the play of emotions which traveled across her face. Terror was the last thing he thought he would see, not from her. She looked like she was waiting for him to strike her. What kind of man did she think he was? He would never hit a woman. He had wanted to make it clear he would not be manipulated, not terrorize her.

He released her.

Was this all some kind of act? Surely, she was not so talented? He could feel her fear vibrating all around him. He knew fear like this, had lived it. No one should have to feel like this, let alone a woman.

"Countess," he said his tone soft now. "There is no need for all these dramatics. Just tell me."

"How can I tell you?" she bit out, opening her eyes and pinning him with a painful glare. "You, who would sell me up the river as soon as the price was right. You, who have no idea of what it is to suffer a false accusation, to live with a guilt which is not yours, day after day! You, who have not been given a name which breeds fear and loathing everywhere you go! A name which makes little children fear you will peck out their eyes if they do not eat their peas!"

Her voice was near hysterical and Oliver sat, stunned. How was he to react to that? He realized his mouth was open and shut it. Part of him sympathized with her plight and had she been any other woman he may have offered her some kind of comfort. While the other part was a little upset she had such a low opinion of him. But how could she have otherwise? Last night had been a disgraceful display of stupidity. Yes, he needed money, and yes, he had agreed to the damn wager, and yes, he was supposed to be reporting on her to Ashton, but he was not as amoral as she seemed to think. Sell her up the river, indeed!

She was right, though; he had no idea what it was like to be accused of a crime he didn't commit. What was he supposed to do now? If he were her and was innocent of such a crime he would stop at nothing to prove his innocence.

Fireworks went off in his brain like *Guy Fawkes Night* as he realized at last what was going on here. She was trying to find out who killed her husband. Hence the disappearing act, the snooping around in Wainwright's study, the notebook, and even the pistol. He fell back against the swabs and stifled a groan.

Dawn was so very bright after such a dark night.

He lifted her chin and spoke softly and directly to her. Those eyes of hers were huge with uncertainty. "Despite what you think of me, you chose me for a reason. If you are truly innocent, then I will help you find out who killed your husband."

She gaped at him. Her disbelief etched in her every feature confirmed he had guessed right.

Well, damn me! His intuition had not abandoned him completely it seemed. This changed the game considerably.

"Shall we start over?" he offered. "This time we will be honest with each other, agreed?"

Lisbeth stared at him; she couldn't believe it. Doom fell on her like a lead blanket. It was too late to deny it. The shock was written all over her face. If he had figured her out so quickly, would others also guess so easily? She closed her mouth and looked at his large hand that he had offered her. He had strong-looking fingers. Fingers with character—if such a thing could be said of fingers. Little nicks and scars decorated them, and she wondered briefly how he had come across so many. Lisbeth looked up from his hands.

She had little choice in the matter now. She had to trust him. She just hoped she was doing the right thing. Tentatively, she put her hand in his. He brought it to his lips and brushed them over her knuckles. Warmth spread up her arm and rested on her cheeks. Her eyes swelled and she blinked furiously. She would not weaken, not now, not in front of him.

"I am afraid I cannot accept your kind offer, Bellamy."

"I don't know how you will be able to stop me."

"This is none of your concern. *I* am none of your concern. I appreciate your offer, I do, but I will not allow you to be put in danger on my account."

"Glad to hear it, Countess, but I am afraid my mind is made up. I am stubborn like that, you know."

"Foolhardy, more like."

He shrugged his shoulders. "Perhaps, but understand this, I can no more let you snoop around strange men's… rooms than I could let my poor Aunt Petunia go off to far exotic India with nothing but a miniature of *Mad King George* in her pocket."

"How chivalrous of you, Bellamy. I'm impressed, really, but I'm not your Aunt Petunia. If you are going to help me, you will have to remain out of the way. You are to be my escort not my protector. I made it quite clear last night and do so again now."

"Hmm yes, as renowned as I am for my gallant nature—and

perhaps because I am particularly attached to my head and it to my shoulders, I cannot let you conduct some misguided attempt at an investigation without me to protect your far prettier neck."

"I will not let you walk all over me, Bellamy. This is too important to me. I will defend myself with whatever information I have at my disposal, you *must* know this. I will not hesitate to use the information I have on you, should you betray me."

He smiled. A charming half smile. She hated when he did that. Hated what it did to her. How it made her heart skip a beat. She didn't have time right now to analyze what those tingling sensations meant only that it happened every time he smiled at her.

He inclined his head in acceptance. Although, she knew he would not play by her rules.

"I wouldn't expect any less from the Black Raven," he said.

Lisbeth raised a brow. Perhaps he did understand, a little. Was it enough, though? "Then *you* had better eat your peas, Lord Bellamy."

CHAPTER SIX

THE COUNTESS OF Blackhurst was the kind of woman who made a sane man run as fast as his legs, or better yet a horse, could take him. And yet, here he was. He already knew he naturally gravitated towards dangerous situations and now, apparently, to dangerous women. This was not something he would brag about at his club.

The countess was to be his new mission, but he would wager he would be far safer on a battlefield than in her company. Oliver's main worry was how to keep her hands out of places they shouldn't be. He had no wish to see her swinging from a gibbet or walking a gangplank in irons bound for New South Wales.

Oliver glanced over at the Black Raven. What was he to do with her? How was he to handle a potential powder keg of doubtful substance? The last thing he could afford was for this all to blow up in his face.

He crossed his arms over his chest. "So, what are you looking for, a bloody trail? A confession written in ancient Greek? The murder weapon?"

She gave him an impatient sigh. "Must you be so tiresome? I suspect the weapon has been sold ten times over by now or is at least at the bottom of the Thames. I am at this time only trying to confirm association. If I can prove my husband had business dealings with certain people, I will put them on a short list of suspects."

"Ah, so the list in your notebook is for suspicious persons?"

The disbelieving look she gave him was enchanting. She began frantically rummaging around in her small bag, her eyes never leaving his.

He sat back, happy. "Yes, I have it." He answered the unspoken question in her eyes. The kiss to get it had been worth it in so many ways. He pulled it out of his pocket and handed it back to her. "You have lovely penmanship, by the way."

She snatched it back and held it to her chest. "How did you steal it from me?"

"Steal? That is rather harsh. I simply borrowed it."

"You took it without my permission, therefore it is stealing."

"I had every intention of giving it back, therefore I borrowed it."

"But how?"

"I have very skillful fingers," he confessed with a smile. "I have many other skills as well, which you may find… beneficial."

She rewarded him with a most terrifying scowl.

"To the investigation, of course," he added.

He loved that his having obtained the notebook from right under her nose shocked her. He loved that she was shoving the notebook back in her little bag with such force that he could imagine she was picturing the notebook as his head.

"Do not take my notebook from my reticule again."

He grinned. "You have my word."

She did not smile back. "Why am I still not convinced?"

"Ouch! Impugning my honor? That's low."

"Can we not concentrate on the matter at hand, please?"

"Fine. I would think Blackhurst was closed-lipped on the fact he was in trade," Oliver said matter-of-factly.

Her head shot up. "He was not *in* trade," she insisted. "He only invested with those who were and according to my sources he sometimes invited others to participate. It is not like he would be the first gentleman to do so."

"How charitable of him to want to share the wealth," he said in a sarcastic tone, thinking of his brother. "Nevertheless, these others would not have been eager to make their *participation* general knowledge."

She nodded. "You understand the difficulties I am up against. I have to be careful what I do and how I gain my information. Someone here in London seems to be willing to jeopardize their own reputation to ruin mine, continuously. I have no idea where the gossip and rumors come from. I would have thought this whole business extremely dull scandal broth by now."

"Murder and money are two things that never become dull, I assure you, Countess."

"So it seems," she replied.

For a moment she looked tired, fatigued beyond what sleep could rectify. She had been battling her demons for years, he suspected, but she was determined not to show it.

"Are you sure Blackhurst was not in debt? Perhaps he owed at the tables or—"

"My husband rarely played games of chance and when he did he was usually successful. He was clever with numbers and had a good memory. I suspect there were not many who wished to play against him. He always said they held little challenge for him, in any case. He liked to gamble with much bigger stakes. As for debts, I can think of no reason why he would be. I have more money than I could ever spend in this lifetime or the next."

"Well, how nice that must be for you," he bit out between his teeth. Did she truly have no idea what her husband's investors lost? How his demise and the breakdown of the speculation had ruined lives, including Oliver's own? His indignant scowl was wasted, he saw, as she again began her ritual. A look at her pocket watch, her schedule, and then back to the watch before looking out the window of the carriage. He felt like flinging that damn watch out the window.

Lisbeth peered at her schedule. *This is all too much,* she thought. *I need to keep myself in control.* She knew what was on her schedule, of course, but it was the reassuring feeling of knowing what was going to happen next which kept her pulling it out of her reticule. It also gave her reason to avoid looking at Bellamy and his all-too-knowing eyes. She knew he was frustrated with her, and he had shown great restraint so far. That did not mean she meant to push him further, but she didn't want to share everything with him either. He already knew too much.

Now Bellamy knew of her plan, everything had changed. Men were used to taking control but this was her fight, no matter what sort of crusade Bellamy thought he was on. He could think himself heroic all he liked, but she had to maintain her course to truth and justice.

"He never spoke of his business affairs," she said now. "And I was rarely introduced to his friends. However, I do have my sources of information, as you now know."

"Indeed," Bellamy said. "Planned out, eh? Why does this not surprise me? I do have another question for you. Do I continue to commit to wagers regarding the Black Raven? Or do you intend to pay me in some *other* form?"

"You may continue to gather your wagers, sir. I am happy with our arrangement as it is. I gather you have a list of these wagers?" She was not desperate to see what stupidity had been made up but she would like to be prepared for the worst.

Bellamy smiled and sat back against the swabs, crossed his arms over his chest, and tapped at the breast pocket of his jacket.

"May I have it please?" She put out her hand.

"No. Are you not worried that some may find it peculiar if I am winning money off your reputation when you are my mistress?"

Her hand fell back to her lap, her expression incredulous. "I am not your mistress! I am not your anything." She tapped her pocket watch open, frowned, and then snapped it closed again in agitation. Why did she let him do this to her? He did it on purpose. He was tricky, manipulative, annoying, and she wished that he would not keep trying to challenge her authority.

"That can be easily amended, my dear. You need only give me the nod." Bellamy moved his arm across her shoulder but stopped when her pistol jabbed his ribs.

She shook with nervous energy. Lisbeth had tried to forget about the pistol but he was moving too close and she panicked. She wanted to give him the nod, all right, with something hard. He made her mad enough to scream but she must remain cool, detached, and in control. The Black Raven must keep playing her part.

"I need only pull the trigger to put a nasty hole in your lovely jacket and your list."

"You, madam, are a very difficult woman," he complained.

"Not difficult, Bellamy, just determined. You must keep your hands to yourself. I told you I will be leading this investigation; you are merely assisting. Is that understood?"

"Absolutely." What was wrong with him? He couldn't stop looking into the deep, inky depths of her eyes. He did not want to be involved with this woman and yet... confusion warred with desire while sanity seemed to sit back and laugh.

He wanted to take her in his arms and kiss all the stiffness out of her, and he had no doubt where that stiffness would end up. He also knew this woman held him in low esteem, somewhere under the coal boy, probably lower.

His mental meanderings needed to be reined in because while he was swimming about in her eyes and bemoaning his status she had slipped her hand into his jacket and retrieved his list.

A whisper of a smile passed over the corners of her lips as she tucked the list in her bodice and lowered her pistol.

"Cheeky minx." She was just getting him back for the notebook, he supposed. He looked at her bodice. Was he really feeling envious of a piece of paper? Oliver smiled to himself as he watched her looking entirely too pleased with herself. "You may think yourself the cleverest of thieves but it will do you little good."

"Don't be a bad sport, Bellamy. Ah, we are here. Shall we go in or do you wish to sulk for a moment?"

"Oh, no, let us go in. I am exceedingly excited by the prospect of gaining a headache."

"Do you not like music, Bellamy?"

She asked the question with such an innocent expression and yet he knew she was cheered by the prospect of torturing him.

"It isn't that I dislike music or singing. What I dislike is music played badly and singing which leaves one's ears near to bleeding. I despise caterwauling amateurs who do little but posture about playing a badly tuned violin like a two-year old." *I much prefer a good opera, where the singing is in tune and the girls are pretty.*

"I'm glad you will be enjoying yourself then."

He laughed, for what else could he do?

They were led into a large room which was decorated in rich golds and greens. Large French doors led to a conservatory and many of the various plants had been moved inside for the evening, their exotic blooms releasing a sweet honeyed spice into the air. An assortment of chairs and sofas were arranged around the room, at the end of which a small platform, just large enough for a handful of musicians and a singer, had been created. The musicians were already tuning up their instruments and Lady Costello looked panicked as to where to put the infamous Black Raven and her companion.

Lisbeth tried to ignore her hostess's stricken expression and informed her, "We will sit here."

Lady Costello appeared to nearly swoon with relief and no wonder; many of the women had their fans held up to their left ear indicating they did not want the notorious Black Raven sitting next to *them.*

A familiar pain invaded Lisbeth's body. A feeling one would think she would be able to control by now. In the ballroom earlier, crowded and overheated with bodies, she had been able to pretend they were not truly there, just a sea of people she would not focus on. Here, there were too few guests. She had let her guard down for just a moment and she had let their twitters creep in. Let their judgmental whispers penetrate her defenses, pressing and straining against the walls she had spent so many years building. She pressed back. She would not give in. She would not let them know how their actions affected her.

Their seats were aptly at the back of the room and as soon as the lights dimmed and the music began Lisbeth took out Bellamy's list of wagers. She scanned it, frowned, and then looked sideways at him.

"I can't read this," she said into his ear.

He smiled and closed his eyes. "I know."

"Bellamy!" she whispered in agitation. "Is this the real list?"

"Actually, it is a shameful and wicked list of all the things I'd like to—"

She elbowed him in the ribs. "Bellamy!"

He opened one eye and chuckled softly. "Yes, it is the real list."

She was perplexed, which made him look very smug, she saw. "Then why can't I read it? What language is it in? It isn't ancient Greek, is it?"

His lips lifted at the sides again. "All in good time, Countess, all in good time." He took a deep breath, and relaxed. "Remember," he muttered. "It is bad form to shoot someone while they are sleeping."

Lisbeth looked at him in disgust. "You are a wretched man," she said as she studied his face. He was so handsome, even in profile, and in this pose more boyish. She was tempted to brush a lock of hair away from his eyes. No! Had she learned nothing? This was all a game to him. He was not a child in need of care. Let him be. Ignore him. Pretend he is not there as he is so aptly pretending not to be here.

Now he knew why she was here, did she really need to keep him so tightly shackled? When he had arrived this evening looking so elegant and handsome she had not known what trials he would put her through. Her plan, although well thought out, was woefully inadequate when it came to the complications and consternations one Lord Bellamy would put upon her. He was too much of everything, and she never knew what she would be feeling from one minute to the next. It was like being blindfolded, spun around, and then left to stumble about unsure of one's footing or direction.

"What are you doing?" she asked him a minute later when he continued to keep his position, but all she got in response was a soft snore.

He was asleep? How typical!

Brow furrowed, she looked at the list again. It looked like chicken scratchings with a few pretty drawings thrown in for good measure. Lisbeth glanced at her sleeping escort and shook her head. She thought she had been so clever in gaining the list but now it looked as though the joke was on her. He had let her have it because he knew she wouldn't be able to read it anyway. "Impossible man!"

Lisbeth looked his way again in her peripheral vision. She just wanted to make sure he wasn't in danger of sliding off his chair. He seemed so at peace with himself. She envied him for his ability to sleep in a room full of people and appear not to have a single qualm about it.

He sighed and shifted a little and she focused on his eyelashes, so ludicrously long for a man. It seemed so unfair, both his eyelashes and his slumber. She wanted so badly to be able to sleep with pleasant dreams and happy recollections, but sleep eluded her. All she had were dark corners and shadows, and a life which seemed more like a burden than a gift.

Tucking the useless list into her reticule, she turned her attention to the small platform where the soloist was singing her aria. It had been so long since she'd had the opportunity to enjoy music. She wanted to let it wash over her in pleasant waves of bliss, but she could not. She looked at the heads of the women who had been so cruel to her earlier. She did not deserve to be treated like this. A court had proclaimed her innocent and yet it seemed that gossip was far more convincing than law. It was clear that until she had proven her innocence by finding the real killer she would not be able to enjoy even the simplest of joys.

Bellamy murmured something beside her. She had valiantly tried to concentrate on the performance, but she kept searching out his sleeping form. It would have served him right if he had fallen off his chair. On more than one occasion he had sighed and shifted in his seat, causing her to look at other parts of him. Parts she definitely should not have been looking at. She should not care one whit he had powerful-looking thighs or his legs seemed to stretch a considerable length ending in incredibly large shoes or that about the fall of his trousers it seemed there was hardly enough room for what lay beneath. She'd felt heat rise from her throat to her cheeks and had fanned herself furiously, vowing never to look at him again. After another guilty look she realized how ridiculous her first vow had been and amended it to, *not look at him again until the performance was over.* She failed miserably at that vow too. By the end of the performance her sinful mind had memorized every inch of him.

What was she doing to herself? As much as he was here beside her, she knew she was very much on her own. She was used to loneliness. It was a cloak she wore daily. Now, being among people again, she felt it wrap around her like swaddling. Constricting, choking and contracting around her.

Oliver felt Lisbeth nudge him awake with her fan and reluctantly opened one eye. He quickly assessed his position and remembering where he was, grinned sheepishly, straightened in his chair, and joined in the clapping when the soloist had finished.

Ironically, he wished the performance had gone on a little longer for he was having the best kind of dream. The fact Lady Blackhurst had been the subject was perhaps not as surprising as it should be. Hadn't she been just about to shoot him only an hour or so ago? His lips twisted and he looked briefly towards the countess. She was fussing with her small reticule, no doubt taking inventory of all her various time pieces, notebooks, and firearms. He really wouldn't be surprised if she were to pull out a vial of arsenic. It had been that kind of evening, and it was far from over. What she didn't know was he quite fancied a challenge. Part of him wanted her to pull her pistol on him one more time and give him an excuse to set her straight about a few things.

As if sensing his eyes upon her, she turned her head slightly and raised one fine dark brow. He smiled and resumed, perhaps a little too enthusiastically, his clapping.

"She was brilliant," he said, nodding at the others around them who were all commenting to each other on the singer's performance.

"The last singer was a man, and I hardly think *you* are qualified to comment," she said, her tone wry, as they stood up and followed the others to the late supper which was being served in another room.

"Not true. That was one of the best musical nights I have slept through this season."

"Oh, for heaven's sake." She shook her head.

He laughed as he continued to steer her towards the refreshments. "You'll soon get used to me, Countess. You might even get to like me."

"But I don't want to like you, Bellamy," she replied, to put him in his place. Drat the man, he didn't even blink at her insult.

"Ah, but you will, my dear. You will."

His dark eyes sparkled, and his teeth gleamed in the candlelight. She wanted to kick him for being so… him. Her reactions to him were strange and varied. One moment she felt safe with him and the next she was all too aware of him and the danger he presented to her. The rest of the time she just wanted to push him off a cliff.

She watched as he moved about the room. He was a marvel to her really, such a nicely put together man. It surprised her more than she was willing to confess. Why wasn't she repulsed by his masculinity? Physical exertions were not new to him by the muscular look of his arms and the strong and sturdy breadth of his shoulders. If only he were not so lackadaisical in his habits and have such a fondness for wastrel gambling.

Oliver casually discussed the topics of the day with the other guests, usually Napoleon's exile or the latest exploit of the Prince Regent. It paid to be prepared with a standard comment or two. The unusual weather this year was a topic which was wearing thin. Yes, it was cold, terrible winds, chill one to the bone, bad for the crops, Mother Nature gone mad... He knew the weather should concern him more considering he was a landowner now. He just wanted to get through the next few weeks before having to deal with crops and cattle and the fickleness of the weather. With a heavy sigh he stuffed two lobster patties into his mouth and scanned the room.

He knew she was watching him. What was she planning with those furtive looks? He had displeased her, he knew, with his nap, not to mention his list. It was in code and although he could imagine her and her pinch-faced butler trying to decipher it until dawn, if all of Napoleon's army had not been able to crack it, he doubted she would. It was better she did not know the contents of the list at any rate.

Oliver made for his host, Lord Costello. He wanted to see if he could get anything interesting out of the man. Oliver had met him a couple of times at White's, but they never had really spent much time in discussion.

"Bellamy, have to say I am mildly surprised to see you here. Thought these kinds of entertainments not quite your thing," Costello said when Oliver presented himself.

"It's true, a musical night is not my first choice for sources of entertainment, but my companion wished to come and who am I to deny her anything," Oliver replied, winking.

"Indeed," Costello commented, frowning slightly.

"I believe you were acquainted with her late husband, were you not?" His host being a short stout little man meant Oliver had to stoop over so as not to appear to be talking to the person behind him. Not to mention the glare—this was coming off Costello's balding head from the grand chandelier above them.

Oliver absently patted his hair in appreciation of its staying power.

Costello eyed him for a moment, his brows knitting together. "I knew him," he replied, looking over to where the Black Raven and his wife seemed to be having a rather awkward conversation.

"Never met the man, myself. What was he like?" Oliver asked.

He noted that Costello was laboring over his answer. Finally, he came up with, "He was… tall."

Oliver wanted to laugh. Anybody would seem tall when you were Lord Costello. "Really? Tall, you say? Not very helpful. Could you try a bit harder?"

"Do you really want to know?"

"Yes, of course, makes it easier to compete when one knows his adversary," Oliver said, taking a sip of his drink and making a face. *Punch, vile stuff.* Thankfully his host did not see. He quickly tipped the offending liquid into the plant next to him. The poor thing was liable to be withered by morning, but better it than him.

"But the man's dead, Bellamy!" Costello explained.

"Apparently so," Oliver replied. He looked around him, already bored with the way the conversation was going. "Buried and everything, I heard."

Costello gave a little snort and after a moment's contemplation finally said something worth listening to. "He was a shrewd one, though. Blackhurst, I mean. He knew how to make gold out of nothing at all."

Oliver raised a brow. "I had not realized he was so inventive," he said with a smile. "Is it too much to hope he has passed on his secrets to his wife?"

Costello snorted again. "Doubt it, but by God he knew how to make money." He lowered his voice considerably and Oliver was forced to bend closer to hear. "I'd invested with him a few times and always thought him a strange sort of fellow but sharp as a tack when it came to money, until the last time." Costello took a large swallow of his drink.

"The last time?" Oliver prodded gently.

"When he was killed, the scheme went belly up, too, but I'm sure you already knew that. Cost me a fortune, he did, I was luckier than most. I didn't invest everything I owned, although some did and lost it all. It was not a pleasant time for any of us."

His tone was bitter, and Oliver raised a brow in interest. "These other investors, the ones who lost everything, what happened to them?"

Costello shrugged. "Wakehurst blew his brains out, Bristol took a bath with a bottle of brandy and his shaving razor, Simons fled to the Continent or the Americas, I cannot remember which. Your brother jumped a fence for no apparent reason. Is that what you wanted to hear?"

Oliver narrowed his eyes on the little man. He wanted to put his hands around his neck and shake him, a lot. "You think my brother committed suicide, Costello?"

"I didn't say that; you just asked me what happened to them, and I've told you."

"You and those still with us did not go to such extremes."

"Some of us were lucky enough to be able to go on, but it wasn't easy. Everyone was shocked and angry and wanted answers. Answers that to this day we have not found out."

Costello didn't say any more, so Oliver let it drop.

Oliver caught Costello flicking his glance towards Lisbeth. Oliver looked up and watched her too. It was an enjoyable scene. "How is it, then, Lady Blackhurst survived any financial hardships?"

"Told you, Blackhurst was shrewd, made sure everything was in her name, or perhaps it was she who insisted it be so. Some of us tried to get back our deposit but Lady Blackhurst would not take any submission. It didn't help her cause I can assure you. Some say she did it, you know."

"Did what?" He asked the question even though he knew what the answer would be.

"Killed him for his money or had him killed!" Costello whispered. "Not that I think that, of course, but one never knows with women." Costello took a sip of his drink and turned his eyes away from Oliver.

It seemed he had said more than he had wanted. It was nearly enough for Oliver. "Yes, women are such strange creatures, but such beautiful ones too; however are we to resist them?" Oliver watched the countess as she excused herself and made her way towards him.

"I agree and none more so than her. Enjoy yourself, Bellamy, but a word of warning, be watchful. There's many a deadly weapon concealed in a pretty case," Costello said before moving on to his next guest.

Oliver was still frowning when Lisbeth reached him and he was startled when she put her hand on his sleeve and said, "It's time to go."

CHAPTER SEVEN

D UES MUST BE paid when one has only one living relative, especially when that one relative is a woman of significant age and health.

Dear Aunt Petunia.

His aunt's long-suffering companion, Mrs. Turner, greeted Oliver in the hall. "Lady Whitely says she is dying, my lord. The doctor assures me she is not, but she is convinced. She insisted that you come here straight away."

Oliver nodded and handed his hat and gloves to his aunt's butler and followed Mrs. Turner down the hall. "I'm relieved to hear that her health is not as dire as she has imagined. I am so glad you are here to watch over her. Although I know she can be trying at times," he said in a good-natured tone.

She smiled. "It is an honor, sir. You know I have been her companion for near on twenty years. I am quite used to her ways."

Mrs. Turner was a small woman, with light silver-streaked hair and intelligent hazel eyes. Oliver liked her very much, always had.

"In any case I would make it known to you that I am very grateful to you."

"Thank you, my lord." She blushed.

Oliver patted her hand as he left her in the hall and entered his aunt's dimly lit parlor to be immediately set upon by three small yapping fur balls who took to jumping up on his legs. He sighed with the knowledge that his boots would be all but ruined by the dogs' small claws.

"Ah, Bellamy," his aunt called from her chair by the fire. "You have finally come to me. Must I be on death's door for you to visit?"

He bowed and she waved him farther into the room. "I was here but the day before yesterday, Aunt," he replied, placing a kiss on her cheek.

Looking a little confused, his aunt Petunia squinted up at him over the rim of her spectacles. "Were you? Surely I would have remembered that," she said. Then, "Oh, do sit down, Bellamy, you are far too tall. Give me a crick in my neck looking up at you all the time. Anyway, it does not signify, for I am dying."

"Really, Aunt? Dying?" Oliver took his usual seat.

"Yes! The dear doctor said so."

Oliver raised a brow. "Mrs. Turner said the doctor concluded you were *not* dying."

"What would that old charlatan know? He's not me," she said in a superior tone, chin up in the air.

Oliver stifled a chuckle. "Aunt…"

His aunt began fussing with her shawl. "Bellamy, there are things that must be said before I curl up my toes."

Oliver took one of the small pug dogs, who kept leaping up at him, onto his lap. "I am at your service," he replied.

"Good. Now, is it true you're marrying the Black Raven woman?"

"No!" Oliver's eyes widened. His voice rose to an alarming and ungentlemanly-like pitch. The poor dog on his lap whimpered, and Oliver realized his fingers had squeezed the poor creature. "Where did you hear that?"

Aunt Petunia looked disappointed. "The doctor mentioned you were the talk of the *ton*. I had hoped there was a smidgen of truth to it."

"Old charlatan," he muttered, letting the dog lick his hand in forgiveness of his rough treatment of a moment ago.

"Bellamy!" Aunt Petunia reprimanded, albeit with a smirk.

"The Countess of Blackhurst and I…" *How to explain something he was yet to quite understand himself.*

His aunt sat forward. "Yes? You do know my dying wish is to see you married, don't you?"

He watched her as she looked at him with pleading eyes. She reminded him of one of her dogs whenever there was a treat on offer. Oh, his aunt was at her mischievous best today. "Are you not worried about her reputation?"

She flapped her hands around in a dismissive gesture. "Reputation? Oh, you mean about her husband? Henry said he was a shockingly rude fellow with no sense of propriety."

"Did he indeed? Some say she killed him or had him killed. What do you say to that?" Oliver watched as his aunt processed all this information with little more than a raise of her graying eyebrow.

"Do they? Well, he probably deserved it, like my Harold."

"Harold?"

"My first husband. He was like a petulant child. Always wanted everything his way. Never happy to wait. Always had to butt in where he shouldn't. He was killed by a wine cork, you know."

Oliver sat back in disbelief. "No, I didn't know."

"They wanted to blame the poor footman, but I was there as and so were several others. Harold had been an impatient man. He grabbed the champagne bottle off the dear boy and popped that cork right into his own temple. He was gone from this Earthly plane before he even hit the Persian rug." She looked off into the distance for a moment before redirecting her eyes to him.

Shocked, Oliver shook his head. He had never known any of this. He had just assumed that Uncle George had been her only husband. "So, then you married Uncle George?"

"George? Heaven's no."

"No?"

"After Harold there was Charles. He had an unfortunate

reaction to something and hiccupped himself to the other side."

Oliver shut his mouth and wondered how such a thing was even possible. "How… awful," he replied, horrified. And yet he had to swallow a bubble of laughter which threatened to escape.

"Oh, it went on for months," she went on. "We were all quite relieved in the end, including Charles, I suspect."

"I'm almost afraid to ask if there are any others."

"I think seeing three husbands to the grave is more than enough for any poor woman, don't you?"

"I agree. So, you think Lady Blackhurst did kill her husband then?"

"If she was not found guilty then she must be… not guilty."

Well, he supposed that made sense but…

She frowned at him. "So, are you going to marry the girl or not? Henry fancied her, you know. Were he still alive you might have had a fight on your hands. He would talk of no one else. Her dark hair, her lovely eyes, her complexion. It was quite nauseating, I have to say."

Now it was his turn to frown. "I had no idea he and Lisbeth had met."

"Is that her name? That is pretty." His aunt smiled, happiness evident on her wrinkled face.

A face that was a constant in his life, the only constant he had left. He would not even entertain the thought of her not being part of his life. "What did he say?" Oliver asked.

"About what, dear?"

"About the Countess of Blackhurst?"

"Who?"

"The lady I am not marrying? The Black Raven?"

She stared at him for a moment, a look of pleasure sweeping over her face. "Are you getting married?"

He shut his eyes briefly and took a breath. "No." Her face fell in disappointment, which made him feel like pond scum.

"Bellamy, you are confusing me on purpose. Do not be cruel. I am dying, you know."

"You are not…"

She grabbed at his hand, which made the dog jump from his lap. "I want you to settle a small cottage on Mrs. Turner when I go. Somewhere near her daughter would be nice. I can give her a small allowance."

"I will do my best, but, Aunt, you are not dying."

"I am and I will see our dear Henry again, and George, and no doubt Charles and Harold, too. Won't that be a jolly party? I do hope that Henry will be in a convivial mood. He was so peculiar before he passed." She looked over at the fire and seemed to be mesmerized by the goings on in the grate.

"In what way, Aunt?" He reached out, touched her arm. "Aunt?"

She looked over at him and appeared to be surprised to see him. "Eh? Oh, Bellamy. Do I have to be ready to go to my reward before you visit me?" She looked over at the window. "Strangest weather we are having lately. It is almost as if the sun had decided to go on a holiday."

He smiled. He should have known this conversation was doomed to run amok sooner or later. Oh, but he wanted to know more about Henry and his peculiar mood.

Aunt Petunia's chin was already dipping towards her chest, he noticed, indicating that she would be snoring within moments. This was the first time she had been specific when talking about Henry. Usually, she just reminisced about them as children. The news about him knowing Lisbeth was intriguing. If his aunt's ramblings were true, how did they know each other? Lisbeth had told him she had not known her husband's business partners. He assumed this included his brother.

He looked around him, looked at his aunt, and wondered what he should do. He had the urge to bang down the countess's door and demand answers. This would be impulsive and pure folly considering the source. No, he must bide his time. Study her. Get under her defenses and into her confidence if he were to find out about Henry and her part in the speculation.

He gave his aunt a kiss on her forehead and left her to rest. In the hall Mrs. Turner met him and followed him to the door.

"She seemed well today, considering her diagnosis," he remarked.

"Yes and no. She says the strangest things to me some days, but I cannot make out whether they are memory or imagination."

"She said some strange comments to me today as well, about Henry."

"I would not take too much stock in what she says, my lord."

"No, well, I suppose you are right. I'll take my leave now, Mrs. Turner, and bid you a good day." As he walked away, despite what Mrs. Turner had said, he could not stop his thoughts from turning to his brother and the woman who would be on his arm tonight.

IT WAS COLD, again, but this time Oliver didn't have the benefit of a flask of brandy to keep him warm, nor did he have the heated affections of the woman sitting opposite him. Despite the warming bricks at their feet, the cold seemed to be seeping in from every crevice of the carriage. He was sure that Rollands had something to do with his missing flask, no doubt perpetrated by *Madame le No-Fun* sitting opposite him. Perhaps her icy demeanor was making the carriage seem so chilly.

"Is it really necessary to go to Lady Fortesque's tonight?" he asked. "Can we not write something more entertaining in the schedule than wasting an evening with that critical old battle-axe? There is a masquerade at Covent Garden which would be infinitely more diverting."

Lisbeth looked at him, her eyes huge with shock. "No, you cannot just write something better in my schedule! Besides, that old battle-axe is my grandmother! Goodness, Bellamy, next you will be proposing that we attend a gaming hell or a… boxing match!"

A choke of laughter escaped him before he could control it. "I would, actually, but not with you. I suspect you would take too much pleasure in causing a scene."

Pure astonishment came over her features. "Me! Cause a scene? I've never heard such a ridiculous thing in all my life!"

"Would you go to a boxing match… if it were on my list of wagers?"

She turned to look out the window again. "Certainly not!"

"Ah, but, Countess, you did say I could collect on any and *all* wagers, did you not?"

Lisbeth paled. She had agreed with those terms. They were, in fact, terms she had made up herself. What if he insisted that she go through with the wager? Looking back towards him, she saw his self-satisfied smile and realized he was bluffing. There was no odious boxing match on his list at all! Scoundrel!

"I believe I said within reason. I would, of course, honor any wager as per our agreement."

Oliver laughed again, his chest rising and falling in the rhythm of comedic exercise. "Liar! You have yet to see the list but still you seem so confident."

"Correction, Bellamy, I have seen the list. I simply could not read it. A legible list will present itself in short order, I expect, or I will march into White's Club and gain a list of my own."

At this point he knew her well enough to believe her mad enough to do just that. As humorous as it would be to see her bodily removed from White's, it would also effectively put an end to his chance to make any money out of this debacle. Although everyone seemed to know what he was doing they did not realize that the countess also knew or that she condoned it. He had to keep it that way.

"I should have known you and the battle-axe were related," he said on a heavy sigh. "Well, won't this be fun?"

They entered the house on Grosvenor Square and were ushered through a mirrored hall to a large rectangular room furnished in blue, white, and silver. It was a stunning room. Full to the brim with small but expensive antiquities and bric-a-brac that Lisbeth explained had been her grandfather's passion.

Part of Oliver wanted to stop and study each piece but, he reminded himself, he wasn't on a trip to a museum. Plaster moldings framed arches in white with the interiors the same blue as the outer walls. More molding in the shape of silver grape vines connected each arch. A brilliant fresco occupied the entire scope of the ceiling depicting a confrontation of ancient Greek gods, all vying for their immortal positions. He spared a glance at Lisbeth, wondered if she would miss him if he were to lie down on the floor somewhere, and just study the ceiling for the night. He had seen many marvelous things while traveling with the army—some that he was trying diligently to forget—but he did like a good piece of art.

Fascinated by the architecture and decoration, Oliver hardly noticed the occupants of the room at all, until one of the guests bowed in front of him. He bowed in return, smiled, but did not stay to have a tête-á-tête. It was then that he saw couples dancing and others playing cards.

Above the din of the music and conversation he could hear the battle-axe's voice. It was husky, harsh, and full of authority. The kind of vocal pattern which could only develop over years of constant ordering about and belittling of lesser beings. Lying on the floor, even though it would completely ruin his jacket, still seemed the best way to pass the evening. It would be worth his valet's wrath.

As soon as Lisbeth heard her grandmother's voice, her legs faltered and refused to move another step. They mirrored her feelings exactly. She did not want to be here. Her heart seemed to be hiding down somewhere near her liver, quivering with anxiety. She wanted to turn and run out of this house as fast as she could. Pretend she had not accepted her grandmother's surprise summons.

It was far too late to turn and run, and besides, she had not done anything wrong. It was not *she* who had abandoned her own flesh and blood. Her grandmother had turned her back on her when Lisbeth needed her most. Disowned her, thrust her from her life like an unwanted burden, without even bothering to ask if the rumors were true. She had simply chosen not to acknowledge her as her granddaughter. It had been a hard lesson to learn. Lisbeth had tried several times to contact her grandmother for support during those early days but had been denied at every turn. It had stupefied her. Did her grandmother actually think her capable of murder? The dawning of this realization had made her weep with a shame she had no reason to feel.

Lisbeth had grieved for the loss of her family, defeat colliding with hopelessness in an all-consuming terror. Had she really lost them? Lost them all?

When she thought of the tears she'd shed, the pain she'd felt, the days she'd spent waiting to wake from the nightmare of her life, the old anger welled up inside her and threatened to choke her. However, Lisbeth was no longer that weak woman who had hoped and prayed they would come to realize their error and come back into her life and want to love her again.

If her grandmother now wanted to repair the ties she had so viciously severed, she would have to beg for her forgiveness on her knees before Lisbeth would even consider such a thing. Even if she could forgive, she would never forget.

"Are you all right?"

Bellamy. She'd forgotten about him. She closed her eyes for a moment, fearing he would see, from her tears, the torment she was suffering and realize how close she was to teetering over the edge.

"Of course." She took a deep breath. A sob rose in her throat. Panic took over. Her whole being began to shake.

I can't do this.

No! She was not going to collapse and make a fool of herself. Not here. Not now.

Damn her. Damn her. Damn her.

Behind her she heard, "Perhaps you should have a drink first. Lord knows I could do with one."

She felt Oliver's hand curl around her elbow, warm, strong, supportive. She could see nothing in front of her as he led her to the side of the room, to a shadowed corner where he could shield her from the inquisitive eyes of the other guests in the room. He handed her a drink and guided it up to her lips.

"Drink," he commanded softly.

She obeyed and choked on the strong liquor as it burned a trail down her throat. "What in God's name was that vile concoction?"

He steadied her and took the glass away, searching her face. "Trust me, you don't want to know. Feel better?"

He always seemed to make her feel too many emotions, too often. In any other circumstance she would have resented his actions. This time, however, he made her feel protected. Safe. Something she hadn't felt for a long time. She nodded.

"Good," he said. "You were as pale as a ghost, and I couldn't have you swooning on me."

Lisbeth looked up as he adjusted a small curl, tucking it behind her ear. His eyes held concern. Concern for her? Surely not. And yet, somewhere in the chocolate depths of his eyes she saw a flicker of something else too. Compassion? Pity? She couldn't bear to look any further in case she saw something worse than pity in his gaze.

"I'm not practiced in the art of dealing with fainting females, you see," he said in a soft whisper.

She looked at him and his ridiculous sideways grin. Lord help her, but she wanted to kiss him. Kiss his lips and pretend nothing else existed. Kiss him and let him kiss her, let him take her away from this place, both body and mind. She realized she was staring at his lips when she felt a finger under her chin and her eyes rose once again to his. They were warm, brown, and steady in their regard.

"Do not let her best you. You are the Black Raven," he said. "Act like it." Then he turned her back towards the room.

He was right. She was the Black Raven. She was the woman who turned young men gray overnight and made children eat green vegetables. The woman who made people cross themselves as they crossed the street. Lisbeth would forever be grateful to him for reminding her to play the part she had been given.

He offered her his arm. "I'll be right here if you need me."

Shaking her head she said, "I won't need you. There is no reason why you should be hauled into this any more than you already have. In any case, I daresay this won't take long."

"As you wish, my lady," he replied. "I am sure Venus and I shall get along famously until you return. Although, I must admit, she does not look much of a conversationalist,"

Lisbeth nodded her thanks, flung her shoulders back, tilted her chin up, and walked off in the direction of Lady Fortesque.

Her grandmother was a woman of considerable age, but even so Lisbeth was shocked when she saw her. She had lost weight, and her hair had turned completely white. Her skin seemed paper-thin and fragile. It was inconceivable. She couldn't imagine her grandmother ever being fragile. Her eyes were the only thing that seemed not to have changed. They now narrowed on her and Lisbeth took a breath and held it as she took the last few paces to put herself in front of the woman. She curtseyed, more out of habit than politeness.

Her grandmother was sitting on a sofa with her favorite whippet panting by her side. Her other guests were soon shooed away, and they were alone. Lisbeth's heart hammered as if she was standing before a judge.

Lady Fortesque looked her up and down.

Lisbeth held her gaze. She would not let her see any weakness.

Her grandmother's eyes narrowed. "So, it is true. You have returned. I have to say I'm surprised."

"I can't see why. It has been two years."

"Yes, two years. One would think you have been mourning your husband, but we both know that would be untrue."

"One might think many things whether they are true or not."

"Indeed."

"Why did you summon me?"

"I wanted to see for myself if the rumors are true."

"To which particular rumor do you refer?"

"Yes, there are so many to choose from, are there not? Your presence here answers one of them. The other, I see, is standing by the statue of Venus, pretending not to listen. You may call him over now."

"No! He is not to be brought into this," Lisbeth said.

"And why not? Is he not part of this little game you are playing?"

"There is no game."

Ignoring Lisbeth's request, Lady Fortesque pointed at Bellamy calling him over with a bend of her finger. Lisbeth looked over her shoulder to see Bellamy making a *who-me?* gesture to her grandmother's imperious finger pointing.

Lisbeth wondered briefly if Bellamy would try to charm the woman he referred to as the battle-axe or simply act the idiot. He took his time sauntering over, like he had all the time in the world. He oozed confidence, nonchalance written across his handsome face. Her grandmother huffed behind her, and Lisbeth could not help but let the corners of her mouth lift a little.

"And this is Bellamy, I suppose?" her grandmother asked of Lisbeth but looked at Bellamy.

"He is."

"I am." He bowed. "Your servant, Lady Fortesque."

"Have you taken my granddaughter as your mistress?"

Lisbeth held up her hand to stop Bellamy from answering. "Lord Bellamy has kindly offered to be my escort for the season. That is all," Lisbeth explained.

Oliver stood beside Lisbeth and watched the two women stare at each other like commanders of opposing armies. It was like a military standoff where neither side wanted to concede defeat by giving even an inch of territory. A battle of the fiery stares. He would have enjoyed it more but for Lisbeth's comment.

That is all?

Was he nothing but a means to an end to her?

To be fair, she had never given him any indication other than he was an annoyance at best. So, why did her comment burn? He was confused by his feelings. This may be due to how much he had wanted to kiss her only minutes before when she had looked more miserable than a child told there was no more pudding left. He could have sworn that she had wanted to kiss him too.

His protective instincts had come to the fore when he had seen how she was about to collapse. He didn't know why but he wanted to protect her from the wagging tongues of the guests.

"Bah!" her grandmother said, dismissing her explanation of their relationship. "It is not what I have been told. You do realize that he is winning wagers off you. That his intentions are for the purposes of gaining money from your reputation?" She said this to Lisbeth but focused on him.

Ah, now we come to the crux of the matter, he thought.

"I am aware of the wagers," Lisbeth replied, her voice flat and composed.

He was glad this was a private meeting otherwise this information would be even now making its way around the room.

"Oh, you are, are you? Well, sounds like someone is trying to make a pretty penny out of the *ton* and I'm guessing it isn't you, young lady. So, while Bellamy here lines his pockets with the King's coins you gain an even worse reputation." Lady Fortesque threw a disgusted look at Oliver.

Well, that was certainly a direct shot.

"I am also called the Black Raven by those same people. I have ceased to care one whit what they think. Lord Bellamy is…"

"Annoying and irritating in the extreme? A wastrel and a fool?" Oliver supplied.

She flung him an angry look. "I was going to say a gentle-man."

"Oh." Oliver wanted to laugh at that one. He was sure she wanted to say at least one of his suggestions.

"You two may find this all a great lark to pull the wool over the eyes of the *ton*, my dear, but believe me it will not only be you that ends up hurt by this prank. I would have thought you would know better by now that what you do reflects on all of us, especially your sister." She peered at the both of them over her patrician nose as they stood together. She humphed. "You should marry; you look well together."

Lisbeth and Bellamy shared a confused look.

"Yes, a June wedding, that will put things to rights."

"I don't think…" Lisbeth began.

"Why are you shaking your head, Bellamy? Are you saying she is good enough to bed but not to wed?"

"I won't be marrying Bellamy. Or anyone for that matter," Lisbeth answered.

Lady Fortesque did not seem surprised by her denial and pinned her gaze on Bellamy. "Leave us now. I have things I need to discuss with my granddaughter."

"With all due respect, Lady Fortesque, I will leave only on Lady Blackhurst's request."

Lisbeth turned to him, took his hand. "I'm all right, Bellamy. I will join you shortly."

"Are you sure?" he asked eyeing Lady Fortesque.

"Yes."

He gave her hand a squeeze, bowed to the two ladies, and left to take up his post at the side of the room.

"He seems very protective of you. It would do him good to be settled and seeing, as he is the only man you have let come within a foot of you in years, I thought… Oh well, it matters not now."

"No, it matters not. You gave up any right to counsel me. You have no say in who I do, or do not, marry."

"You are right. What you do is on your head, which is why we must remain distanced from you. Do you have no inkling of what you put us through?"

Lisbeth held her tongue. Every fiber of her being wanted to scream at the woman before her. She knew that the shame of her accusation had caused a scandal. How could it not? But, she was innocent. A court of law had decreed it for all. Where had her family been then? Their lack of support at that time only fueled the flames of scandal that she had somehow gotten away with murder.

"And now you want to pull poor Bellamy through your muck as well? Not that he seems to care. I may not have met him before tonight, but I know of him, of his family. He deserves better but he has no one to direct him, does he?"

"What do you mean? Are you talking of his brother?"

"I was talking about what happened to his parents. He lost his mother, father, and younger sister in a shipwreck over a decade ago. The poor boys, and that's all they were, had nothing to bury either. Such a pity. Lady Bellamy had been such a beauty too."

Lisbeth instantly searched for a glimpse of Bellamy. "I only knew of his brother's accident a few weeks ago. I had just assumed… He is all alone?" Why did she feel the need to go to him, wrap her arms around him, and comfort him? Was it because she knew what it was to be alone too?

"There is an aunt, Lady Whitely. Although, she may have passed too."

"No family at all," Lisbeth said in a whisper.

"This seems to have surprised you. Did he not tell you?"

No, he had not told her, and she had not asked. She had not asked him anything personal. To do so would be to invite intimate conversation. She did not want such converse with him. It was hard enough to keep him at a distance. She was better off not knowing about him, wasn't she? Oh, but it was too late now.

She knew. She felt. For him.

"I know you resent me for the decisions I made. I'll tell you, I don't regret it. I did what I had to do for the greater good of the family. If you had been in my shoes, you would have done the same."

Was this her grandmother's attempt at a backhanded apology? Her face gave nothing away. Cold old fish.

"I am nothing like you," Lisbeth said with conviction. "I would never have abandoned one of my own. I would have ridden out the storm, held the faith, and protected what was mine."

Her grandmother studied her for a moment. She nodded. "And you have done so, admirably. I wasn't sure you had the gumption, but it seems you are stronger than even you yourself thought."

"A compliment? It is ill-timed. None of it matters—for I have lost everything!" Lisbeth desperately wanted to leave.

"We have lost too," her grandmother said in a whisper.

"Do not speak to me of loss."

"If society accepts you after this farce you are playing at, then there may be hope of you returning to the family."

Family. This woman may be her blood, but she was no longer her family. "I only want to know of my sister."

"Marie is well—married Lord Fenwick last June."

"I know. I read the announcement. Is she happy?"

Lisbeth remembered clearly the day of her sister's wedding. It had been a bright June day, warm but with a cool breeze that sent the gowns of the female guests flapping against their legs. She had hidden within her carriage across the street to watch the bride and groom emerge from St George's Church in Hanover Square. Lisbeth should have been on the steps with the other guests, offering hugs of congratulations, and sharing in her sister's joy, attending the wedding breakfast and toasting to the happy couple. Instead, she had spent the whole morning worrying that Lord Fenwick may not be the man he purported to be. Was he a good man? A gentle soul who would never lay a finger on Marie? Would he treat her with respect and kindness? She did not want

Marie to suffer the same fate as she had.

Tears had streamed down Lisbeth's face, and she cursed the fates that had put her in such a position. She should have been shedding tears of joy but instead it felt more like Marie was being torn from her heart a second time.

Her grandmother frowned at her now. "Her husband appears to be doting towards her and really, she could not have hoped for a better match, considering."

"Considering she is related to me you mean?" She flashed her eyes to show her anger but the woman before her did not react.

"You put us all in a position where we had no choice. Don't you see?"

Was she pleading for her to understand? She knew it would not have been easy for them. Who would want to marry the sister of a suspected murderer?

She looked over to where Bellamy was standing, drink in hand and gazing at the ceiling. He may have no family, but at least they had probably loved him.

"Be wary, my dear. There are still those who would wish you ill."

"I am used to looking after myself," she replied. "I would hate for you to lose sleep over me. Do have a good evening." *Tell my sister I miss her...*

She was proud as she walked away. She had not let it show how much her grandmother's cool reserve had hurt her, ripped her heart to shreds. What had she expected this to be? A sweet family reunion? It was better this way she told herself. This way she wouldn't be lulled into thinking the old woman still cared for her.

Oliver studied the countess as she excused herself from her grandmother and began the walk across the room towards him. She was looking directly at him. Odd! He felt no burning sensation anywhere in the region of his forehead. He was beginning to feel warm in another region though. He took another sip of his drink and rolled it on his tongue as he continued to hold her gaze.

He swallowed. Lord, she was perfection! She was artless in her movements and yet the sway of her hips told an ancient story that his loins understood completely.

He must look away.

He couldn't.

He watched her watching him.

His heart pounded violently. Her every step was grace; her breasts moved up and down slowly in her bodice like music for the eyes. Every shimmer of the emerald material as it moved around her body was like whispers of an enchantment. He was mesmerized by her. Every painful breath he held told him he was mad to think of her this way. Every beat of his heart told him he was a fool.

She was nearly in front of him and he blinked. What an idiot he must look. He had to remember they were nothing to each other—she had made that clear enough. Just partners in an arrangement that was starting to show more holes than a match girl's shawl.

That is all.

"Did you take your fill of half-naked statues, Bellamy?" She took the empty wineglass out of his hand and gave it to a passing servant.

"Pardon?" All he'd heard was the word *naked.*

"The statues, did you find them entertaining enough?"

"Oh, the statues? Well, you know, seen one, seen them all," he said with a grin. "I'd like to know where all their arms went, wouldn't you? There must be a vault somewhere in Greece full of lost limbs." If she only knew what he had been thinking while looking at those figures.

Lisbeth took his arm and began leading Bellamy away from the statue of Aphrodite. "I am feeling I must grant you a boon... for having put up with me this evening, not to mention dealing with my grandmother."

"Really?" Bellamy looked more than shocked, and Lisbeth

wanted to laugh but nothing seemed to come out.

"Yes," she continued, pulling out his infamous list from her reticule. "I thought we should complete one of your wagers."

"Oh, I see," was all he said in reply.

She was not sure if he was happy about her suggestion or not. "So, which one shall we complete? This one?" She pointed to an incomprehensible scribble about halfway down the list.

Oliver looked over her shoulder at the one she had selected then frowned. "No! Not that one. Choose another."

"Why? What does it say?"

"Just choose another."

"All right." She looked down the list and pointed to a shorter scribble.

"Definitely not," he said.

"This one?"

"No!"

"Oh, for heaven's sake, Bellamy!"

"This one," he said indicating one towards the top of the list.

She sighed loudly in irritation. "Fine," she said, relieved that he had at least selected one.

"Good." He took her by the hand and led her towards the other side of the room. "What? Where are you taking me? Bellamy, I insist on knowing what you have chosen."

"It is nothing too torturous, I assure you. If you try not to trample on my toes, I'll try not to step on yours."

"Trample?" She dug in her heels and stopped. "One moment please, is this by chance a waltz?" They were not quite at the dance floor. "I told you—"

"I know, you don't waltz. That is why we are doing a cotillion."

"Bellamy!"

"You do remember the steps, don't you?" he asked as he pulled her onto the dance floor.

"Of course, I remember the steps, and why is it I trample and you only step? That hardly seems fair."

The music started and with a satisfied smile on his face he positioned her in the line and took up his place opposite. As the music started he gave a double eyebrow wiggle.

Lisbeth rolled her eyes.

He laughed.

It had been some years since she had danced and yet as soon as the couples around her began, the steps just seemed to happen on their own. Her feet moved into the steps and turns without fail, no doubt due to her mother who had insisted she dance flawlessly before being allowed to go to London for her season.

Bellamy was very agile and confident, light on his toes and, thankfully, skillful enough to keep his promise of not stepping on hers. At first, she did not want to enjoy the dance, but too soon the music and laughter around her drew her in and every time she touched hands with Bellamy her heart sped up. She enjoyed it a lot more than she had thought possible though she told herself she most certainly did not.

"You dance very well," she said to him through a turn.

"You seem surprised."

"Not really, well, maybe a little."

He laughed. "Even in the army there were social occasions which necessitated the officers to dance with various female guests. You may be surprised by other things I do well."

She blushed and was reminded that this was Bellamy she was talking to. They parted, clasping hands with other dancers before coming back together.

"Those things do not concern me, no matter how well you do them," she said with a smirk.

He laughed.

Again they separated and came back together.

She found herself longing for the steps that brought them together, if only for the briefest of moments. When his hand touched hers, she felt a strange kind of warm tingle go right through her. She was right to keep away from waltzing with him. If he were to hold her too close, in the circle of his arms, she may go up in flames, for her thoughts and her cheeks were warming shockingly. Surely, it was the exertion of the dance or the stuffiness of the room and nothing to do with him. Then he smiled at her and the tingles swept through her body like an inferno.

She felt herself wanting to smile back. Why couldn't she just let go?

It would be so easy to let him charm her. To woo her with his sad past and his seductive quips. She felt sorry for him, she decided. It was the only plausible answer to her reactions. It was nothing more than sympathy after hearing how he had lost his parents. Any woman with a heart would feel the same, wouldn't they?

He winked at her with such amusement that she missed a step. Lord, was she doomed to fall for the same tricks that had hideously ruined her life only seven years ago?

Nathaniel had been a good dancer. Smooth with his words and compliments and yet… and yet that had not been him at all. If only she could turn back time. She would play her cards differently, that would be for certain. The deceiving words of a man who promised her the sun and the moon would not play her for a fool again. How could she have forgotten the tricks men played to get what they want?

It wasn't like Bellamy was here by choice. She had made him come here tonight. It was quite clear to her that he found this whole thing a game which he was playing along with. At every turn he was aiming for higher stakes, just waiting for his cards to turn and take the advantage. Is that what he had been doing at the beginning of the night when she had been upset at seeing her grandmother? Had he seized the opportunity to take the trump card by playing the concerned lover?

The pain she carried with her increased, and she found herself fighting tears again. Was there no one whom she could trust? Lisbeth slowly turned the hurt to anger. It was the only way she knew how to cope with what was happening. She still had need of him and was not ready to let him go but she would be prepared to defend herself against him with everything she had.

The dance ended and Bellamy offered his arm to escort her off the dance floor.

"You think too much," he announced. "I swear I could see cogs moving in there." He made as if to look in her ear. He grinned.

She gave him one of her burning glares in warning and he stepped back, shocked. "Surely it wasn't so bad?"

"You tricked me." She began to walk towards the refreshment table with determined strides. He did not immediately follow.

Any man can be kind, she told herself, when he was after something. What if she were to give in to him, then what? Then who might he turn out to be? Someone like Nathaniel? The thought was too terrible to contemplate.

"Are you all right?" he asked her, his smile long gone. "You look… upset."

"I'm fine." She picked up a glass of wine from the table and took a sip, closing her eyes for a moment.

"Are you sure because—"

Setting her glass down with trembling fingers she turned to face him. "I said, I'm fine!"

He raised a brow. "Countess, if that is even remotely true then your definition of fine and mine are very different, indeed."

"Bellamy—"

He took her elbow in a strong grip and escorted her to the end of the room with quick strides. So different from earlier, he was not protecting her now. It just went to prove her point.

"Unhand me, now!" she hissed.

He pulled her around to face him. She gasped at the dark look in his eyes.

"I was going to wait for a more private moment but now I am just going to ask you. Were you and my brother lovers?"

Lisbeth's shocked confusion did not seem to give him the

answer he wanted, for he said something under his breath before he scowled at her even darker.

She said, "Why would you think I knew your brother?"

"Because he knew you."

"And when did he tell you this?"

"He didn't."

"Bellamy, I cannot be responsible for the imaginings of men."

"Henry talked to my aunt about you… in detail it seems."

So, the aunt was alive. Not completely alone then. "I can't imagine why. I met him but once."

"Only once?"

Her eyes grew huge with indignation and anger. "Yes, once! Why are you questioning me like I am somehow responsible for a wrong done to your brother?"

"Aren't you? You and your husband both?"

"The speculation had nothing to do with me," she replied.

"You were the sole benefactor of its collapse."

"Benefactor? Benefactor! I got no benefit from that accursed speculation. It ruined my life." Lisbeth walked off but Bellamy caught up to her in two strong strides.

"You are rich as Croesus. Do not tell me you did not benefit."

"Financially, yes, but it was not my choice. I never even knew until the reading of the will. It has not given me one day of happiness I assure you."

"Why didn't you give the investors back their money?"

"Oh, if only it had been that simple. There were… legal reasons but I am not about to discuss them with you." Tired, sad, and sick to her stomach she began to walk off. Bellamy appeared in front of her. Damn his long legs.

"Henry was my brother. For some unfathomable reason he gambled the family's money on a speculation. A speculation that didn't exist. I have every right to know why he'd be fool enough to do such a thing."

"Gambled is the word, Bellamy. And you have no right to question me. However, if you can produce the paperwork that states how much money he put into the speculation, I will gladly refund the debt."

She watched him as hope flared in his eyes. It made this whole night even more depressing because she knew no such paperwork existed. He would no doubt turn his house upside down looking for it—all for nothing.

Lisbeth signaled a footman, handed him a glass of wine, and picked up her own. "Here is to finding the un-findable." She clinked her glass to his.

Bellamy watched her for a moment, a small crease between his brows. She knew exactly when understanding dawned on him because his shoulders slumped a little and his lovely eyes seemed to dim. She wanted to say she was sorry, sorry for everything, but what difference would it make? It would not bring back his brother, nor put his family finances back in place. It would not help anyone, least of all herself. Yes, she too was looking for the seemingly un-findable—the truth.

CHAPTER EIGHT

O LIVER ALWAYS THOUGHT of himself as a man who could handle any situation with tact and decorum. Now he knew better, and it was not better, it was worse, so much worse than he could ever have anticipated.

Women, he decided, were the most infuriating creatures. The Countess of Blackhurst the most infuriating of all.

Rollands, Lady Blackhurst's butler, had kept every card that had ever entered her house if the collection which had been scattered across the dining room table earlier this evening was anything to go by. Quite a useful hoarder was Rollands. However, seeing his brother's card among the pile made Oliver realize Henry was only one of many who'd been deceived by the Earl of Blackhurst. Sir John Selbourne was one such gentleman. His card had aroused suspicion due to its cryptic note on the back—a hefty amount followed by the words, *I'm interested.*

"Tell me again why you have dragged me from the ball below and lured me into Sir John's bedchamber?" Oliver said from under an ornate writing desk in said bedchamber.

"To find evidence, of course."

"You do not seriously think I will find something under his desk, do you?

"If we do not look, we will not know if there is anything to find, will we?"

Oliver frowned. *How contradictory of you, Countess.* Her jibe about the un-findable last night, still fresh in his mind. There was no way he would ever admit to her he had searched high and low for those damned non-existent speculation papers. What a desperate fool he was and yet, he'd had to try. Like she just said, if one does not look how will one find, or not find, what one is looking for? Pity his frantic search had produced nothing. He knew Henry had taken out the massive bank loan for something, the speculation presumably, but there was no proof he used it for that specific purpose, and that purpose only.

The countess put her hand on his shoulder. "What's that?"

"What's what?" He was still searching for a hidden panel or a key or some small scrap of parchment which said, *"Yes, it was I who killed Nathaniel Carslake, with a pistol, in the study, because he was a dirty rotten scoundrel—Sir John,"* knowing all the time he would never find it. Another un-findable to add to the list.

"I think I hear voices," she whispered in his ear.

Oliver closed his eyes. He liked her husky, sultry voice vibrating into his ear. "Why does this not surprise me?" he drawled as he straightened up.

She gave him a slightly confused expression then looked around her before saying, "Quick, in here."

Before he could protest, he found himself stuffed into a large armoire.

They stood then, chest to chest, in the darkness surrounded by men's jackets, breathing louder than a pair of postal horses who had just done the London to Dover run.

"Ah, now *this* is cozy, wouldn't you say?" he said through the arm of a jacket, wanting more than anything for their heavy breathing to be the product of some rather more inspired recreation. Like kissing. He wanted to kiss her very much indeed.

He found himself obsessed by her lips. Her shapely top lip. Her full bottom lip. The dents at the corners of her mouth that hinted at the marvel of a smile. Yes, her lips were consuming a lot of his gray matter these days. It was not a habit which was good for one's wellbeing, he was sure.

He knew what Ashton would tell him. *"Stop looking at her damn lips and get the information."* He would be right, and that fact only made things worse. He had done his duty to Ashton by sending him a missive about the nonexistent legal papers and the countess's willingness to pay the investors if they could produce evidence of their investment. He knew it would not appease Ashton, nor his client, for it had not satisfied him either.

Her unique fragrance filled the small space around them, and he groaned. Was it not bad enough he had to be in her presence every night and not be able to do more than have her hand on his sleeve or help her down from a carriage?

"Shh!" The countess turned away from him, elbowing some more room at the same time, and peered through the keyhole.

"I think it's safe but I can't be sure," she said.

Safe? Not for him and certainly not for her if she didn't get out soon.

"We had better stay here then, until you are sure, of course. There is nothing quite like an unsure woman to ruin a perfectly good hiding spot."

"Bellamy, kindly shut up." She peered through the keyhole again. "I can only see the edge of the writing desk," she whispered.

Oliver smiled in the dimness of the armoire where he could just make out her outline. For all her squirming, her lovely little derriere was now conveniently placed in front of him, and he had to resist the urge to reach out and touch her waist and pull her hips closer to him. He'd been aching to hold her, kiss her, and convince her he was not as repugnant as she seemed to think him. He wanted her to look at him like she had last night when she'd been upset, like she had when she had granted him the boon of a dance. He wanted her to smile at him. He didn't really know why, he just… did.

He decided he needed to test whether or not she was truly immune to him. If it failed, he would be in the same position as he was now, only hopefully not in an armoire.

"You smell nice," he said through the darkness.

"What?"

"Like a spring meadow, just before it rains," he announced.

"Do not be ridiculous. I smell of no such thing," she retorted, moving so he was pushed farther to the side of the wardrobe.

"Ah, but you do." *Torture me.*

"Bellamy—" Her tone held more than a little annoyance.

"I know, but you see your hair is tickling my nose and the heat of your skin is making my skin heat, therefore, my body is reacting in the most... amusing manner."

Lisbeth rolled her eyes and attempted to count to ten. His body was reacting? Oh, Lord! Thankfully, it was dark in the armoire for she did not want him to see how his words were affecting her.

"When a man's body reacts," he was saying now, "there is often a need to—"

"Bellamy!"

"Yes, Countess?"

If there were enough room, she would have tried to slap his hand away from her hip. "If you do not desist with your ranting, the only thing your body will *need* is a doctor," she hissed.

He gave a soft little chuckle. "Promises, promises."

Fuming and face burning, she turned towards him, well, as much as she could with all these infernal jackets in the way. She tried to push him farther away from her but he stood fast. He laughed again.

"Shhh!"

He seemed intent on ignoring her as he continued, "I'd wager, had I a lamp, you would be blushing most becomingly."

"Had *I* a lamp, I would find a cravat and gag you with it."

"My, my there is no need to be nasty." He reached out, touched her cheek with the back of his fingers. "You *are* blushing!"

"I am not! And kindly keep your hands to yourself, if you please."

"Yes, definitely have you all hot and bothered, don't I? Perhaps we should have jumped into an armoire earlier. I have a particularly large one, you know." When she snorted he qualified, "And an armoire, too. It would accommodate two people a lot better than this old thing. I'd even toss out all my clothes to make more room. My valet would make a fuss, but I'd do it for you. What do you say, Countess?"

She pushed against his chest, knowing it would do no good but wanting to wipe the, no doubt, smug grin off his face.

"I'd say, regardless of how big you *think* your armoire is it will never be large enough to tempt me." She put her ear to the door, trying desperately to ignore his disturbing presence beside her. "Do you hear anything?"

"I believe that sound is my heart breaking."

Scoffing, she turned towards him and replied, "Men don't have hearts to break, though they do spend a great deal of their time trying to break ours."

"Not true," he whispered seductively in her ear. He grasped her hand and placed it over his heart, keeping it there, despite her efforts to remove it. She could feel the warmth of his body and the steady rhythm of his heart beneath her palm.

"You see? Just like yours," he said.

Lisbeth's whole arm tingled, just like last night during their dance. Her fingers flexed, glided over the woolen fabric of his jacket. She wanted to explore under the fine lawn of his shirt to the hard planes of his chest, but this was Bellamy. Despite the strange things he made her feel, the extremes in emotions she felt when he was around, the fact was he was a man who was only to be in her life for a short time. A man who would pocket as much as the foolish gentlemen of the *ton* would hand him and disappear from her life. What would be the use of letting herself like him, desire him—fall under his spell?

He placed his other hand on her left breast. "Your heart has considerably more padding, which is just as it should be."

"Bellamy!" She swatted his hand away.

"I know, I know, but, Countess, would it be such a terrible thing? You and I in an armoire, giving each other pleasure?"

His fingers were tracing their way up her rib cage towards her breast again and she realized her other hand was still on his chest. The heated tingling sensation was spiraling through her body and doing strange things to the thumping of her heart. If she hadn't been blushing before, she was now. Her breasts were already swelling. Her nipples were painfully erect and straining against the tight corset. Her body may be reacting but not in an amusing way.

Why was her body being so disloyal to her? Or was it her body knew what she wanted and was straining for his touch, even as her brain articulated all the reasons why she should end this right now. It had been an age since she had been touched with any kind of tenderness. Not a hug, nor kiss in years. Part of her rejected the need but her heart yearned for comfort and affection.

His hand brushed over her breast, and she gasped. She hardly knew what her body was doing, for she found herself pushing forward against his hand, as if wanting him to do more, press harder, release her from the confines of her bodice.

She could feel him come closer to her and realized with dread it hadn't been him who had taken the step but she who had pulled him closer. His fingers were now toying with the edge of her bodice. Part of her wanted him to hurry up and free her, kiss her, here, in the dark where there was no way he could see her.

The real her.

The desperate her.

The lonely her.

His fingers hovered over her skin, mapping their way in the dark, up her arms to her shoulder, collarbone, the column of her neck.

"I'm going to kiss you now, Lisbeth," he announced, and it was a dark and dangerous sound. It thrilled and scared her.

So like Bellamy to tell her of his intentions, not like a request but a warning. A warning, which had her whole body quivering in anticipation of his touch. He kissed the hollow behind her ear and gooseflesh covered her body, like her skin had been woken after years of being asleep. She gasped at the feel of his lips on her neck, warm and soft. When his tongue flicked out to wet a small patch of skin before putting his hot open mouth there, she trembled. Her fingers dug into his jacket.

Her eyes closed as he kissed her chin, the corner of her mouth. *My lips. Kiss my lips,* she silently pleaded. It seemed an age but finally his mouth did come down on hers. She tasted the wine he had consumed earlier and wondered if he could taste the champagne she'd had. Soon all such ridiculous thought of who drank what was far, far away. His soft and unhurried way of kissing gave her time to relax. Tentatively she kissed him back, letting him deepen the kiss as he pleased because it pleased her too. She heard him groan low in his throat and would have smiled but that her mouth was otherwise delightfully occupied.

She was enjoying the dizzying feeling he created with his lips. She had always thought he had a clever mouth on him; how right she was, but for much better reasons than she had originally thought. The smell of his shaving cologne and the starch from his cravat filled her nostrils, only to be outdone by the heated scent of the man himself. Lisbeth breathed it in, reveled in it, and wanted to inhale it like an opium smoker breathed in the bittersweet poison of the poppy.

Bellamy's lips left hers to make their way down her neck again and lower to the tops of her breasts. He kissed from one side to the other while one hand smoothed down the side of her ribcage to rest on her bottom, pulling her hard up against him. The other hand pulled down her bodice and was palming her breast with a tender but sure hand. She couldn't breathe, or was it she was breathing too much? Whichever way, she felt delirious.

"Lisbeth," he rasped in her ear.

Oh God! His voice was low, dark, and heavy. *Keep talking,* she thought to herself. *No, stop talking and kiss me.*

"I want you, Lisbeth. I've wanted you from the first moment

I saw you. You are so soft, so lovely. You're perfect."

Perfect? Her? She'd been called many things, unsavory things, but never perfect, never lovely. He kissed her then with a determination which gave her no chance to resist him, even if she'd wanted to.

Oh, Lord, his whole body was pressed against her, and it felt so unexpectedly good, but he was still not close enough. She wanted more. She was a greedy child in a sweet shop. One hand gripped his jacket while the other tangled in his hair, and he whispered her name again before taking advantage of her open mouth. His tongue plundered as his body rocked against her. She gloried in the press of his erection against her. Consciousness was giving way to a sweetest oblivion. She didn't want to think, just for a moment or two.

"I knew it." He growled in her ear, and she turned towards him.

"Don't talk, please don't talk," she said and put her lips to his. He took her invitation without hesitation. Deepened the kiss further.

She vaguely felt his hand on her leg, gathering her skirts higher, lifting her leg to his waist, fitting himself between. Tension was simmering low in her belly and moving lower.

Yes! Yes!

No! Why had he stopped kissing her? Was it possible for lips to feel bereft?

Now his lips were at her breasts which were now exposed and swollen and wanting. She liked his mouth hot on her.

His hand was between her legs, touching her softly, confidently. It was the sweetest kind of torture. She had not experienced a man's fingers there before, even on her wedding night. Was this how it should have been? It was shockingly delicious.

As much as he was slowly, exquisitely, driving her mad, she held no illusions as to what this was. This lustful seduction had been his intention all along. *He probably seduced women every other day like this.*

Part of her didn't care any longer. She just wanted more. Part of her cried at the injustice of the reality of what this really was and where they were. In an armoire of all places! The knowledge she had let this happen was painful. What was she doing? More importantly, what was she doing with Bellamy? She had decided she would not give in to him and become just another woman who had warmed his bed, hadn't she? It was too dangerous; he was too dangerous—to her heart. For why dabble in something that could not ever be?

She pulled her hand away from his crotch sharply, causing her elbow to bang loudly against the side of the armoire. The pain was sharp and intense. It was hard to believe her hand had been there at all. She could not remember putting it there, but it would be a long time before she forgot the feel of him hard beneath her palm. Lisbeth bit back the dull ache that throbbed up her whole arm.

"Lisbeth? Are you all right?" His voice was a combination of concern and frustration.

He had asked her earlier would it be so terrible, them together. He had no idea how very bad a thing it could be. There were things about her he should never know. Shameful, ugly things. All of a sudden the armoire felt stifling. The sides seemed to shrink, closing in all around her. She had to get out, away from him. For both their sakes.

Lisbeth frantically began moving jackets out of her way. "I… I can't do this."

She burst out of the armoire with a gasp and landed harshly against the desk.

"Lisbeth!" She heard him call after her again, but she ignored him, pulling her bodice back into place with desperate shaky fingers. Seeking her reflection in Selbourne's shaving mirror was a mistake. The woman who looked at her was horrifyingly tousled. Dark hair sticking out at all angles and lips wantonly plump. She looked like a Covent Garden doxy. What had she done? Shame washed over her and left her gasping and angry.

Oliver stepped out of the armoire slowly, tucking in his shirt and pulling on his jacket sleeves, adjusting his neck cloth. "I take it you came to your senses?"

"How could you do that to me?" she blasted at him, humiliation washing over her and making her feel ill.

His brows rose to his hairline. "A lesser man would be demanding you finish what you started. Perhaps you should be asking yourself the question, how could I do that to him?"

She spun to face him. "Oh, how typical! How like a man!"

"How typical of a woman to say no to her own desire. Let me remind you it was you who suggested we enter the armoire in the first place." He gave her a sad little smile which only made her angrier with him because she wanted to say yes to her desire for him more than anything.

"I'm leaving," she announced, having hastily pinned her hair back into something resembling respectability.

"Of course you are." He gave her a mocking bow, making no effort not to look at her.

She spun around from the mirror again, struggling to make her bodice stay in place. "What do you mean, of course I am?"

"I mean you always leave, when things get a little… uncomfortable. You run away to your little schedule and your infernal pocket watch. You hide behind them. It is no way to live."

"I lived my life well enough before you came along, thank you very much."

"Did you? Did you really?" With a mocking salute he left her.

Damn him! she thought with fury. Who was he to tell her what she should do? He knew nothing about her, about what she had been through, nothing.

OLIVER WAS ANGRY, with himself and with Lisbeth. He entered

the overheated ballroom and wanted to immediately leave again. Too many bodies, too many eyes, and the drone of too many voices was like an assault to his nerves. Nerves that were already stretched to the limit. Things had gone way beyond a kiss. He could still smell her on his clothes, on his fingers. She had been more passionate than he had anticipated, and it had shocked and delighted him. His body had taken her tokens of encouragement and charged ahead. Her response, initially so promising, had suddenly gone cold. For what reason, he had no idea. The puzzle which was Lisbeth was both complex and multilayered.

She desired him, but something was holding her back. Surely she knew she was free to do what she wished as a widow. The whole of London was convinced they were already lovers. Perhaps she really did dislike him or simply distrusted him. Perhaps Blackhurst had been a bore in bed or just simply a boar.

"Bellamy, penny for them?"

Oliver turned towards the voice. "Dalmere, how long have you been here?"

"Long enough to know you have been gone from this room for some time and only just returned." Dalmere gave him a knowing wink.

Oliver smiled in reply. *If only he knew…*

"Where is the lady who has so captivated your nether regions lately? Honestly, I don't know why you even bother coming to these events at all if you don't actually stay around to attend."

Oliver laughed. "What can I say? The lady is… demanding." *And that was no lie.* "She will be here shortly, I am sure."

He looked around the crowded room before turning back to Dalmere. "Tell me, what was Henry like before he passed? My aunt said he was much changed in the weeks leading up to his untimely death."

Dalmere took a sip of his drink before regarding him. "He was changed."

"How so?"

Dalmere looked away. "I hesitate to tell you."

"Why?"

When Dalmere looked back Oliver saw anger in his eyes. "Because you loved him."

Oliver tensed. "I don't quite get your meaning."

"I do not want to alter your memories of him. I loved him too; he was my friend. You are better to remember him as you do now."

"He was that bad?"

Dalmere ran a hand through his golden angelic curls. "Do you really want to know? Once I tell you, you cannot undo what has been done."

"I have to know."

Dalmere sighed. "Very well. Your brother was in love with the Countess of Blackhurst."

Oliver closed his eyes. He knew this. Why then did it hurt? Shouldn't he be happy Henry had fallen in love? Even if unrequited? It wasn't like the countess was his wife. Yet it felt so much like betrayal. He didn't understand his own feelings when it came to Lisbeth. "Were they lovers?"

"I don't think so, although he would have done anything for her. Anything! He *hated* Blackhurst," Dalmere said with a shake of his head. "We all did in our way. Henry, however, once saw the aftereffects of Blackhurst's temper in the form of bruises and such on the lady and went into a fury."

Oliver's blood stopped. Blackhurst had beaten Lisbeth? Disgust filled him with a fury that made his head throb, his gut clench, and his fists tighten. Henry had always been softhearted towards women. Oliver could imagine him wanting to come to her aid like Sir Galahad on a white steed. It answered quite a few questions and yet left so many unanswered. "What did Henry do?"

"He was going to call Blackhurst out. He told me he was going to put a bullet between the Earl of Blackhurst's eyes and send him to hell where he belonged."

Oliver gasped. "Good God!" This he could not picture his

brother doing.

Dalmere shook his head. "I managed to talk him out of it, but the damage was done. Henry became like a man possessed. He cursed Blackhurst to the devil at every opportunity. He said he told her of his feelings and vowed to keep her from harm."

"And?"

"And what? I don't think she took him seriously. Either that or she was happy to be slapped around by Blackhurst. Would it surprise you to know that what she gives to you, she never gave to Henry? Yet, he was her slave, ready and eager to do her bidding. I worry he may have gone too far and committed the ultimate crime of passion—for her."

Oliver leaned against the wall for support. No! Henry would never have done such a thing. What Dalmere was implying was impossible, improbable, and completely mad. He felt like casting up his accounts.

"I see I have upset you. I have no proof, of course, and I, myself, am disgusted I could even think it of him. But really, if you could have seen the murder in his eyes that day."

"And you told no one of this?"

"Why would I? The duel never happened. No one else but I knew of his feelings towards Blackhurst or his wife. Who would have believed it of mild-mannered Henry Whitely? It is possible Lady Blackhurst had him under the thumb though. He seemed consumed by dark thoughts before Blackhurst's death and plagued by paranoia after."

"Do you think he was capable of murder?"

Dalmere shrugged. "I don't know. A desperate man will do anything under the right kind of pressure and with the right kind of incentive."

Oliver paled.

Dalmere looked at him thoughtfully. "I shouldn't have told you. I have no proof, and I do not think you should delve into this issue any further. It will only make your memory of your brother tainted. The fact is Blackhurst was an arse. A manipulative,

Machiavellian genius with brutal tendencies. He deserved what he got."

"I just can't imagine my brother like that. He was a gentle, dependable, steadfast sort of fellow."

"Yes, yes he was," Dalmere said. "It is how you should remember him." He gave Oliver a pat on the shoulder.

Dalmere left Bellamy frowning into his drink. How quick the fool had been to believe his brother possibly capable of murder. Dalmere could not stop himself from smiling as he headed towards the card room.

A seed, once sown, was bound to grow with the right tending.

CHAPTER NINE

L ISBETH HAD A newfound admiration for actors. Not for their lifestyle, but for their ability to play a part and sustain it. She too was playing a part. Her alter ego, the Black Raven, was used to stares. Used to the finger pointing and the whispered conversations as she passed. It was a part she'd been forced to play by the *ton*. A part she no longer wanted to play but had to, for just a little longer, though it was getting harder to pull off, especially in front of Bellamy.

Lisbeth saw him standing alone, deep in his thoughts at the side of Selbourne's ballroom. She walked over and stood next to him, taking in the sights and sounds of the crowded room before her. She didn't really know what to say to him. What could she say? He knew she was there, but he did not look at her or acknowledge her presence.

She looked around at the other guests. They all seemed to be having a grand time. Laughing and chatting and dancing. At this moment she hated them all.

Then Lisbeth saw her, just a flash as she moved in and out of the crowd, but she would recognize her anywhere. Marie! Her sister was here? A frenzy raced through her veins urging her body into movement. She took two steps before she even realized and was able to stop herself from picking up her skirts and sprinting across the crowded ballroom. Her eyes frantically searched for one more glimpse of her beloved sibling. Tears pricked behind her eyes, her throat closing around her sister's name, but she was gone. An ache invaded her chest, like a steel band pulled tight around her heart.

Marie!

She turned to Bellamy. He only raised a brow at her. "I just saw my sister," she said, her voice filled with barely held back excitement.

He cocked his head to the side. "You have a sister?"

"Yes, younger by nearly five years… and she is here."

"Then by all means, do not let me stop you from speaking with her." His voice held more than a little annoyance.

"I can't. Not here."

"I would think this the perfect time," he said but he was looking over her shoulder to the room beyond. "I would give anything to talk to my brother right now," he said, his voice oddly strained.

"You don't understand. There are too many eyes here."

His gaze returned to her. "The Black Raven cowering to the mob? You should go to her."

"I would not wish to upset her."

"How long has it been, since you saw her?"

"Five years, seven months, and a dozen or so days."

He looked shocked and waved her away. "Don't waste this opportunity. You may not get another."

"Like the opportunity you didn't get? To say goodbye?"

Bellamy's eyes narrowed. "Yes. And to ask him questions, about the speculation, Blackhurst and… you." He looked at her with such a searching look. Heat took over her body and sizzled all the way to her toes. She broke the contact, uncomfortable with the way he made her feel. When she chanced another look at him, he was frowning.

"It seems your sister is not the only member of your family here tonight."

Lisbeth turned and gasped as her grandmother came limping towards them. Despite needing the aid of a walking stick she was moving at an impressive speed towards them. Her face was a mask of grim determination.

Bellamy bowed. "Lady Fortesque, what a pleasure." His tone sarcastic.

"Bellamy," her grandmother acknowledged. She gave no indication she had noted his tone.

She turned towards Lisbeth. "Marie is here."

"Yes, I just saw her."

Her grandmother's eyes narrowed. "You spoke to her?"

"No, I have not spoken to her. I merely saw her in the crush."

"Good. You and Bellamy must leave," she said, waving her arms in a shooing motion.

Bellamy stepped forward. "With all due respect, we will leave when we are ready."

"Do not make a scene," her grandmother hissed, turning towards Lisbeth. "Your coming back among us is already bad enough."

What other kind of response did she expect? "Does she know I am here?"

"Not to my knowledge, and I want to keep it that way."

"I think it should be up to her whether or not she wishes it."

"I agree," Bellamy said.

"Stay out of this, Bellamy," Lady Fortesque said, before she looked around her quickly then turned back to Lisbeth. "Do not be a fool and ruin it for everyone. I will try and organize a meeting... at the opera... next week. I cannot guarantee your reception."

Lisbeth was dumbstruck for a moment. Her grandmother was offering to set up a meeting between her and Marie? "Thank you. I would never make a scene or do anything to hurt her."

Her grandmother studied her for a moment, nodded, and walked away.

"You shouldn't let her dictate terms with you. Seek out your sister on your terms." His tone was irritated.

"I would if I thought it would be the best way, but my

grandmother is right, in this at least." Lisbeth looked down at her hands clenched in her skirts. She had an overwhelming want to sink to the ground and sob her eyes out in despair and happiness. But the Black Raven would never do such a thing.

Without a word, Bellamy stepped forward and offered her his arm. She took it and together they left the ballroom, her sister, and Selbourne's armoire behind.

LISBETH WAS THANKFUL for the silence in the carriage. However, there was an energy in the air, of issues unresolved, that had her sitting tensely in her seat. Bellamy said not a word, just kept staring at her. Was he still angry about the armoire? He wasn't usually the type to hold on to his anger for long. Still, he kept his gaze on her. What was he looking for?

Her nerves stretched like the fine hair on a violin bow, and she wondered how much more she could take before they broke into disarray. Seeing her sister, being warned off by her grandmother, and the unquenched sexual tension between Bellamy and herself was not doing her anxiety any favors. To make matters worse, she could still feel his kiss on her lips and remember the heat of his hand as it glided up her thigh… to her….

She felt the warmth of a blush on her cheeks and glanced over at Bellamy. He was still looking at her. She wished he would stop. It was doing strange things to her insides. Silly, girlish things.

The silence stretched. The only sound in the carriage was her breathing and the rattle of the carriage wheels on the cobbles below them. She was tired of constantly battling her emotions. It was difficult trying to maintain indifference when what she felt was so much more. Anger, desire… shame. What a terrible combination.

Yet her body thrummed with the awareness of his body being

opposite her. If she moved her leg a fraction she could touch him. Had he liked her hands on him? He certainly seemed to. He hadn't liked it when she had burst out of the armoire, halting his seduction. Neither had she, but she'd had little choice at the time as her brain had argued for rational retreat. She had liked him touching her and so had her body. Oh, but there were so many reasons not to complicate this relationship any more than it already was.

He is going to leave you in two weeks, when the season is over.

Yes, but why not enjoy yourself for this short time? Why must you always deny yourself?

Because I am scared.

Lisbeth closed her eyes—longing for some relief from all she was feeling. When she opened her eyes, it was to find Bellamy still studying her with a slight frown upon his handsome face.

"I'll take you home," he said.

"No, that won't be necessary. I am quite prepared to go on to our next engagement."

"Countess, there is no use in exhausting yourself."

"So eager to be rid of me?" she retorted in a manner which disgusted even herself.

"With all possible haste," he replied.

Lisbeth tried to hide her shock and hurt at his comment. So, he *was* still angry with her. Well, she was angry with him too. It wasn't like she started the incident in the armoire, *he* did.

She had to remember her purpose for re-entering society and his part in it. She had tried so hard to keep to their agreement and yet after the dance at her grandmother's soiree he had not asked her to do another wager from his list. She could not lose sight of her goal now. Neither could she let him forget their agreement. It was business, not personal. Both of them had let their baser instincts shadow their focus. It couldn't happen again.

She needed to prove her innocence beyond doubt. If she didn't, all her self-worth would be lost, and she would have nothing left but this cynical shell which she despised.

"Well, I'm afraid you will have to wait to be rid of me until after…" Digging out her schedule with shaking hands, she attempted to read it in the dark.

"Phelps is next on the list," he said, his tone bored. "I'm surprised you don't remember. You must surely have memorized it by now—you have looked at it so often tonight."

Ignoring him, she tapped on the roof and instructed the coachman to stop under a streetlamp.

Oliver tried to keep his annoyance under control, but it was difficult when she kept doing irritating things like leaning half out the window with her backside absorbing his view. Did she have any idea what kind of picture she was presenting him? Was she doing it on purpose? What he couldn't see in the dimness of the carriage, his mind was more than willing to make up. He had contemplated her backside more times than was healthy as it was. He had held it in his hands tonight and that was something a man did not forget in a hurry. He doubted he would ever forget what happened in that infernal armoire.

"What are you doing?" Oliver asked with a sigh. The urge to get his foot and give her a little assistance out the window was tempting, especially after her little pantomime in Selbourne's boudoir.

"Why do you… not have a… lamp in your carriage, Bellamy? This is most awkward."

"I've never had need of one. I may perhaps have one installed tomorrow just so you won't be teasing me by wiggling your derrière in my direction in a most distracting manner. It is deuced awkward… for me!" He put his hands on her waist, his fingers sliding deliciously over the dark-emerald satin.

"I… the schedule… I have to…" she said.

He pulled her back in the window before she injured herself. "Forget the stupid schedule," he growled, grabbing the vellum.

"No, you don't understand," she said, wrestling with him over it.

"I understand… you're being completely ridiculous," he

muttered while trying to avoid her flailing hands. "You could have fallen out of the window and broken your neck. Although I see my concerns about your safety do not, for some reason, concern you." He had her under control, but she still did not realize her fight was lost.

Oh, how he wanted to kiss her again. The fury in her eyes just made it harder not to.

"I have to go to the Phelps's, it's on my schedule," she bit out, giving up on getting back her schedule and digging into her reticule for her pocket watch with shaky fingers. He grabbed it too and her eyes grew huge with shock and disbelief. "Give that back!" she yelled.

"No, I'm taking you home," he said, before giving his coachman instructions to return to Blackhurst House.

When he looked back at Lisbeth she had her pistol out. Blast! Her eyes were now full of panic, her breathing erratic. He knew she would do it, silly woman.

"Put it away," he said in his most serious voice. He was sick of this particular threat.

"Give me my watch," she demanded with her hand outstretched. "Please!"

He crossed his arms over his chest. "When I have you safely in your door, I shall return it to you." He kept his eyes directly on hers, trying not to look at the pistol at all. "I promise."

"Now, Bellamy! I want it now!" she demanded.

Oliver grabbed the barrel of the pistol, gave it a twist and a tug, and gained command of the gun.

The look on her face was priceless. She had gasped, her mouth a perfect O. Obviously, she had not expected his efficient removal of the pistol from her possession. "Now, sit down and be a good girl," he said, trying to speak as softly and calmly as he could without grinning.

Her face was flushed, her breathing rapid and heaving, then her eyes rolled back in her head, and she fell forward, knocking Oliver back against the back of the seat.

"Lisbeth?"

No response.

She fainted? Well, this was certainly something new.

Pinned underneath a beautiful woman would normally have Oliver in good spirits, but this was hardly the same situation. He was used to women passing out *afterward.*

The carriage pulled up outside Blackhurst House. He maneuvered around so he could gather her in his arms and on his lap, then pocketed the pistol. *And she had the hide to say men were dangerous with pistols! What a grand end to the evening,* he thought as he gazed down at her angelic face. Quiet like this, she seemed no more than a child.

This whole situation was ludicrous. What was he doing here, with her, on this fool's errand? There was no way they would find Blackhurst's killer. Frankly, he didn't care who killed the bastard. *Even if it may have been your dear departed brother?* Oliver shook the thought away.

He was meant to be collecting wagers, making money, paying off Henry's debts. Instead, he was obsessing about Lisbeth's lips and her backside—of putting his lips on that sweet backside—and mauling her in confined spaces. Mauling her? She'd been mauling him! He'd be damned if she hadn't planned the whole thing, luring him into that farcical oak box to have her wicked way with him. He laughed out loud in the carriage because if he didn't he just might yell in frustration. John Coachman opened the carriage door.

Oliver carried Lisbeth up the steps and kicked the door a couple of times with the toe of his shoe. Lisbeth's head lolled on his shoulder. She moaned his name and her eyelashes fluttered as if trying to open but she stayed unconscious.

Rollands opened the door. When he saw his precious countess lying so still in the earl's arms, he looked perplexed, then horrified.

"Good Lord! What has happened?" the butler asked, still standing in the doorway.

"Let me in and I'll tell you." Oliver followed a red-faced Rollands into the parlor and deposited Lisbeth onto a soft peach-colored sofa.

"Is she ill? Should I call for a physician, Lord Bellamy?" Rollands asked, looking apprehensive from his position behind the sofa. Mrs. Rollands, the housekeeper, was hovering in the doorway, her face a mask of concern for her mistress.

"No, I don't think it will be necessary. She fainted, is all; some smelling salts would be handy if you have some."

"Oh, yes, of course, my lord. I will get them immediately." Her butler scrambled out of the room like Aunt Petunia's dogs were nipping at his heels.

Oliver perched himself on the edge of the sofa. He removed a dark wayward curl from over Lady Blackhurst's eyes and then rubbed the back of his hand over her soft cheek. *By God she is beautiful,* he thought. Beautiful despite the dark smudges under her eyes which indicated she was not sleeping well. It seemed these last weeks had worn her down at least as much as they had worn him. Oliver was not sleeping well either these days. It had been a frustrating few weeks in more ways than one.

Their investigations had yielded very little in the way of physical evidence, but a disturbing picture of her husband was beginning to form, and her list of suspects capable of his murder had grown to terrifying proportions.

Oliver looked down at Lisbeth. Her lips were relaxed and opened slightly. He was taken back to when those lips were on his, hot with passion, not so very long ago. His eyes moved lower to where her breasts strained against the fashionably low-cut bodice. He remembered the feel, the weight, of those glorious globes in his hands, of having said breasts squashed against his face only moments past. It should have been an occasion worth celebrating. Alas, it was not to be, and taking advantage of an unconscious woman was not his style.

Instead, he put a cushion under her head and adjusted her skirts so she was the picture of unconscious ladylike composure.

She was not as unflappable as she always put on, it seemed.

He looked up to see Rollands re-enter the room. He passed a small vial of smelling salts under the countess's nose and very effectively brought her back to consciousness.

"Rollands?" Lady Blackhurst asked, in a confused voice and then looked at the woman. "Mrs. Rollands?" She then focused on Oliver her expression still a little wistful, as if she thought she was dreaming.

"Bellamy?" she queried, in a wispy voice. "Bellamy!" she repeated but this time her eyes were wide open and accusing. "Where is my watch?" she demanded, sitting up.

"Right here, Countess," Oliver replied, placing the silver watch, with the Blackhurst crest, in her palm.

"Oh," she said, looking at the watch. She put her other palm up against her forehead as if dizzy.

"I'll get you some nice warm milk, you poor dear," Mrs. Rollands said, patting Lisbeth's hand before she and her husband left the room.

"Do you faint like that often, Countess? Perhaps your corset is too tight. I could—"

"No, I do not and no, you definitely cannot," she said vehemently. "And don't you ever interfere with my schedule or my watch again." She crossed her arms over her chest.

"I think you depend on your schedule far too much," he countered, crossing his arms over his chest in imitation.

"I don't care what you think, Bellamy."

"Oliver, my name is Oliver."

"Well, how very nice for you," she shot back.

Her eyes were flashing like crystalline daggers and by rights he should have stab marks all over his chest or at least in the vicinity of his heart. He supposed, in hindsight, he should have let her have her silly schedule and have done with it, but she'd been driving him crazy with it for weeks.

"I'm sorry, I had no idea you would get so upset." He could see his apology wasn't gaining him much ground. Not the forgiving kind, apparently. What a surprise! Not the rational kind either but that was an altogether different thing again. "You looked tired. I thought I was doing the gentlemanly thing."

"Then don't," she said, shuffling a little farther up on the sofa.

The urge to smile was tugging at his lips again because she was so incredibly easy to tease. "I wouldn't go putting ideas in my head, Countess," he warned, shuffling up the sofa too.

"Oh, for God's sake," she said looking more uncomfortable by the moment, crammed as she was up against the edge of the sofa.

Shrugging his shoulders and sighing as if it was a nasty job she had just ordered him to do, he moved closer still. "Well, if you feel so strongly on the matter," he whispered, just before he lowered his head and put his lips to hers.

Lisbeth's eyes closed involuntarily as she let the pressure, the heat of his lips, consume her. There was a strange light that lit behind her eyelids, and she felt like sighing. She wished she didn't like his kisses so much. She wished he wouldn't keep doing this to her—it was hard enough to keep him under control, keep him at arm's length, keep him from getting too close to her and her teetering heart. Oh, but the kiss was so soft, so sweet. Why was it he could make her forget everything but his lips on hers, the taste of him in her mouth where his tongue explored with searching, searing strokes? She sighed, despite herself, and put her arms around his neck, pulling him closer to her. And, oh, how she wanted to forget, just for a little while.

This was so unfair. They had been tangling words and wills for so long it seemed, and now he knew she was nothing but a swooning female. Now, in his arms for the second time tonight and with him kissing her so pleasantly, she hardly knew what to do.

All she really knew was when he kissed her she felt free, free of everything she'd been before. Free of the Black Raven and its clutching claws. He made her… *feel.* Like a woman who was desirable and deserving of passion. She had been deliberately cruel to him and yet he would not let her deter him. Instead, he just kept chipping away at her. If he knew how close she was to shattering into a million deadly shards he would possibly reconsider his determined efforts and move far away—Scotland perhaps, or the North Pole.

"Stop thinking," he rumbled near her ear as he kissed her neck.

"Oh." All thought deserted her. How obedient her mind had become to his demands. If only it would listen to hers the same way.

His mouth was caressing her jaw and neck. His kisses burning their way towards her collar bone.

It was so nice to be held… but no, she must concentrate and make him understand he could not do this to her. He could not sweep her away completely. Her heart couldn't take it.

But he was so very good at distracting her, the cad. So she did the only thing which was sure to make him see it was foolish to keep trying to seduce her.

When her hand connected with his cheek he was quick to take it prisoner. He smiled. "If you are going to slap a man for doing what he has just been dared to do, then you should really put a little more power into it—make the effort worthwhile."

She raised her other hand but saw the look of challenge in his eyes and let it fall to her side.

"Giving up so easily, Countess? Tsk, tsk, I would have expected more of a fight than that."

Fighting against his superior strength? She already knew how fruitless an effort it would be. Her past was full of unsuccessful attempts to fight off a stronger opponent. But Nathaniel was dead now and could no longer physically hurt her. Still, wrestling with Bellamy in the carriage had also proved he was far stronger than she.

"Go home, Bellamy."

He smiled again and leaned closer. "I know you are all bluff, Countess," he whispered, and then kissed her on the nose.

Stunned, Lisbeth gaped at him. Then he chuckled, damn the man.

She was about to speak when Mrs. Rolland's wide form arrived with the warm milk.

"Would you like some, my lord?"

He gave her grin. "No, thank you, Mrs. Rollands. I think I will leave Lady Blackhurst in your capable hands. She has had a… trying night." He stood, turning towards Lisbeth who was still watching him warily.

"I look forward to seeing you again soon, Lady Blackhurst." He gave her a bow and kissed the hand that had slapped him. He straightened to his full height again and turned towards the parlor door leaving her aching in his wake.

Lisbeth fell back against the sofa.

Mrs. Rollands handed her a cup and smiled. "Lord Bellamy is very handsome, if I may be so bold as to say."

"Yes, he is," she replied, tired, confused and defeated.

"He seems very attentive. He looked so worried when he brought you in."

Lisbeth glanced up at her housekeeper. "Did he?"

"He made a great fuss of making sure you were comfortable. I was watching him from the doorway."

"Oh," Lisbeth said. She was surprised he hadn't just tossed her on the sofa like a discarded coat. Especially after the way she had acted tonight.

"Just to make sure he wasn't taking advantage, if you get my meaning."

Lisbeth did know what she meant. And he had taken advantage. She could still feel his lips on hers. Warm, soft, confident. Where had Mrs. Rollands been then?

If only Bellamy knew about her past, about what had happened between her and Blackhurst, surely he would want nothing to do with her. He would know her deep shame and be disgusted, just as she was of herself.

"He was very attentive. Such a gentleman." Mrs. Rollands

sighed, wistfully. "I'll let young Millicent know you are home. Would you like a bath?"

She nodded. The housekeeper smiled, picked up the tray, her many keys jingling as she moved. Lisbeth had always found it a comforting sound.

So, he had charmed Mrs. Rollands? Typical. Even her butler seemed to have thawed towards him. Her own emotions were in turmoil when it came to Bellamy, and she didn't know what to think.

Lisbeth sipped her warm milk.

Oliver, he'd said his name was Oliver.

Why had he told her his name? He seemed to know hers and use it. She had not given him permission to, but neither had she objected at the time.

"I know you are all bluff," he'd said, and he was right. She also knew she had just lost any advantage she might have had over him. Did he feel something for her? To use her name as he had, call her *perfect* and *lovely* and kiss her like he actually wanted to. More than once at that. Not an act then, not just playing the part of the lover for the spectators of the *ton*? What did it all mean? What did he want from her? And, could she give him what he wanted without losing herself completely?

CHAPTER TEN

O NE'S MEMORY IS all one has of the past but how to know if it is faulty? Could memory be altered by time or circumstance? Or the angle in which one viewed it?

Oliver sat at his brother's desk, palms down on the cool wooden surface. The leather chair he sat in was well worn too. How many times had his brother sat here? The room looked the same as when his father had occupied this space. It looked as if Henry had not done anything to make it his. Had he felt, as Oliver did now, that it was not his to change? Or could Oliver simply not remember how it had been?

Shaking off his mental cobwebs he opened the first drawer, which was full of credit notes for tailors and bootmakers, and general correspondence from the land steward begging funds for repairs to tenants' homes. Had the repairs been completed? Not that he had the money to do them if they were not. He clutched the letters tight, crushing the papers in his fist. Had Henry felt as useless as he did? To ease his nerves he uncrumpled the papers and placed them in a pile.

Next, he took out the household ledger and flicked through the pages. Column upon column of figures. His brother had not lived an extravagant lifestyle, which to Oliver pointed to a financial situation which was in crisis before the speculation. Had Henry hoped for a miracle? Was that why he had risked everything?

Opening the next drawer, he found his own letters to Henry, a dozen at best, all bound together with string. Was this all there was? His gut churned, an uncomfortable knot forming low in his belly at the realization. So few words had passed between them in all the years he had been away, and he had not kept even one of Henry's letters. Had his brother worried about him? His letters had never implied that he had. Nor had there been anything of merit discussed in his correspondence, certainly not finances. But neither had Oliver. Mostly because he could not but also, how to explain what he did? Yes, he was a soldier but as a code breaker he was often summoned to travel to some unexplained place or woken up at odd hours to pore over important missives by candlelight. It was not the life one put in a letter.

The more papers Oliver found and stacked into piles, the more his heart descended into darkness. "Damn you, Lisbeth." Fire boiled his blood in that now-familiar feeling of injustice. He had wanted to prove her wrong. Had wanted to ride over to her house and slam the evidence down in front of her and say, "Ah ha! Now pay up, Countess."

He hated that she was right. The truth is unfindable.

He hated that there was nothing here to explain his brother's state of mind, his thoughts on Lisbeth, or indeed her husband. All he had was Dalmere's less than cheerful remembrances of his brother on his last days and his aunt's less than reassuring ramblings. He was more lost than ever.

Oliver tilted back in the chair, his head flung back, eyes closed. What to do now? *Help me, Henry, give me something. Anything.*

One drawer remained. Probably empty or simply more bills, but he was nothing if not thorough. He opened the drawer and jerked upright. Instead of more papers, a wooden box sat inside. Would this hold what he had been looking for? His heartbeat sped up as he put the box in front of him. Using a skill learned many years ago he picked the lock and opened the lid. What lay inside felt like a slap.

Sketches of a woman shook in his hand. Not just any woman. It was Lisbeth, a little younger perhaps, but it was her. There was a half-dozen drawings on different sized pieces of paper. His brother, and he had to assume they were by his hand, had captured a vulnerability in her eyes. When had he sketched them? Aunt Petunia must have been correct when she said Henry had romantic ideas or even love towards Lisbeth. One was dated 1810 and had to have been before she had married Blackhurst. He spread them on the table in front of him trying to organize them into some type of timeline. Had she lied about their relationship? Or had Henry simply had an infatuation that had never manifested? He could not blame Henry for sketching her; she was an intriguing subject, and he found himself searching out every detail his brother had missed.

A loud knock at the door had his heart nearly leaping out of his chest. He dropped the sketches back into the box and slammed the lid shut.

His butler appeared. "Lord Ashton is here. He is in the parlor."

"Thank you, Kinsdale." Should he tell Ashton about the pictures? He looked around at the mess on the desk. "I will be right down."

He swept the piles of bills and invoices back into a drawer, even though he was tempted to throw them all in the fire, adjusted his cuffs, and schooled his features before leaving the room.

He found Ashton lounging on the sofa, reading *his* paper. Tony looked up, did an infantry-style inspection of Oliver's person, and then went back to the paper.

Whatever had he been looking for? Bullet holes? Oliver walked farther into the room and took a seat.

Tony remained silent, which grated on Oliver's nerves. "How kind of you to come here to read my paper. Does your brother, the duke, not share?"

The blaggard had the hide to laugh. "I am simply reading of

your latest adventures with the Black Raven. You cannot blame me; it is riveting stuff."

Oliver stood. Agitation had become his constant companion these days.

"I assure you," he poured a drink for each of them and handed Tony a glass, "I take my life in my own hands every time I step out with that woman but… I must also confess that I find her as fascinating as I do irritating." *And she kisses like a goddess.*

Tony raised a blond brow and bent the paper with deliberate folds. "You sound smitten. Should I be worried?"

"Ha. Hardly." He sat and made a show of swirling his drink. Smitten. Was he? She *was* extremely attractive and part of him loved the challenge of her. Or was it the danger of her that was so alluring? Perhaps it was something else entirely and he was not going to delve any deeper into those thoughts.

"Has she disclosed anything interesting to you? You spend a great deal of time together so you must discuss something."

"Oh, we converse on many things." Like their debate that first night of the validity of her owning a handgun, and the delicacy of keeping time, not to forget missing earbobs and the art of telling the truth. None of that would interest Ashton, but it would amuse him, and Oliver wasn't in the mood to be the brunt of the joke that was his current predicament. "She has not had it easy, you know, since her husband was murdered. She told me she took to her house because she could not cope with the whispers and stares."

"I would think it not an easy thing to carry around the guilt of murdering one's husband and would stay at my residence too. It surprises me that she did not beat a hasty retreat to the Continent." Tony leaned forward. "But now she has no qualms about it. Indeed, she seems to flaunt herself about the *ton's* ballrooms without a care in the world. Do the whispers suddenly no longer affect her?"

"At first, I too was curious as to why she would want to reenter society if everyone had been so awful to her. I have watched her closely and I assure you the whispers still upset her, but she puts on a brave face. Like one would wear a mask at a masquerade ball. She hides behind the façade of the uncaring Black Raven. Then I discovered something."

Tony sat up his face having suddenly lost the pretense of boredom. "And what was that? Is she blackmailing half the *ton*?"

Oliver shook his head. *Oh, how Tony would love that.* It was so easy to think the worst of her, but last night he had seen a new side of her, and he was unsure she was worthy of her slanderous reputation. "I believe she is looking for evidence."

"Evidence?" Ashton looked as if he were just offered porridge for dessert.

Oliver took care to try and phrase his reply so that Ashton would not laugh. "The countess swears she is innocent of her husband's death and is trying to find out who did do it."

"And you believe her?"

Well, yes, he did but he was not sure why. "I cannot say right now. I will keep my judgment until I know more."

"Just remember, she is a possible killer. She cannot be trusted. Don't let your head be turned by her pretty face." Tony put down his drink and sat forward, clasping his hands together. "I don't want you to forget how dangerous she is."

"As if I could forget. There are whispers everywhere, but then there were murmurs about Henry too. Should I believe them as well?"

Tony frowned. "What do they say about Henry?"

Could Tony not have heard them? He must have. "That he was much altered before his death. I cannot believe it. I will not believe my brother would have even contemplated…"

"Contemplated what?" Tony glared at him intensely.

Oliver did not like it at all. It reminded him of the countess and her withering death stare. "I hesitate to say, only that he was not himself. Dalmere said as much."

His friend closed his eyes as if bracing for unwelcome news. "Bellamy, what did he do?"

He would be damned if he would tell him exactly what Dalmere had indicated. "That is the thing. I cannot believe my brother would even entertain such thoughts, let alone act on anything."

"What thoughts? Bellamy!" Tony was up in a flash, pacing in front of him.

Putting his hands up in surrender Oliver said, "Only that he hated Blackhurst."

"Well, that is not new. Everyone hated him."

"Before he was dead, and the scheme was revealed as fake?"

"What are you intimating?" Tony had stopped his pacing now and glared at him again.

Oliver glared back. "Dalmere said that Henry wanted to kill Blackhurst. He said that my brother, my steadfast, never impulsive brother, was in love with Lisbeth. That he took offense to the way Blackhurst treated his wife."

"And you believe this to be wrong?"

"You knew Henry from Eton. Was he the type to challenge someone to a duel? I mean, yes, he did invest in the speculation, which was also out of character, but he was not usually emotionally reckless."

Tony took up position by the window and peered out. "No, he was not. However, we cannot ignore the possibility."

"Lisbeth said they met only once."

"Debatable. We cannot rule out some kind of arrangement between them."

Oliver wiped a hand down his face. "I don't know what I believe." Should he tell Tony about the sketches? That would only make his brother look guilty, and deep down in his gut Oliver knew his brother was not a killer.

But did he know the same when it came to Lisbeth?

CHAPTER ELEVEN

*B*LURRED FACES. FAR-OFF *voices taunting. Dreadful names, chanted at her as she descended from the prison carriage for her trial. Hurtful words, as clear and sharp as a razor's blade, cutting her over and over.*

She had not expected this reception. She had not been prepared to be pelted from all angles by rotten fruit, have her hair pulled, and her gown ripped. Who were these people and why did they hate her so?

The crowd was a cresting wave of hatred, looming all around her, ready to crash down and drown her. Shouts of, "hang her, hang her," echoed off the stone walls as she passed on her way into the courtroom. "Murderous bitch, sinner, pox-ridden harlot!"

Lisbeth looked desperately for one friendly face, one set of sympathetic eyes in the crowded courtroom. It made her dizzy. Was there not one person in all of London who cared if she was innocent?

Nathaniel's family was there, united in a group of vile looks. These people had been her family, had loved her as a sister, or so she had thought. They knew her; how could they believe she had killed her husband? Where was her father, her grandmother, her sister? Was there no one here who loved her?...

Lisbeth blinked furiously upon waking. Tears fell in relentless streams down her cheeks to stain her pillow. She had learned long ago, it was better to weep in the privacy of her room than to let others see her weakness.

It was always just before dawn that she felt the most alone. Surrounded by all the worldly goods she could ever want, and yet her life was empty—meaningless. There was nothing and no one to love her. She could hardly expect less when she had ceased to even like herself.

It wasn't until she was undressing for bed last night she realized Bellamy, dratted man, had stolen her pistol. Not that a pistol could protect her from him. Not any longer. Oliver Whitely had shaken her to her core, and she had not a clue how she should feel about it.

She had to concede everything that had happened last evening she'd deserved. Acting like a Bedlamite over a silly piece of paper was bad enough, but to faint over a watch? A watch she hated because it had belonged to Nathaniel. She only carried it to keep her focused on her task of proving her innocence.

Having decided she must stop this destructive behavior she had tried *not* to write her schedule for the next day. But at four this morning, candle in hand, she had found herself heading for her desk in the library to do just that. Some habits were just too hard to break.

She had avoided Nathaniel's study like the plague. His room was more than the place where he had died. Dark shadows had haunted it long before the ghost of her husband. It had been his private domain, his place of secrets, as well as his place of hatred. She knew it was silly to be scared of a room, but she *was* afraid. Afraid of the memories there, the nightmares they evoked, and her weakness. More than anything she was terrified of what she might find in there about herself.

She could hardly read her own handwriting the first time she had attempted to write out her schedule. Her hand had shaken so violently it was amazing the scribble even resembled words.

Perhaps a few more days grace, then I might be strong enough to venture where devils danced, she'd thought.

No!

A demon faced is a demon vanquished, her father used to say. Lisbeth was sure it wasn't going to be so easy, but she had to try. She could no longer put it off. It would only play on her mind as it already had for weeks. She must do it. She must do it tomorrow!

She wrote that dreaded schedule out again and again and again until it was neat as a pin, satisfied at last the staff would be able to read it without making judgment on the state their mistress had been in while writing it. She placed the schedules on the hall table, as usual, and went back to her room. The top one addressed to the Earl of Bellamy.

STANDING AT HER bedroom window she watched the gray haze of dawn blush to pink with the promise of a new day. The dawn always called to her, offering her a chance to try again. The glass was cold from the frost of the early morning, and she used her forefinger to draw an O in the fogged-up pane.

Oliver.

To know his name evoked a certain intimacy that she was not yet ready for. Intimacy demanded a certain expectation of truth, of friendship. She needed a friend. She couldn't deny it. Although, it was not likely the kind of friendship he was hoping for. Was it so selfish of her to want his friendship, knowing she would not be able to offer him the same? While she accepted that she needed him, she also acknowledged that she needed to protect him, just as much, from herself.

Her blackness.

Her curse.

Her worthlessness.

So many things could go wrong and yet he refused to try and accept her schedule. He could not understand how it had helped her survive the foulest of days. How she needed it, still.

The problem was she'd been prepared to use him when things had been all on her terms. Now, Lord I-know-you-are-all-bluff was trying to play Saint George to all her private dragons. She had not asked him to champion her. It must be a family trait, as his brother had the same sense of chivalry. She wondered how different things may have been for her if she had taken up Henry's offer to buy her passage to the Continent and away from Nathaniel.

Lisbeth knew what would happen if she let herself give in to Oliver. Inch by inch he would steal her resolve, her will, and her very thoughts. Until one day, she would not know what she was doing or why. He would convince her this quest was foolish and she should abandon her plan, live a quiet life, become his mistress, and dismiss all hope for a future of her own making.

It was not enough. She would not live like that; she couldn't.

Dawn had broken, the clouds had rolled in, and rain now splashed against the glass pane in fat drops. Lisbeth knew deep in her heart that today would make or break her.

LISBETH HAD HER hand poised over the door handle of Nathaniel's study. It was late afternoon and rain fell steadily outside, a constant hum layering the silence of the hall in which she stood. She felt a fine sheen of perspiration on her upper lip and brow. Her heart was beating a tattoo that was making her lightheaded. She'd stayed in the same position for nearly ten minutes with her hand hovering ridiculously over the handle.

Her housekeeper wasn't helping by standing to her left twisting her apron in her hands and saying, "I've done nothing but dust in there. I never moved a thing 'cept to dust."

Lisbeth wished she were alone but was at the same time comforted by Mr. and Mrs. Rollands's presence. Had they not been there, she may well be thumping her head against the door by now. Still, the nervous twitching of Mrs. Rollands was pushing her already frazzled nerves to the breaking point.

Lisbeth gave her housekeeper an imploring look which only made Mrs. Rollands twist her apron more. Lisbeth's eyes burned with unshed tears, not only because she didn't want to do this but because Mr. and Mrs. Rollands had always been so kind to her. Because she cared about them, because they were as upset as she was about this whole ordeal. And it had yet to even start.

Her stomach lurched up to her throat again at the thought of entering the room, of making the first step. She had put it on the schedule and that was that. Rollands's look of surprise and then concern this morning had been enough to gage his thoughts on the subject. She almost wished he'd at least tried to talk her out of it. It might have made her more determined to face the demons she felt lurked behind this solid oak door. Time was ticking away and with every tick-tock of the grandfather clock, Lisbeth felt her courage drain away.

Be strong! It's just a room. Put your hand on the knob and turn it. Come on, do it! She stamped her foot in a fit of temper with herself, which made her housekeeper jump, murmuring, "Oh, my lord."

Lisbeth closed her eyes. Put her hand on the door handle. It was cold, icy and condemning. It was so cold it seemed to burn her palm, like touching snow with no gloves on.

She pulled her hand off the handle again.

She paced around in a circle with her palm to her forehead and the other hand on her hip, trying to both compose and lecture herself. She was just about to seize the handle again when the front door knocker banged loudly, echoing like thunder down the hall towards her. This time all three of them jumped. Lisbeth's hand came up to cover her heart; she was sure it had stopped for a brief moment.

The Rollands looked at Lisbeth.

She stared back at them.

Rollands coughed. "Shall I answer it, my lady?"

She couldn't imagine who it would be but found herself nodding. Her mind was still on the study door and what lay behind it. She could see her reflection in its highly polished surface, and it was a coward's face. Her lack of courage was a slap to her flagging spirits. She tore her eyes away and turned towards the door Rollands was opening, relieved, even if only for a moment, for the reprieve.

The gust that flew down the hall towards her was in the shape of a man. For a split second she thought it might have been

Nathaniel's ghost come to mock her. The man seemed enormous in a greatcoat and hat. He threw off his hat as he advanced and she gasped.

Oliver!

Her hand flew to her heart in relief, but his face was thunderous. She stepped back from the door as he continued towards her.

"What is the meaning of this?" He waved his copy of the schedule around erratically over his head. Confused, Lisbeth looked from Oliver to her gathering staff then back to Oliver.

He growled at her blank look and shoved his soggy schedule in her face, his finger at a line. "There will be no need of Lord Bellamy's services today? Services?"

Stunned into silence, she remained staring at the schedule in front of her. This is what had so upset him? It was written clearly enough, so where did the confusion lie?

"Are you trying to punish me for last night? Is that it?" he said, his voice dangerously low. "Well, I don't care. I will not apologize."

She did not like his tone at all. Did he have any idea what she was going through here? No, of course not. How could he? It was why she had decided to do it alone, but perhaps she had been wrong to exclude him.

Watching him as he impatiently shrugged out of his coat and tossed it negligently towards her butler, Lisbeth couldn't help but be reassured by Bellamy's presence. His body had never scared her, even though he was a good head and shoulders taller than she. He usually held himself in such a way that it presented no threat to her. Now, worked up as he was, she couldn't help but notice the power he held at bay. The width of his shoulders and the leanness of his waist and hips all seemed so much more dangerous today. His muscular legs were encased in buff-colored breeches and finished in a pair of top boots. Large boots.

Why was it she was so fascinated with the size of his feet? He seemed awesome in a way she had never bothered to notice before. It shocked and thrilled her.

"Well?" Oliver asked.

Lisbeth's head snapped up from his feet.

"Because if you think for one moment I am going to—" Bellamy looked around and saw everyone in the hall was looking at him. He scowled. If his expression was meant to make her staff scatter, it didn't work. Mrs. Rollands moved closer to Lisbeth and Rollands also took a step towards him.

"What the devil is going on here?" Bellamy ordered.

"My lord," Rollands said, "I'm afraid I'm going to have to ask you to leave."

Oliver replied in a flat tone, "I'm not leaving."

"My lord, you are not on the schedule. You were not needed today. Surely—"

"Really? Are you sure, Rollands?"

Rollands's confusion showed briefly on his face. "Yes, my lord, I am."

"Show me." Oliver put his hand out to Rollands for the schedule.

Lisbeth watched as Rollands slowly took out his copy of the schedule, still crisp edged and folded neatly.

Oliver took a pencil out of his jacket pocket. "Thank you. Mine was a little soggy. Now… one hour spent in Nathaniel's study," he read, then leaning on the wall, added, *"with Bellamy,"* and handed it to Rollands.

Bellamy then turned, glaring at Lisbeth.

Having recovered somewhat from her shock, Lisbeth was now throwing him her most disgusted look. "You can't do that!" she said, hands on hips. The nerve of the man!

"I believe I just did, now—"

"No!"

"No? But, Countess, it's on your schedule," he mocked with a raised brow.

"Just because you write it in doesn't mean anything! Now, get out!"

"Is this about the armoire?"

She gasped.

"You're not going to faint on me, are you? Threaten to shoot me? Oh, that's right," he smiled for effect, "I have your rather pretty little pistol, don't I? In case you were fretting, it is safely out of *harm's* way." He then leaned a little closer to her, whispering, "You are *harm*, by the way."

"Oh! How dare you! How dare you come in here and… and… come in here and… my schedule… in my own house!" she heard herself screech. She knew none of that had even made sense. She was so angry and so confused by the fact he had just ruined her schedule with such ease, she didn't know quite what to do with herself. Part of her was waiting for lightning to strike her down. The other part just wanted him to leave but he kept looking at her.

She looked at the clock in the hall. In the silence it ticked over another minute so loudly it reverberated in her head like a gong.

"Damn you, Bellamy—" she began.

"You are not shutting me out, not now, not after all you've put me through."

She gasped again because she really couldn't move or think. What was he talking about?

She had to make him leave, but how? She could feel perspiration gather and trickle down her back. She looked at the clock again.

When she made no further argument or movement, he made that strange growling sound in his throat again, looked around him once more, and raked his fingers through his hair. It seemed he had made up his mind for her when he grabbed her arm, cautioned Rollands with a finger, and grabbed the knob on Nathaniel's study door.

She felt somewhat unreal as he propelled her through that door, like stepping back in time, like reliving a nightmare only with the wrong man. She looked around the room and her head began to swim.

Oh Lord, protect her!

Her legs wobbled when he let go of her arm to close the door behind them. She stumbled to the desk and looked frantically around the room to get her bearings. Or was it to look for an escape? All she knew for certain was she did not want to be here.

Lisbeth felt her eyes fill. The gentle spill of her tears as they made their way down her cheeks tickled her flesh, but she was too distraught to wipe them away.

Turning towards Bellamy and seeing his frown still in place on his too handsome face was the last vestige of reality she felt before she was swept away to a time and place she had never wished to visit again.

Memories whirling, she crumbled to the ground.

...NEWLY MARRIED, SHE had entered her husband's study expecting her stunning smile to be gifted with a kiss or a smile but instead Nathaniel's fierce scowl advanced upon her. He slapped her. The slap so hard it sent her head spinning. The shock of his unexpected attack made her stare at him with wide eyes full of confusion. She could feel the sting of his handprint on her cheek. What on Earth had she done?

"I asked you to see me a half hour ago," he yelled in her face.

"I...I was just finishing off our thank-you cards..." Her eyes burned as she battled to contain her tears. His summons had not said he required her urgently.

"I am your husband, and you will do as you are told when I tell you to do it. Is that clear?" The chill in his voice made her shudder, but he was not quite finished with her yet.

"Yes, of course, but I have done all you asked. I simply didn't know you needed me immediately," she replied, shocked and confused by this sudden change in him.

Her answer did not please him, and he gave her another savage slap that sent her to her knees.

"You will do as you are told!" Nathaniel yelled. He moved closer until they were face to face. "And you will do it to the letter. My word is law in this house, little wife. I decide everything. You are my property now and no more worthy of my attention than my dog. Do you understand or do I need to beat it into you?"

"I am your wife. You took vows to protect me," she whispered, still unable to comprehend what was happening.

"And you took vows to obey me. Now take off your clothes. I wish to see the marks I make."

She scrambled back against the door. "No! Have you gone mad? What have I done to you to deserve such treatment?"

He laughed then, and it was to be the last warning he would give her. He ripped the clothes from her body while she fought him with all she had, but he was so much bigger and stronger than she. He beat her with his fists, his booted feet, and when they were tired, he used a crop he had in his drawer.

While she was cowering on the floor in agony and terror he calmly sat down on a chair and looked at her, laughing. "Why is your kind always so stupid, eh, wife? Thinking you are worthy of being treated like some kind of queen, expecting it, as if it is something you deserve simply because you are a lady? I won't tolerate disobedience in my wife so learn to do as you are told, when you are told. Understand?" He stood, stepped over her like so much rubbish, leaving her huddled in her humiliation.

THE MARKS HE so wished to see were to be constant reminders to her in the next few months until she learned neither to be seen nor heard unless he asked for her.

He didn't love her. He didn't even like her. He wanted a plaything, something he could control.

Something he could break.

His betrayal cut her to the bone even as his beatings bruised her flesh. She became like a mouse, scurrying around to avoid notice and yet ever vigilant, waiting for his summons. After those initial beatings she knew there was no hope for her future or of an escape from his brutal treatment.

Lisbeth was vaguely aware of her surroundings now, but her misery had taken a merciless hold of her senses.

Sounds seemed to come at her from everywhere, shouting her weaknesses, branding her for her failings. She put her hands over her ears to shut them out. It did no good. Why would they not go away? Why couldn't she push these memories out of her head?

She was adrift on an angry sea of emotions and grief. Grief not for her husband but for the young girl she had been, for the trust he had wrenched from her heart. She mourned the young woman who had thought so naively that she was about to start a new and exciting life, only to find it was to be the end of her innocence, her dreams, and her hope in a future that was not to be hers.

For so long she had taken the blame for her husband's anger, for his brutal treatment. For was there anyone else to blame? She had searched in vain for an answer to so many questions but in the end, she had felt only numb, unable to function without his instruction, without his fist forever poised and about to strike for the smallest, faulty step.

Her mind spun and dipped and swayed in an effort to bring her back but all she could see was the darkened room, smell the metallic aroma of blood, and something else she didn't quite understand, of her hand reaching out and finding Nathaniel's body cold and staring. Her shaking hands on the...

"Lisbeth? Lisbeth!" Oliver didn't know what to do. He'd turned from locking the door to find her doubled over on the floor crying and making a horrid keening sound that almost stopped his heart it was so soul-wrenching. The sound of pure misery. He'd heard it before, too many times before. The sound of grief and despair. It was the sound of one's heart shattering into a million pieces.

He'd seen women crying over the bodies of their dead, screaming their anger at a hazy smoke-filled sky. At the time he had been glad there was no woman who would have to suffer such a fate over him was he to fall in battle. He'd seen this at too many battlefields, too many dead, too much needless grief. He wished he could forget but some things burn into one's memory like a tattoo.

He blinked several times, which didn't help at all. His eyes still burned. What had he done?

Dealing with women in such a state was beyond his experience. Did he dare touch her or offer her comfort? He'd tried that once and she had threatened to blow a hole through his ribs. She didn't have her precious little pistol now so perhaps if he… just…

He knelt down beside her and took hold of her shoulders. She jerked away from him, her eyes filled to overflowing with tears—unseeing. He swallowed the smart remark meant to make her laugh. Instead, he pulled her towards him. She resisted for a few moments, fighting him with her small fists. Then focusing, as if recognizing him at last, she practically threw herself into his arms, weeping uncontrollably until his jacket and shirt were quite soaked through.

He sat on the floor with her in his arms and for a long time just rocked her. He smoothed her hair, crooning comforting words into her ear until he was nearly hoarse. He apologized profusely, and multiple times, for he knew to some extent her tears were a direct result of his thoughtless actions. If only he had not charged into her house like an imbecile demanding to know why he had been left out of her schedule. If only he had not been so upset by the thought that she was leaving him out of something important, he may have been able to process the fact that this was something she had needed to do herself, without him. She was in no state to tell him, so he guessed he would just have to wait.

It seemed like days she wept, intermittently hitting him in the chest, and squeezing the breath out of him. Finally, she released him. She had developed the most adorable hiccups, and he took this to mean that this particularly puzzling play of emotions was over with, for now.

Oliver stood, pulling her to her feet, and guided her to one of the stiff-looking chairs by the window. He gave her his handkerchief, for what it was worth, and went to open the door.

Now the entire household staff was waiting in the hall. He smiled. "She's perfectly all right. Just had a bit of a…" Bit of a what, complete breakdown? "Turn," he decided. "Spot of brandy I think, Rollands, if you please," he requested. The butler raised a brow for a moment in surprise but then nodded even if he was still looking rather peeved.

"Oh, and some tea… for your mistress," Oliver added. Well, by the looks on their faces that didn't earn him any popularity points with her staff. He retreated back into the room and sighed loudly.

"It's official. They hate me," he announced as he walked over to her. She hadn't moved an inch. "Look, Lisbeth I'm sorry… again for… whatever it is that I did."

She lifted her head and looked at him for a few moments. Then she laughed a sad little laugh that indicated that she didn't really want to laugh, but he was obviously so pathetic at apologizing that it had caused an involuntary reaction. It was a start, if nothing else. The start of what, though, he wasn't sure. Hopefully, not the start of more crying.

Oliver offered her a small smile in return.

"You have been very kind," she said in a whisper.

"I have? Oh, the hair-smoothing technique was quite effective, granted. Learned that from my mother, God rest her soul. The words of comfort, though, were all mine, except for maybe, 'don't cry, precious,' which I *think* I stole from my nanny."

She smiled tremulously. "You are ridiculous."

He looked at her through lowered lashes. "Yes, sorry."

"Stop saying sorry. I'm beginning to believe you." Lisbeth gave another weak smile and wiped her eyes again before offering back his handkerchief.

He looked at it. "Keep it as a memento… or twist it into an impossible knot, whatever takes your fancy," he said as he watched her hands do just that.

"Thank you." She stopped twisting his handkerchief and looked around the room. "It is I who should apologize. I am so sorry that I… wet your shirt. It is just that I… I hate this room!" she announced.

"Really? I would never have guessed."

"My… husband was not a nice man. He was… mean and

cruel and…" She stood, turning away from him.

"Countess, Lisbeth, please, there is no need for explanations if they upset you… Really." He had a good idea exactly how mean and cruel Blackhurst had been.

"Do you not wish to know why I was so upset? Why this room so unsettled me?" She had commenced pacing around the room touching small items now, her brow creased as she looked for the right words.

He watched her, as always, with a growing admiration he wished he didn't have. He had heard about Blackhurst from Dalmere last night, but he had not wanted to believe him. Perhaps Dalmere had been on the mark. He remembered Blackhurst's portrait above the mantel in the parlor. A bitter taste formed in his mouth. Was it bad of him to want to dig Blackhurst up and pound his bones into dust?

"I assume there are bad memories in this room?" he asked, taking a seat to watch her. He loved watching her move. She had such an easy grace, the kind that came naturally and could not be taught no matter how many books may be placed on one's head.

"Yes, bad memories." She pushed one of Nathaniel's pictures off-center on the wall. "I should thank you really."

Oliver's eyebrow shot up to his hairline.

"I had been standing outside this room for nearly fifteen minutes." She paused then and looked around her before locking eyes with Oliver. She pushed a glass paper weight off the desk where it smashed into a hundred pieces. After contemplating the pieces of glass on the floor, she continued.

"This was the room where we found him, you know. Right there, under your feet."

Oliver brought his feet up immediately and looked at the wooden floorboards expecting, what, blood, to still be there?

"Don't worry. It has been thoroughly cleaned so there is little chance of you catching anything… deadly." She pulled out a drawer and tipped its contents onto the floor. "He would have hated this. Disorder was his enemy, among other things."

"Including you?"

She nodded. "Including me."

"Then he'll probably be rolling over in his grave just like he deserves," Oliver replied, stepping over *the spot*, and propped a hip on the end of the desk. "Think he'd like me sittin' on his desk? No? Good! Now, what else can we do to upset him? Shall we have some fun at his expense, Countess?"

Lisbeth looked at him, so handsome, so alive, so aggravating, and somehow… also wonderful. She realized that she had been the one that had involved him in her nightmare. If she had just left him on her steps he would have gone home, eventually, and she could have spared him all this.

He didn't deserve to have to put up with her and yet she needed him, now more than ever. He was somewhat endearing, she had to admit. Most men would have simply walked out at the first sign of tears, not to mention the scene she had just put on.

She should have known it would affect her so strongly, coming in here. She *had* known, which was why she had found it so difficult to open the door herself. Her reaction was regrettable. If Nathaniel was rolling in his grave over her abuse of his study now, then he would have been laughing up a storm in hell to have seen her earlier.

"Yes, let's," she replied, knocking an inkwell to the floor.

He laughed, strolling around the room. He toppled some books off a small table by the window.

They continued in this fashion until the floor was littered with books and other assorted bits and pieces. Every picture was put off-kilter and when it was all done Lisbeth looked at the small mantel clock and then at Oliver.

"I think you should do it," he said.

"But it was his father's."

"He's hardly going to be worried about it, is he? Besides, isn't that even more reason to do it?"

She knocked the clock off the shelf and stepped back as it smashed to the wooden floor, springs and cogs flying every which way. And it did feel good. It felt very good. She wiped her hands together and regarded her partner in crime.

"Well done!" he praised. "There is perhaps *one* more thing you should do before we end this."

"Oh?"

He nodded towards the door. "Call off your watch dogs. They are no doubt standing in the hall ready to attack me with soup ladles and feather dusters."

Shaking her head she repeated, "Soup ladles and feather dusters?"

"I suppose you would rather pitchforks and fire pokers?" Oliver pretended to be deeply offended but was happy to see a slight smile around the corners of her rather lovely lips. Could it be that they were finally on the same side? That perhaps he would begin to know the Lisbeth of BC—Before Carslake?

He was a little disappointed when Rollands knocked on the door a minute later and entered with a tray of brandy, closely followed by Mrs. Rollands with another tray containing a teapot and cups and some little cakes.

Rollands made a jolly good show of not noticing the state of the room as he placed the tray on the now clear desktop, unlike his wife whose eyes grew huge at the sight of the mess. She immediately looked Lisbeth over for any signs of mistreatment. Typical that she would think the worst of him but, upon reflection, he could perhaps understand their reaction. The pair retreated, leaving him alone again with her.

She poured herself a cup of tea and then smiled at him over the rim of her teacup as she sipped.

Lisbeth Carslake, Countess of Blackhurst was more an enigma to him now than ever.

She intrigued and fascinated him, and he couldn't wait to know her better.

CHAPTER TWELVE

OLIVER ROLLED OVER and tried to smother himself with his pillow. It didn't work. Then he kicked off his blankets and lay there letting his body cool. Why could he not stop thinking about Lisbeth?

Her lips, they were so soft and plump, like a feast for a starving man. Her magnetic blue eyes could burn a man's soul, and he would gladly die in the inferno. Her breasts… yes, her breasts could burst a man's blood vessels, and still he would smile while bleeding.

Lisbeth, Beth, Lizzy. He chuckled. She'd hate being called Lizzy—he should try it on her sometime.

He was asking for trouble.

He was doomed!

He was ten types of a fool to feel like this about her. The worst being: stupid fool, idiotic fool, insane fool, and of course, bloody fool. He was sure there were more than ten types and if so he would still fall into whatever category they might represent. Ashton could probably come up with fifty but that was because he would find perverse pleasure in reciting them to him one by one, probably for days on end—without a breath.

He had to keep Lisbeth on a shorter rein. Huh! *Add, naive fool to the list, if you please, Ashton.*

If he had learned anything in the last couple of weeks, it was the Countess of Blackhurst was a determined little baggage.

He got up, washed, and dressed for the day, but his mind was full of the woman with the incredible eyes. Eyes that could make one suffer both pain and desire.

He was so confused, especially after yesterday. Now he knew there was so much more to her story, and damn if he didn't want to read the whole book. Her cold beauty masked a woman who had endured more than her share of ugliness. He understood masks. He wore one too, but now he felt like his reasons were far more trivial than hers.

He took on the façade of one who was in control, who cared little for financial matters, like he did not have a huge debt and potential failure looming above him. He wanted to make Henry proud, make his parents proud. He wanted to prove he could come rising out of the ashes of this financial debacle like a phoenix rising—wings spread wide and ready to fly once more.

Oliver was determined he would not put his aunt through the scandal of having his pecuniary state exposed to all and sundry. If he could just pay back the bank and show that he was capable of repaying his debts, he may have some hope to rebuild his legacy. He was under no illusion; it would take years to gain any real profit from his estates. He would just fade into the shadows of the *ton* and reside in the country until he felt he was worthy to take a wife.

A wife! Where had that come from?

Oliver moved from the window overlooking the road below and sat behind his brother's large desk. Lord, he missed his old life. Gaining his title had lost him more than just his brother. He'd lost his sense of being something useful, his sense of control. It was a sad state of affairs.

His position as a code breaker under *Scovell* had been an important but unglamorous position, but because he had shown skill in the fighting arts, he'd been assigned under Captain Markham, writing or breaking a coded message by spluttering candlelight at midnight. It was how he'd reunited with Ashton. It was because of Ashton that Oliver had become an unofficial member of *The Ring*, a small network of specialty agents who work for the King.

He laughed remembering Lisbeth's whispered words of confusion when she couldn't make head or tail of his list at Costello's musicale. Only a handful of people in all of England could read the code. However, that part of his life was over and now here he was, in his brother's house, surrounded by things that were not his and never should have been.

Picking up Lisbeth's little pistol, he glared at it as if it represented his life—shiny and impressive on the outside but empty and useless on the inside. He'd been furious upon finding the gun was neither loaded nor primed. The worst she could have done with it was hit him over the head. He put it in the box that held her sketches. He had looked at those sketches too many times to count but it seemed a fitting place to put her puny pistol. Picking up his coded note from Ashton he deciphered.

Client wants you to dig deeper, get closer. He warns not to fall for her manipulations and falsehoods. There are many who would take matters into their own hands. Beware.

I would like you to bring Lady Blackhurst to my sister's coming out ball. My mother and Warrington have agreed. I want to meet her. Make sure she attends.

Ashton.

Oliver stood, threw the missive into the fire, and wiped a hand down his face. He had hoped Ashton's *client* would give up on this madness. Obviously not. He knew things looked bad for Lisbeth, especially considering what had come to light yesterday regarding her marriage to Blackhurst. She had every motivation to kill the bastard. But then, so did a dozen more—including his own dear departed brother. What a mess this was all turning out to be.

Returning to his brother's desk, he picked up Lady Blackhurst's schedule—Mozart's *Don Giovanni* at the opera. It looked like her grandmother came through after all.

OLIVER. LISBETH COULD not stop thinking about him. Part of her didn't want to but she couldn't help it. The way he had held her, whispered those ridiculous endearments in her ear, and helped her vent some of her anger on Nathaniel's study was something she would always be grateful for.

She felt her face flush red at the thought of what had happened in Nathaniel's study. Such an embarrassing display would have made most men run for their lives and not stop until they hit Portsmouth and yet Oliver had stayed. Not only stayed but comforted her and asked for nothing in return. It was strange.

Stranger still, he had not even tried to kiss her. It was unlike him not to at least try. It was unlike her to be disappointed by the fact, but she was. She wanted Oliver to kiss her. She had thought she would never want to kiss another man, not ever, not after Nathaniel. So this was quite a revelation.

She picked up her quill and let the feathered end whisper across her cheek. She wondered briefly if Oliver had inherited his strong jaw line from his mother or his father's side of the family. Were his warm chocolate eyes a Whitely trait? Henry had brown eyes too from memory, but she could not remember him specifically. He may have looked similar to Oliver, but her memory of his brother eluded her.

She heard the knock and glanced up to see Rollands come into the room.

"Is it strange, Rollands, to want to know everything about him?" she asked when he deposited her afternoon post on the table.

"About who, my lady?"

"Bellamy, of course."

"Oh, him," Rollands replied.

She looked up at him, surprised by his tone. "I thought you liked him."

"I am unsure of my exact thoughts on the matter at this time, my lady."

"Is this because of yesterday? He didn't know about my fear of Nathaniel's study, you know."

"Yet he man-handled you into the room by force. It was not his place."

"You are right. It was not his place, but I cannot be angry with him. He did me a great service."

"I wish you had let me accompany you into that room instead. It would have been less… messy."

Lisbeth stifled a laugh. "I agree, but it was most cathartic. Was Mrs. Rollands terribly upset with us?"

"She has been in a mood for some time and has the poor maids in fear of their lives."

"Oh dear. Should I have a word?"

"I have already spoken with her."

"And?"

"She is now in a mood with me." He smiled. "I am quite used to her moods, my lady."

"Oh, but Rollands, I cannot be the cause of your marital misery."

"I assure you her mood will pass. Do not worry. You might, however, want to worry about Lord Bellamy."

"Why should I worry about Lord Bellamy?"

"It has come to my notice that he has not collected on any wagers."

She gasped in surprise. "None? That cannot be!" She stood and stalked over to the window to look out at the busy street below then turned back towards her butler, a frown between her brows.

He shrugged. "Perhaps he has another reason for aiding you."

Shock made her seek a chair. "He cannot have known why I let him in back then, that I had needed his assistance to re-enter the *ton*. He cannot… I thought he was without funds?" None of this made any sense. How had he been living all this time without claiming his wagers? She did not want to think he was deceiving her about his financial standing. She did not want to think ill of him. Not now, not after yesterday.

"Odd, is it not?" Rollands asked. "Especially as my source tells me Lord Bellamy is racking up debts as we speak."

"It does not make sense. Why would he continue to carry out the wagers and then not collect the money? Does he plan to pauper the *ton* all at once?"

"He may still be living off the money he received when he cashed in his commission."

Yes, of course. "You are right. Perhaps he has just been too busy."

"Too busy? To collect money?"

"There has to be a reason." She sat back down at her desk. She needed to be still, to think why he would not have collected the money owed to him. They both looked at each other for a moment, both thinking.

"Have you considered his pride?" Rollands suggested.

"His pride? No, I had not considered it because I thought him a man who possessed neither sense nor pride." She tapped the letter opener on the table. "I was wrong about his sense. Perhaps I am wrong about his pride as well."

"I will look into it further. I should not have mentioned it until I knew for sure."

"Yes, please do." She bit down on her lip, wondering why Oliver would not have taken what was his. There must be a logical reason. Perhaps it was his pride, just as Rollands said. In that moment she decided this revelation would not ruin her night. She said to Rollands, "In the meantime I must get ready for the opera. Millicent will no doubt be already waiting for me. That will be all, thank you, Rollands."

Rollands nodded and backed out of the room, leaving her alone with her thoughts. She refused to think anything negative about Oliver, not unless it was proven to be otherwise. Still, what would make a man act in such a manner if not to deceive? He was already deceiving the *ton* by hiding his financial standing. She could not fault him for that. What was it that bothered her so much about his actions? He was entitled to do what he wished with the money he won from the wagers. If pride was stopping him from collecting his winnings, who was she to tell him otherwise?

She shook her head and stood. It was time to get ready.

It was too important a night to be worrying about Bellamy or his pride.

LISBETH WAS BEAUTY personified tonight, Oliver thought. She was wearing a bright crimson evening gown that highlighted the flawless expanse of flesh at her neck and shoulders. A most wonderful set of rubies and diamonds adorned her ears and throat. This was quite noticeable considering she usually only wore a small golden cross and a pair of golden earrings.

His eyes hurt from looking at her, trying to keep this image stored away in his brain. She was like a goddess come to steal his soul. He could hardly breathe for the effort of suppressing his desire for her. She had even smiled at him. It had been more than a smile but not quite a grin. It was an odd experience that he wanted to re-live over and over until the end of his days.

He could not say with any certainty what was going on in her head but there was a certain agitation or excitement around her tonight that was unnerving. She was always such a picture of stillness, but tonight she fidgeted, sighed, and spent a lot of the trip to the opera with her gaze out the window. What was she thinking? He wished she was thinking about him.

When the carriage jerked to a halt her eyes flew wide open and focused on him. He expected her to pull out her pocket watch, but she did not. He expected her to pull out her schedule, but that did not come out of her reticule either. *Interesting.*

"I'm sure it's nothing," he reassured her.

"Of course." She smiled at him again.

It was dazzling, sent his heart thudding, and made his mouth dry. Oliver stuck his head out the window. One, to gain some air and restore his equilibrium and two, to briefly ascertain where they were.

"I'm afraid it may be a bit of a wait," he said. "The usual crush has started, and it could be a half hour before we get anywhere near the steps."

"That is fine. We will wait." She placed her hands back in her lap and looked out the window again. "The city looks so pretty at night. You can't see the dirt and despair for all the twinkling lights and stars."

"You may not be able to see the dirt, but you can still smell it." He looked out the window again. "We could get out here and be inside before the champagne runs out," he offered.

Her eyes returned to him. "Really, Bellamy, is that all you think about?" Then she did the most amazing thing. She laughed. A sweet, tinkling sound. It vibrated merrily around the interior of their carriage like bird song. "Do *not* answer that question," she quickly added.

"Come on, it shall be an adventure." He needed to put some space between them before he leaped across the carriage and kissed her senseless.

Lisbeth shook her head at him. "My gown will be ruined and no doubt you are hoping I shall trip and break an ankle on the way so you have an excuse not to go."

It was his turn to smile. "I would never do such a thing. I am actually looking forward to *Figaro Gets Married*."

"That is the *Marriage of Figaro* and we are seeing *Don Giovanni* which I suspect you know and are playing the fool just to tease me. I think I am beginning to see through your ploys, Bellamy."

He laughed. "So you are, Countess, so you are."

Lisbeth may have seen through this particular ploy of his, but she was far from figuring him out completely. There was much to learn about this man, and she hoped to start tonight if all went well with her sister.

The house lights were blazing when their carriage finally made it to the steps. A cacophony of gaiety and excited conversation spilled out onto the stairs leading to the Opera House. Ladies in their finery displayed gowns hemmed in gold. Intricate beading adorned their dresses, shot through with silver thread and precious gems. Their gowns were made from various exotic materials sourced from far-flung corners by means better worth ignoring.

The picture was dazzling and confronting. The poorest of lords and the richest of merchants vied alike for the right to be most envied when really all they did was envy each other. One, for the riches a title could not guarantee, and the other, the social acceptance that only marrying a title could bring. And so, publicly, they politely excused each other's faults for their own ends while secretly hating each other as only rivals can.

Here, in this place where the entertainment was only as important as the people who attended it, Lisbeth hoped for a new beginning. To once again have the warmth of her sister's smile fall upon her.

Marie's new husband, Lord Fenwick, had looked handsome enough when she had watched them emerge from the church a married couple, but Lisbeth knew not whether this man was worthy of her wonderful and generous sister's heart. She hoped tonight to find the answer.

If she could only put her mind at rest and be assured of her sister's happiness, all then would be well. Nerves made her stomach lurch and her head ache. If only she could be confident of her sister's welcome. Better still, if only she could turn back the clock and make things right. Never marry Nathaniel or leave the security of her family. Regrets, she knew, were a waste of time. In order to make her life worth living, she could depend on no one but herself. After all, she could blame no one but herself for marrying Nathaniel in the first place.

The *ton* had become accustomed to Lisbeth's attendance to their varied entertainments but still there was a mixed reaction among the crowd who gathered in the foyer drinking their champagne and showing off their precious assets, whatever they may be. Lisbeth simply sailed on regardless. It would take a Spanish armada to stop her from seeing her sister tonight.

Oliver felt a certain sort of angst come over him. He knew what it was, he could smell it—danger. Someone was not particularly happy about the Countess of Blackhurst being here tonight. He scanned the crowd but could see no one being specifically aggressive. Still, the feeling nagged and niggled at him, and he wished he had brought a weapon with him. A small dagger would have been sufficient.

It was strange, for this was the first time he had felt this way and he had escorted her to many functions over the last few weeks. Not even that very first night at Wainwright's had he felt any need to be wary. Why was tonight so different?

He picked up a glass of champagne and handed it to Lisbeth, looking fleetingly her way.

"Is there something wrong?" she asked.

"Wrong?"

"Yes, you seem distracted. Are you ill?"

He turned towards her then and regarded her. "Do I look ill? Not that illness has anything to do with being distracted—which I am not."

Lisbeth raised a brow. "It is only that you have not smiled once since we got here. Nor have you even attempted to tease me." She sipped her champagne and watched him.

"It is also very unlike you to be concerned about my welfare. That you even noticed is very flattering, I suppose."

He saw her wince, for she knew he was right.

"The truth is that there are many people here tonight who do not like you. I am being cautious."

"Cautious. I see. Is it *very* painful?"

A smile cracked at the side of his mouth. "More than you will ever know," he said. "Which side did your grandmother say her box was?"

"The eastern side. What are you looking for?" she whispered in his ear.

He wished she hadn't done that, as much as he wished she would do it again. "Suspicious persons."

She looked around the assembled crowd. "Oh, and what do suspicious persons look like?"

He looked around too. "Shifty, among other things."

"Shifty? Like your friend, Dalmere?"

He looked at her surprised. "You think Dalmere looks shifty?" He laughed.

"Actually, I think he is too handsome for his own good. However, he gives me a peculiar feeling. I know he does not like me but nor does anyone else. Have you known him long?"

Oliver was stunned by her confession. "I met him a few days before I met you. He was my brother's friend. He befriended me when I felt I didn't have or deserve a friend."

"Well, I for one, am glad he did, otherwise you would not be here looking out for suspicious persons on my behalf."

They started to ascend the stairs. "One would think that you are saying you forgive me for the other night, when I took your schedule, and may actually be starting to like me. Considering all that concern and gladness you are currently feeling towards me."

"One would be thinking wrongly then."

Her tone was suitably cool, but he saw her lips twitch. Oliver smiled, pulled the curtain to the box aside, and bowed her through. "I do believe you have developed a sense of humor, Lady Blackhurst."

Lisbeth passed through and smiled to herself. Suspicious persons aside, she felt safe with Oliver around, and she was grateful for his presence. Bellamy may have distracted her for a while but sitting here in the box brought back the reason for this visit to the opera. She closed her eyes for a moment and prayed that Marie would have matured enough to hear her out.

She heard them before they entered. Marie's voice rang sweet with excitement and Lisbeth could only hope it was because of her. When they were behind the curtain, she could clearly discern their words.

"And Mrs. Merryweather said that I sang like an angel with a face to match. Martin was so proud, and he bought me this gown and said that I may have whatever trimmings I pleased and—"

The curtain was pulled aside, and Bellamy rose to face the women. Lisbeth found herself shaking but could not stand.

"Oh, hello," her sister said when she saw Bellamy.

Lady Fortesque made the introductions. "Marie, this is the Earl of Bellamy. Lord Bellamy, my granddaughter, Lady Fenwick."

"A pleasure to meet you, Lady Fenwick," Oliver said as he bowed. Marie smiled and did a small curtsey but it was obvious she was a little shocked at his presence.

Lady Fortesque then took control of the situation and bustled Lady Fenwick farther into the box. Lisbeth stood and turned towards them.

"Hello, Marie." She hoped the quiver she felt in her throat had not come out in her voice.

They stood, both staring at each other. Marie gasped and took a step back, bumping into her grandmother. Lisbeth too was shocked. Marie was all grown up and beautiful. So like their mother. Her dark hair was piled high into a ring of curls with a large lower curl lying over her shoulder. Small beads had been threaded through her hair like raindrops. Her deep blue eyes were wide with confusion. The pain that settled around Lisbeth's heart made it hard for it to pound in its usual rhythm. Oh, how she had missed her sister! Her arms were aching with the need to hold her.

Finally, Marie looked away from Lisbeth and turned towards her grandmother. "How could you do this to me?"

CHAPTER THIRTEEN

"Listen to me." Lady Fortesque stared at her granddaughter, Marie, a ferocious frown marring her features. "It was against my better judgment at first, but I think you should at least hear your sister out," she urged.

Marie shook her head, glancing around her as if looking for the quickest escape route before returning her stare to her grandmother. "I must leave immediately. If Fenwick knew… he would never let me out of his sight again."

Lisbeth let her gaze drop to her lap. She should have prepared herself for such a reaction. She had let blind optimism rule her heart tonight. It was a foolish mistake. She understood Marie's concerns. Her baby sister did not wish to displease her new husband. Lisbeth could not fault her for that. Still, there was an ache within her. It had been there since their estrangement began but now it threatened to consume her in a flood of pain and sorrow.

"Pish posh. Fenwick will do no such thing." Lady Fortesque pulled her granddaughter farther into the box. "Greet your sister as you should."

Marie whirled around, confusion written clearly on her face. "As I should? And how is that, Grandmother? With open arms? After everything we went through because of her?"

"Do you not think I have pondered the matter thoroughly? If I did not think it right, I would not have organized this meeting," she said, her tone matter-of-fact.

"Fenwick will forbid me to ever leave the house again," Marie said in a hushed voice. She peeked over her shoulder at Lisbeth, worry and confusion etched on her face.

"Thank you for trying, Grandmother," Lisbeth said, standing up. "I will leave. I do not wish to be responsible for any unhappiness between Marie and her husband."

Her sister turned a tear-stained face towards her. "I'm sorry, Beth, but I can't."

Lisbeth felt like casting up her accounts.

"I will not entertain this business again when you change your mind!" Lady Fortesque warned.

Marie turned away from Lisbeth to face her older relative. "She murdered her husband, Grandmamma," she said in a whisper.

"Do you really believe that, Marie?" Lisbeth asked, in a voice that sounded strangled and off-pitch. Her emotions were starting to overtake her. She desperately tried to rein them in but the lump in her throat grew even larger.

"How could I believe otherwise? It was all over the papers. We couldn't leave the house. It was months before we could even hold our heads up in society. It was horrible!"

Lisbeth took a tentative step towards Marie. "You know me! I am your sister. Do you really believe I could do such a thing?" Lisbeth implored, although she hardly knew why she was bothering. "I am innocent—surely you know that in your heart."

Marie focused on Lisbeth, her lip quivering just like it used to when she was upset as a young child. "I thought I knew you once, but I don't know you, not anymore. You changed after you married *him*." Marie wiped at her eyes. "After Mother died, you promised you would never leave me. But you left me, Beth. You left me…"

She had promised, but how to explain to Marie, who had been only a child when she had married Nathaniel, that it had not been her choice. Nathaniel had kept her prisoner in the house and forbidden contact with her family. If any of them had seen the bruises he had inflicted, the weight she had lost, the fear in her eyes, would they have come to her defense?

"I have already grieved for my sister." Marie's voice cracked on a sob. "I will not do so again."

In that instant, she knew. Her sister did still love her. Lisbeth swallowed past the lump in her throat. Knowing this did not make the situation any easier. She felt the agony in Marie's voice. Nathaniel had taken so much from her, but he could not take away the love Lisbeth felt in her heart. Her love for her family had always been there. Even if she felt they had not loved her back.

Lady Fortesque took Marie by her shoulders and shook her gently. "You must listen to me. I had heard rumors that Blackhurst was a club-fisted fool, and I let her marry him anyway. He was an earl with a good family and a sizable income. I didn't know he would make your sister's life a misery." She looked past Marie to Lisbeth. "I can do nothing to rectify what I have done, except to bring you two back together."

Lisbeth felt her legs go weak. She felt Bellamy's steadying hands at her waist and drew strength from his support.

"Hold fast," he murmured in her ear. The soft, deep timbre of his voice was calming. He would not let her fall. She knew this instinctively. He had proven himself dependable in this respect, even if she had not always appreciated it, as she did now.

"Lisbeth did the best she could under the circumstances," Lady Fortesque said. "I understand that now, and so should you. Marriage is not all champagne and roses, as you well know, young lady. I believe now that Lisbeth is innocent, and I would not say this without having done a lot of soul searching these past weeks. Having said that, I cannot be sorry Blackhurst is dead. He deserved what he got, whoever it was that did the deed."

Marie watched her grandmother with her mouth open. Clearly, she had not expected this confession. Neither did Lisbeth. Lady Fortesque walked away from Marie and was now standing in front of Lisbeth.

Lisbeth looked up, eyes filled to overflowing. Her grandmother took Lisbeth's hands in hers. Studied her for a moment. Gave Lisbeth an odd, sad sort of smile.

"Can you forgive an old fool? I know now that we should have rallied around you, we who knew you best. I did what I thought I had to for the family at the time, but that meant sacrificing you. I regret my actions more than you can ever know. Forgive me." Lady Fortesque bowed her head and waited.

Lisbeth's whole body was shaking with emotions she knew not how to control. She felt Bellamy's hand on her shoulder, warm and secure. She wanted to turn and bury her face in his chest and let him comfort her but there was still her sister staring at her like she could not quite believe this was happening. Lisbeth couldn't believe it, either, but she wanted this so badly. Badly enough to forgive everything?

"Yes," Lisbeth said. "Yes, I forgive you, Grandmamma."

Marie was flushed, her eyes glassy with unshed tears and no doubt confusion and anger. "What can I do? You ask too much." Marie said. "Defy my husband or go with my heart? He will not like the scandal."

"I will speak to Fenwick. He will see reason, even if he does not like it," Lady Fortesque replied.

Oh, to have her grandmother's confidence that everyone would do as she wished. However, Marie's plea gave Lisbeth hope that her sister was not completely opposed to reconciliation. That fear of displeasing her husband, more than anything, was holding her back.

"Do you really think he will listen?" Marie said now, looking between both her grandmother and Lisbeth. Lady Fortesque nodded. Marie bit down on her lower lip, hope flaring in her eyes as she took a step towards Lisbeth.

"Beth, I have dreamed of you so many times. Of bumping into you in the street or in a shop, anything just to see you. Even if I could not talk to you, just to see your face again was all I wanted for so long. On my wedding day I pretended you were there."

"It was my wish as well," Lisbeth said. "And I was there on your wedding day, outside in my carriage. I would never have missed your special day."

Marie released a sob and flew into Lisbeth's arms.

Lisbeth held her for a long time. Her heart was beating so fast she felt faint, but she didn't care because she was so happy.

"I've been such a coward. I'm so sorry, Beth, so very sorry…"

"Shh, my darling. It wasn't your fault. You were too young to understand. I will never leave you again. I promise."

OLIVER HAD WATCHED the scene before him unfold in a great deal of discomfort. He did not belong here. He walked out of the box as soon as he could and finally felt his breath return. Two disturbing interludes in as many days had given him palpitations. All these family reunions were well and good for Lisbeth, even if they were dramatically over-emotional. He was happy for her, but it brought home to him the sad fact there would be no family reunions for him and that he had limited time with the one family member he had left.

He had never felt more alone than at this very moment. He closed his eyes and tried to picture his brother's face, to no avail. He rubbed at his chest, at the familiar ache there whenever he thought of Henry. He'd lost his family; he knew how abandonment felt. But he had abandoned Henry, too. He had run away to war because he couldn't stand being in the way with nothing to do. He should have stayed, helped Henry, learned from his brother, and taken some responsibility. Instead, he had left everything to his brother to deal with. Now he knew how hard it must have been for him.

Lady Fortesque stuck her head out of the curtains and eyed him. "It is quite safe to return now, Bellamy."

He turned towards her and saw that she was smiling. It looked slightly peculiar on her, probably because her face was unaccustomed to the act. For Heaven's sake, this smiling thing was beginning to be a habit for Lisbeth and her relations.

"Are you sure? Because I am not sure I can handle any more tears."

"Honestly, I was beginning to think Marie addled. I am not used to being questioned."

"Young ladies can afford to be addled in circumstances such as this. Don't you think?"

"Quite. And old ladies, too. There is hope for you yet, Bellamy. Come. The lights are going down." She waved him inside.

Lisbeth came and took his arm, looking up at him as if to gage his demeanor. He smiled down at her, wanting to assure her that he was fine, even if it was not what he felt. She smiled and sat him on the left of her. He patted her hand on his sleeve, and she squeezed his arm tightly.

"Happy, Countess?" he asked.

"Yes, very. Thank you for bringing me here."

"It had little to do with me. I simply do what I am told as per your always delightful schedule."

"Since when?" Her eyes were all merriment and joy.

He liked her eyes sparkling like this. He imagined even diamonds of the first water paled in comparison to the beauty of her eyes. "Since… well, fine, you have me there." He gave her his cheekiest smile.

Lisbeth raised a brow.

"Principle, my dear. A man cannot be under the thumb, you know. It's bad for his liver, or is that his spleen?"

"And we can't have that."

"Indeed, we cannot. Now, be a good girl and watch your opera. I will be asking questions later."

She smiled at him and even in the dimness of the box it felt like being hit by a thunderbolt. It was bliss and pain at the same time. He felt it in his liver and his spleen—not to mention other places.

As he sat and stared at the stage below, he realized he could tick off another of his wagers tonight. His list was still in his pocket but with every passing day the thought of carrying out the list felt more and more abhorrent to him. He still needed the money, that hadn't changed. And he still had Ashton on his back about Lisbeth's part in the speculation. His life seemed to be filled with tasks he did not want to do.

He glanced towards the sisters. They were holding hands with their heads close together, whispering. It was an endearing sight. He felt himself smile despite the ache in his heart that he never had the opportunity to talk with his brother before he died. Never got to tell him how much he meant to him, how much he loved him. How much he missed him still.

INTERMISSION CAME TOO fast for Lisbeth. Marie, still hesitant to face the crowd, would not let go of her sister. "I've decided I do not care what Fenwick wishes," Marie announced, her chin tilted up. "Let us go down and get tipsy on champagne."

"I will not have you punished for seeing me, Marie." Lisbeth was adamant that she would protect her sister from any unnecessary pain on her behalf.

"Punished? Nonsense, Fenwick is not that kind of man," Marie stated with a smile. "The worst he will do is mumble that he is displeased, *very displeased*." She grumbled, in mock imitation of her husband, before giggling.

"I'm glad." Lisbeth hugged her sister. Relief swept through her but still she would not be satisfied until she knew for sure that Marie would suffer no ill effects from their reconciliation.

"Oh, he will no doubt sulk for a day or two, but I know what to do to make him happy again." Marie winked and gave a tinkling little laugh.

Lisbeth could only think how she had never been able to make Nathaniel happy, no matter what she had done to try to please him.

"Then this is not such a disaster, after all?" Lady Fortesque asked Marie.

"I am glad of it, Grandmamma. Thank you. I know I have acted ungratefully but it was so unexpected. I would have preferred for Fenwick to be here, but it is done now."

Lady Fortesque nodded. "I will organize a luncheon so that Fenwick can meet Lisbeth for himself. That is, if you do not have any objection?" she asked, turning towards Lisbeth.

Lisbeth shook her head. "I would like nothing better than to meet Marie's husband and, of course, my new nephew."

Marie walked faster down the stairs dragging Lisbeth with her, chattering all the way, clearly excited. "Oh, Michael is the most magnificent child. He has Fenwick's curly hair but my eyes and Papa's chin…"

Oliver didn't like Lisbeth to be so far from him but perhaps he was just overreacting. He could hardly walk faster with Lady Fortesque on his arm.

"You should bring your aunt—"

A startled scream rent the air.

Oliver instantly let go of Lady Fortesque and ran down the stairs but came up short when he saw that a man had bailed upon Lisbeth and Marie. He was whispering something that had made both women look quite pale. Oliver slipped down the right side of the stairs. A small crowd had gathered.

"I do hope you are not insulting these two ladies, sir?" Oliver asked, coming to stand directly behind him.

The man turned towards him. "Oh, look who it is. Lord Bellamy. Come to protect your mistress? How charming." It was obvious he had partaken of more than a little alcohol tonight.

"I have not had the pleasure of meeting you before, but I see you know me," Bellamy said.

"This is my brother-in-law, the new Lord Blackhurst." Lisbeth explained.

Oliver raised a brow. "Well, Blackhurst, you have made your

presence felt, so I suggest you leave these two ladies alone."

Blackhurst's expression was incredulous. His sneer so reminiscent of the portrait above Lisbeth's mantel in the parlor.

"I am not leaving. She should leave. Murderous strumpet. She insults us all by showing her face here."

"She is entitled to be here as much as anyone else," Marie interjected.

"Why should she be able to parade around here? Flaunting herself, dripping in gems. Bought, no doubt, with money that was rightfully mine. If I had my way, she'd be rotting on some ship bound for the colonies. Thieving witch."

Lisbeth shoved Marie behind her in a defensive stance. Oliver watched as she narrowed her eyes on Blackhurst and summoned her courage. It was wonderful to watch, and he knew he was not required to end this just yet.

"These are my mother's jewels, not that it is any of your business. As to your accusation," she added loud enough for the assembled crowd to hear, "you should really consult your memory, Lord Blackhurst." She stepped forward. "I was found not guilty in a court of law."

"Technicalities saved you. Everyone knows you did it. She killed my brother!" he said to the crowd. The gasp was loud and in unison as those gathered around them moved ever closer. "You weren't content just to get rid of my brother; you had to go and pauper us all in the process. You have ruined not only my family but countless others and yet you show your face in public," he spat. "It's disgraceful."

Oliver grabbed Blackhurst's jacket. "That is enough! You have insulted a lady. I demand you apologize."

"Bellamy, let him go, please," Lisbeth said, before turning towards her brother-in-law. "If you wish to dispute the judge's decision you may take it up with the court. My conscience is clear. If you wish to contest the will, you should have done so. In the meantime, I wish you to remove yourself, and your vulgar tongue, elsewhere."

He turned to Lisbeth and pinned her with a dark stare, just as his cronies came to drag him away. "You took everything from me!" he yelled.

Oliver shook visibly with anger beside her. She turned and put out a steadying hand. "Don't, please. I couldn't bear it. Don't call him out."

He looked at her and took a breath, nodding. She knew it was not in his nature to be passive, especially in the face of such hostility from her brother-in-law. She was in no doubt that Bellamy would shoot sure and true. She did not want to see him banished from England, or worse, for defending her.

"The truth will out, you lying witch," Blackhurst shouted over his shoulder.

Lisbeth called after Blackhurst, "I live for that day, dear brother. I sincerely do."

Blackhurst growled an obscenity but was dragged down the hall and out of sight.

Lisbeth wanted to fall to the ground and sob her eyes out. Now, surely, Fenwick will never let Marie see her again. She looked around her, at the crowd of people staring at her, waiting. Their whispers seemed to swell around her. She saw their concerned expressions and wasn't sure what they expected from her. When she did nothing but raise her chin, take her sister's hand, and began to walk, they cheered. She looked at Marie, confused.

"Bravo, dear sister! They love you," Marie said.

"I feel sick," she replied, her hand going to her stomach.

"Well, you were magnificent." Oliver kissed her hand and guided her to a seat.

"I thought you were going to challenge him for a moment there, Bellamy," Marie remarked, still looking pale.

He looked at Lisbeth and then back to Marie. "I'm not one who generally likes to wake before dawn. However, if he had insisted, I would only have killed him a little." He gave Lisbeth's sister a smile and a wink. She laughed. He turned then to Lisbeth.

"Would you have worried for me, Countess?"

She had no chance to answer because her grandmother had finally caught up to them. "Goodness! All those stairs. What was Blackhurst playing at?"

"Nothing really. He dislikes me and thought I should know," Lisbeth replied.

"Those Blackhursts never did have any sense of propriety," Lady Fortesque said a little breathlessly. "Are you two all right?" She was looking them over with concern.

"Oh, yes. Lisbeth gave him a piece of her mind and put him in his place," Marie said, patting Lisbeth on the arm in a show of affection that Lisbeth had dreamed of for so very, very long.

Lisbeth took a sip of her champagne and held Oliver's gaze for a few moments, her heart beating a tattoo against her ribs. The thought of him dueling over her, putting his life in danger, was not sitting well with her.

Would you have worried for me, Countess?

Yes, I would have worried for you, Oliver. I do worry for you.

The second half of the opera was uneventful, and they did not see Blackhurst again. Still, Lisbeth could not concentrate on the activities on the stage. What if Fenwick did forbid Marie from seeing her again? After what had happened with her brother-in-law, Lisbeth couldn't really blame him. What if the consequences of this evening were too much for Marie to bear? For there would be scandal, and it would be in the papers tomorrow. There would be no hiding from it.

OLIVER HAD BEEN quiet on the way back to her townhouse. He was thinking, she suspected. Probably going over the night, trying to see how he could have prevented their confrontation with Blackhurst. He would blame himself; she knew it. He had, after all, been looking for suspicious persons before they had even ascended the stairs at the beginning of the evening. He had sensed something wasn't right, but she had not believed him, not really.

"I'm sorry," Lisbeth said as soon as they had disposed of their coats in the hall. Her confession seemed to startle him.

He frowned briefly. "And what are you apologizing for?" His eyes turned so warm and comforting like the amber on her father's favorite walking stick.

"I put my grandmother and sister in danger. I put *you* in danger. It was never part of our agreement to put you in that kind of situation. Never."

He waved her off. "Blackhurst is nothing but hot air. Air that smelled overpoweringly of gin."

"It isn't funny, Oliver. If he had hurt Marie or… you."

"I have been in danger before. Quite a few times in fact. Soldier, remember? I quite like it—imminent death and all that." He gave her a grin.

This made her smile, despite not wanting to. Her joker, her jester, always trying to make her feel better. "You are such a liar."

His smile turned contrite. "All right. I might not like it *quite* as much as I have made out, but I do know how to protect you. I *will* protect you. I'll just be more prepared in the future."

"I know you will. This is why I am breaking our agreement," Lisbeth said as she walked into the parlor.

Oliver stopped mid-stride in the doorway. "What? I don't think so." He strode in after her.

She turned to look at him. "I think we have to, don't you? What if something happens to you? I could not…" She was surprised by the quaver in her voice. She told herself she was going to be strong but, as usual lately, her resolve was worthless around this man.

"Lisbeth," he said as he walked towards her, "when this is done, when you have your justice—"

"Ever the optimist, Oliver?" Lisbeth said on a sad sigh. She went over to a sofa and sat down patting the seat next to her. "You must be exhausted."

He looked at her intensely for a moment but did not laugh.

"It is one of many such blights on my personality, but what can I do?" He smiled almost apologetically as he sat. It was such a dear smile, one she was beginning to depend upon. She wanted to reach out and cup his cheek, run her fingers along the roughened skin of his jaw, trace his lips…

"I wish I could be like you," she said now. "Smiling and joking all the time. All I feel is worthless…" Oh, why had she said that? She had never meant to say it, at least not like that. Not to him. Tears sprang to her eyes, and it took all her determination to keep them at bay.

He studied her face for a moment then said, "How is that possible when you are as rich as Croesus? Try being me, worthless *and* penniless."

Was he boosting her ego, again? "Oliver, I am trying to be serious."

The smile dropped from his face, and she saw a raw emotion in his eyes that made her want to cry all the more.

"Then try being serious about something worth the effort." His speech was soft and low, and he smoothed his knuckles over her cheek in the softest of caresses. Then he let his hand drop. "My, my, we have become melancholy. Only one way to remedy this pitiful situation—a nice hot cup of chocolate! I'll ask Mrs. Rollands, shall I?"

She grabbed his hand as he went to stand pulling him back down next to her. "No, Oliver, really, I'm fine. I just wanted to say thank you. You have been good to me."

He looked down at his hand in hers. "Well, I'll admit you didn't make it easy for me at times."

"I know. I'm sorry."

"Stop, please. Even *I* am starting to feel sorry for you. Perhaps, if you kissed me I might feel more forgiving?" The lopsided smile appeared on his too handsome face.

He was just teasing, she knew, but she took up his hands and kissed them both on the top, near the knuckles.

He tipped up her chin and with a chuckle said, "Not exactly

what I had in mind, but it's a start. I shall simply have to show how it's done… Like this." He kissed the knuckles of the hand she had been holding his with. He turned it over and kissed her palm, the inside of her wrist, the soft spot inside her elbow, and right up to the top of her shoulder and the turn of her throat.

Lisbeth, eyes closed, had never experienced anything quite like it. She was quivering. She had never quivered in her life, but somehow he had achieved what she had never thought possible. It was more than just what he made her feel, or the tenderness of his attentions. It was so much more than the way he made her heart flutter or her pulse race. He cared. He cared about her. She cared about him too, and she was just beginning to realize how much. It was an ache in her heart that was so painful she could hardly bear it. Could she let this ache for him grow, knowing it could all end soon, leaving her with a broken heart?

Lisbeth should have stopped him. She should have made him go, but she didn't. She couldn't. And for once she let her heart have its way. The hot tingling sensations of his mouth on her flesh were bliss. He was awakening nerve endings that had lain dormant for more years than she dared count. His lips seemed to be mapping every dip and curve on their journey to who knew where. She held out for as long as she could before she sought those lips with her own.

Oliver could feel the tension in her body. She was wound tighter than a clock spring. One false move and she could explode. She was holding so much back. She was afraid. Whether it was of him or of their passion he didn't know. He hoped it was the latter. The thought of her being afraid of him was abhorrent. He was not Blackhurst, and he desperately wanted to show her that.

He knew he should not have put himself in this position or her, especially after the turmoil of this evening, but he simply couldn't help himself. She was like his favorite sweet set down in front of him. He couldn't resist. He wanted desperately to be all over her, inside her, on top of her, underneath her, but mostly just *with* her. To finally be on equal terms, with equal longing and desire, was a dream that he had never thought would come true.

She broke the kiss and put her palms on each side of his face so that he had to look at her. "Come upstairs with me?"

CHAPTER FOURTEEN

LOSING HIS EYES he thanked the fates for their impeccable timing. He kissed her long and hard. Kissed her while his heart beat crazily against his ribs and his lonely soul filled with hope.

"Are you sure?"

In answer she took his hand and led him to the door of the parlor. They walked into the hall, past Rollands, who still held Oliver's coat. Lisbeth nodded towards her butler and headed up the stairs. Oliver spared a quick glance behind him as he followed Lisbeth.

Her butler was gone.

He let her lead him down the hall. When they stopped outside her door, she turned, reached up, and kissed him. Her lips were warm and soft, her kiss slow and lingering, her fingers curled into his hair. It made his insides do a jig and his cock stir from its slumber.

It was the first time *she* had kissed *him* on the mouth. Lisbeth was initiating this intimacy. He sensed her need to be in command of what was to happen. The idea appealed to him, excited him, but he worried about his own control. He had to tread carefully here.

When she broke the kiss and let her hands drop, he felt bereft. He instantly tried to gather her back into his arms, but she had opened her door and walked in. He followed. He looked around briefly.

"The room is a little stark, isn't it?" she said. Her face was sad. He hated seeing her sad.

"It isn't so bad. It is most annoying to bump into a veritable obstacle course of furniture on the way to one's bed. Don't you agree?"

"Such a layout would be troublesome, I'm sure."

"Fraught with all sorts of dangers," he said, his voice lowering to a husky whisper.

She smiled, placing her small hands on his chest and moving them over his jacket. Her questing fingers found the buttons and set to work freeing them. He remembered another time when her hands had been busy at his buttons.

"What? Why are you smirking?" she asked.

"I am hoping you are not simply going to attempt to correct the slowness of my timepiece."

She gave a little laugh, obviously remembering the scene in the parlor on their first night. "I have come to learn that neither time nor you, Lord Bellamy, like to be constrained."

"Time flies when one is having fun. Who am I to clip its wings?"

She nodded. "Sometimes time is your friend and sometimes it's not. In my case I had to learn to use it for protection. I know you don't understand, and I don't want to talk about it right now." Her nimble fingers made short work of his jacket and waistcoat. Peeling each item off his body she placed them on top of the chair by the fire with infinite care. She watched him through her thick lashes as she undid his cravat and placed it on top of his other clothes.

He found he couldn't move. Like a dream, he seemed to be observing his own seduction, and it was fascinating. Not wanting it to end he decided to do nothing she didn't direct him to do. He thought it might be difficult but when she started to kiss his neck, his shoulder, his breastbone where his shirt lay open, he realized it may be impossible to give her what she wanted. A man was just blood, bone, and randy flesh, after all.

Every muscle in his body was fighting not to take her in his arms and crush her against him, rip her clothes from her body, and ravish her within an inch of her life. He also knew such an act would not do, not for this woman.

Not for his woman.

His eyes widened in recognition of his thoughts. The fact that she had her fingers down there, in the midst of chaos, so to speak, wasn't helping. He wanted to stop her, still her fingers, but she brushed them so softly over him through the fall of his pantaloons that his head fell back in abandon with a groan.

He recited his catechism—Lord forgive him for the bits he simply made up. Eventually he could stand no more of her torture, as sweet as it was. He stilled her hand.

"Lisbeth," he warned.

It did not deter her, despite the fact that her name came out more as a growl. She simply moved on. He felt with agonizing clarity the rest of his clothing leave his body, scraping and grazing over sensitive nerves and skin. He kicked off his shoes, thankful that boots were not attire worn to the theater.

He now stood before her naked and proudly erect. The need to be one with her was infinitely more powerful than he had expected. He was hard and throbbing, just for her. He wanted to say things to her, lover's words, but he didn't want to scare her off. As confident as her actions appeared he knew how much this cost her. Was she doing all this for him, so he wouldn't have to be noble? *Sweet, sweet Lisbeth.* He cupped her cheeks and kissed her softly and with everything he had to give.

He lifted his head and looked at her. She took a step back and looked over him with those amazing eyes of hers. Had she felt it too? That rush of feeling, of one's heart filling with infinite hope and joy.

Her expression was changing to... alarm.

Apparently not hope and joy then.

Her expression was dismayed, like she couldn't believe they

were doing this. She looked down at him, looked directly at *it*, standing so proudly before her, and… giggled.

Giggled! Now it was his turn to look horrified. What the hell? Everything looked in order to him, quite impressively in order, actually. Perhaps that was the problem. He frowned and shoved both legs back into his pants in record time. He should have known it was too soon for her.

"No, please!" She grabbed his wrist, and he left his pants unbuttoned. "I'm sorry. I'm… I'm just so nervous," she said, her face blushing a furious red.

"You giggled at my—"

"I didn't! I mean I wasn't giggling *at* it." She tried to pull him towards her. "It's lovely, really."

"Lovely? Lovely! I don't think so. Your breasts are lovely, your hair is lovely, and your eyes are particularly lovely. This," he pointed at it shaking his head, "is not lovely!"

He placed his hands on his hips and gave her a displeased look. A man could only take so much… description.

"Oliver." She took a step towards him.

"Lisbeth," he replied, holding up a hand to stop her from advancing or, horror of horrors, describing further.

She sighed and flashed her eyes at him. "Fine, it is not lovely."

That's my girl, he thought.

"In fact it is rather… cylindrical."

Cylindrical? Oh, please. "That will be enough of that—ever. Are you sure you want to go ahead with this?"

She nodded and put her hand on his chest, curling her fingers into his chest hair.

"I can't help seeing that this situation is very lopsided," he said. "Besides, I am getting damn chilly standing here like one of Elgin's marbles."

"You certainly seem made of marble," she said, moving her fingertips lightly over his pectoral muscles. He made them dance up and down and she laughed. He loved it when she laughed. He wanted to make her laugh forever.

"I've seen the statue of David, you know. When I was thirteen, our parents took Marie and me to Florence for the summer. I loved Italy—the art, the music—but I don't think my parents knew what we were in for when we visited the *Galleria dell'Accademia*. My mother nearly fainted."

"So, now I look like David?" *Could this get any worse?*

"Heavens no, you are much more… impressive."

He burst out laughing and reached for her. "Cheeky baggage! Later you may tutor me in Italian sculpture but for now let us correct this imbalance immediately. I do believe I have a few poetic descriptions of my own to make." He turned her around and began undoing her gown. She laughed again when he cursed at the number of buttons and tabs he found as each layer was revealed.

"There had better not be some kind of medieval chastity belt under here. A man can only perform so many miracles in one night, you know," he growled into her ear.

She laughed. "Oh, I don't know, you seem to be capable of many miraculous things."

"I do have a trick or two up my sleeve, and the night is young."

Then he kissed her from just under her ear to the point of her shoulder, pushing her chemise down her arms at the same time. He marveled at the softness of her skin, the smell of her, the taste of her. Goose bumps rose on her skin where his lips had been. He nipped and licked the slender column of her neck.

"Oh, that's nice. That is very, very nice," she said, with a shaky quiver in her voice.

He liked the way her body reacted to him. Half-undressed like this, she could not hide from him. She could not say she did not want him, did not need him, as he needed her. The evidence was all over her curvaceous body, in the delectable rosy hue that stained her flesh. He could smell her arousal mingled with a subtle hint of roses and lemon drops. It was a scented net set to tempt him. She needed no such traps to snare him. Tonight he gave himself up willingly.

His heart sped up considerably at the sight of her breasts as he exposed them to his gaze. Her nipples puckered in the cool air. He had held her magnificent breasts before, in the darkness of Selbourne's armoire, but seeing was so much better. He sent a quick thank you towards the heavens that he had not been blinded while at war. Then he placed his hands on them. They fit perfectly in his large hands, and he squeezed them with the reverence they deserved. He paid homage to them, licking and sucking until Lisbeth was gasping.

She was better than pudding, he decided, which was a bizarre thought considering the circumstances *and* considering how much he loved pudding! He banished such ridiculous thoughts in quick order. He had a beautiful woman in his arms and a hunger that could only be satisfied by her.

Lisbeth could feel his restraint in every muscle she touched. She'd known he would be magnificent when she beheld him naked but nothing could have prepared her for the truth of him at the ready.

Earlier she had panicked before she'd had a chance to rationalize her thoughts. Panicked at the sheer size of him. Thoughts of Nathaniel had come flooding back unbidden. There had been no tenderness in her husband. No care for tender flesh and virginal sensibilities. He had used her like a common doxy and then left her to sob in fear and confusion while he snored his head off in the next room.

Oliver was kissing her eyelids. Her eyelids! What had she expected him to do? Do as Nathaniel had? Throw her on the bed, rip the clothes from her body, and roughly slap and bruise her until she cried? No, he was definitely not Nathaniel, and she was glad of it. Looking at him now as he smiled at her, his eyes at half-mast as he leaned down to take her lips again, there was little resemblance between Oliver and her husband. Nathaniel had worn his height like a sword, forever ready to strike those smaller than himself. She had seen power in Oliver too, but his was of the protective kind. Nathaniel's eyes had been dark, cold, uncaring, whereas Oliver's were light, warm, and full of humor. She worried about the things she didn't see in his eyes, the things he was holding back from her. He'd said he would not hurt her, and she believed him. He might drive her crazy, but he would not hurt her willingly.

He made her feel things that scared her. This desire was new to her, this wanton fire that spread through her body with every touch of his lips, every caress of his masterful hands, every hungry look he gave her. She wanted him.

Love me! She could feel the words forming in her throat.

Love me! It pulsed from her with every beat of her heart.

Love me, please, her soul implored.

Yet she said nothing, too much the coward to say the words her whole being wanted to scream.

He knelt and removed her shoes, throwing them negligently over his shoulder before massaging her foot. Smoothing his hands up her leg to the end of her stocking, he undid her garters and skimmed his fingers over the smooth skin of her upper thighs. He rolled down her stockings while kissing his way down first one leg and then the other. All the time she watched him. He seemed to be very dedicated to his task, intimately stopping to kiss the inside of her knee or the arch of her foot. She had never felt anything like it, and she never wanted it to end. At the same time, she was excited by the prospect of what else he would do to her.

She had no idea what he was thinking. She hoped he wasn't thinking at all. She so desperately wanted to feel tenderness. She wanted to feel the joy of copulation, not the fear of fornication that she had felt for so long.

"Stand up, my beauty," he said.

She did as he asked. He smiled as he looked up at her, kneeling in front of her, still wearing his pants.

"Just a little tug and…" Her chemise fell to the floor to pool at her feet.

Oliver's mouth went dry. He sat back on his heels and absorbed the naked beauty of her. She was Venus, Athena, and Aphrodite in one. It was cliché, he knew, but his brain wasn't functioning with any great clarity right now. He was running on pure desire. Seeing her like this, naked and reclining seductively against the bedpost, he felt even less worthy of her.

He hoped this would not be his only chance to be with her, to show her how it could be, how it was supposed to be.

She gave him a slow, lazy smile. Encouragement or dare? Was she daring him to stay? If only she knew how needless that look was. He was hers, had been since he first laid bloodshot eyes on her all those weeks ago, even if it was only now that he was realizing it. Even if it was for this night only that he surrendered to her—body and soul.

He was still on his knees, so he kissed the inside of one of her thighs, making his way back up her body while she clutched the bedpost and made the most beautiful of sounds. When he put his mouth to the juncture of her thighs, the place where heaven resides, she simply uttered, "Oh!" Then, "Oooh my God!"

It was music to his ears and he wanted to hear the whole symphony. He was sure the perfect melody was inside her just waiting for him to play the right notes. He held her to him and began to play. It wasn't long before the crescendo began and she writhed above him like an out-of-control violin. Her hands were the conductor instructing him where to place his tongue and how much pressure she desired. Her final note hovered in the air like a ghost and then disappeared as she collapsed back against the mattress, breathing heavily and clutching at her chest, her eyes wide with wonder as he looked up at her.

"I see you enjoyed that?" He couldn't help but feel a measure of arrogance.

"Pardon?"

It seemed she was not quite back from her ascent just yet. "Never mind." He began to kiss her hip, intending to kiss his way up to her mouth and everywhere in-between.

It was on his travels up her beautiful, mesmerizing, and completely enchanting body that he noticed them. They were so faint he wasn't sure he was really seeing them at first. They were small silvery lines across her lower abdomen. He knew what they were, how one got them. He looked up. His question must surely have been clear. She was staring down at him with a grief that quickly filled her eyes. He saw her blink the tears away.

"He died," she said softly.

"How?" he asked without thinking.

"I didn't kill him, if that's what you are thinking!" She put her arms around her belly trying to hide the scars as if cradling the memory of her child. Her face turned away from him.

"Of course not! You must have been devastated."

"Does it really matter?"

Well, no, he supposed. It did make him wonder how she had survived everything that had happened to her and not gone to Bedlam long ago.

"No, it doesn't matter," he said.

"Influenza. It was influenza," she said moving away from him, her voice hitching with emotion. "It wasn't my fault."

"I'm sorry."

"Nathaniel blamed me, of course. I had produced a sickly child. If he had just let me…" She hid her face in her hands.

"Lisbeth?"

She looked at him, hard. "He took my baby away from me, Oliver!"

The look of defeat on her face filled him with such anger. He curled his fingers into fists at his sides to control the urge to punch the bedpost beside him.

"My baby was dying and he… he would not let me see him. He said I was a bad mother. He said I didn't deserve to kiss my son goodbye." The total devastation of her experience was etched in her eyes, in the tone of her voice. It was all there for him to see, the pain, the suffering, and the guilt of not being able to be there for her child.

"I begged to let me see him. I sat outside the nursery and beat my fists on the door until they were bloody," she explained, while silent tears slipped down her cheeks and her hands made fists.

"I listened at the door as his cries grew weaker. I sat there, imagining I was holding his… his little hand in mine. I promised him I would never leave him. I would let no door prevent me from loving him with all my heart. After he passed away, I stopped caring, about anything or anyone—including myself. I shouldn't have, but I did. I think it made Nathaniel despise me more."

Oliver swallowed the rest of his questions and kissed her belly. Laying his head against her stomach, he hugged her lower body. No one should have to endure the death of a child. Between them they shared too much death and grief.

Lisbeth was stunned and moved by his actions. She bent over him and kissed his head. Ran her fingers through his hair. He was kneeling at her feet. He was kissing her stretch marks—all she had left of the little boy she had loved so much and held in her arms for so little time.

He didn't seem appalled, as she had thought he would be by yet another terrible, shameful truth from her past. He kissed her belly button. He looked up at her from his place on the floor.

"What was his name?"

"Daniel."

"I don't care what Blackhurst thought of you," he said. "It only matters how much you loved Daniel while he was here. I am sure he knew how much you loved him, despite everything. How much you still care about him even now. Just like I care… about you."

Tears threatened again but she somehow kept them at bay. She did not deserve a man like Oliver. He made her feel good when all she'd felt for years was sad or mad or both. Lately she had just stuck to mad. How had this all happened? She was naked with a man who was not demanding she fight him off. Or pushing himself into her in the darkness uninvited. He was waiting, even now, for her to give him permission to love her. She didn't know quite what to do. She felt so incredibly humbled. How had she ever thought him stupid and witless?

Physically, she wanted him like she had never wanted a man before. Emotionally, she needed him like one needed safe harbor against a storm. With him she had felt her confidence return. She could battle any storms if he was beside her.

Lisbeth took his hand and urged him up onto his feet. She kissed him, wanting him with every beat of her heart. A heart she had thought would never beat with love again. Love? No, it couldn't be. It was just her emotions getting confused—easily done in such a circumstance. Oh, but he was wonderful, and her heart swelled with affection when she looked at him.

Oliver smiled up at her. "We all have scars, Lisbeth. I'm sure you have seen that I have a few scars of my own." She had noticed, but on him they did not seem as shameful as hers. It was to be expected, she supposed, for a man who had fought in many a battle to have some war wounds.

"See this one here?" he pointed to a rather nasty looking scar on his right side. "Saber." He then showed her a round puckered scar on his shoulder. "Lead shot. Had a fever for three days."

"I want to know all about your time in the military," Lisbeth blurted out, reaching out to caress dent of his shoulder wound.

He looked up, surprised. "Now?"

She laughed. "Not this very minute…"

He kissed the inside of one of her elbows, distracting her completely.

"Good, because I need to make love to you, Lisbeth. Right now, in fact. There are certain parts of the male anatomy that are very impatient."

"Really?" She smiled.

He pulled her into his embrace. "Really." He kissed her long and hard. Less hesitant now, less controlled. He picked her up and laid her on the bed, climbing on after her. She opened her arms to him, and he gave her his cheeky half-smile before settling himself between her thighs.

Oliver framed her face and looked deep into her eyes. "Have you any idea how beautiful you are?" She blushed and shook her head. These were not the type of words she heard in relation to herself. She would not have believed them from anyone else but Oliver.

He rested his forehead against hers and she felt him nudging at her opening. She tensed for a moment but then he kissed her and drew her legs up around his waist. "Trust me."

Lisbeth closed her eyes.

"No, don't shut me out. I need to see that you want this too. Do you want me, Lisbeth?"

She wriggled underneath him, unable to say the words aloud, trying to show him how much she wanted him to press deep within her. When she finally opened her eyes and looked into his, she saw the concern there. Knew it was all for her. Tonight she had promised herself so much, and now she could see it was time to make true on those promises. Tonight he was hers and she was his. She would entrust him with her body and her heart. Just for tonight.

"Yes. I want you. Please, Oliver, make love to me." She clutched at him wanting him closer.

He plunged deep, filling her, and an overwhelming sense of relief washed over her. There was no pain, just the fullness of him inside, as he moved within her, slowly, languidly, building their pleasure. Lisbeth knew then, with a clarity she had never known before, she did love him. She had tried to deny the truth, but the evidence of her feelings drummed through every part of her. It filled up the empty spaces within her, creating something wholly new and wonderful.

Sensation slid over every nerve and fiber. Her skin tingled from her scalp to her toes, centering on that place between her legs that was currently occupied by a man who, at times, made her question her sanity. Sanity be damned! Her body was floating in a bliss that could not be denied. Heat curled within her, her body moving without conscious thought. Climbing and coaxing, yearning and needing what only he could give her.

Sounds escaped her that she had never heard before. Oliver responded to her moans with grunts and growls of his own. Like before, when he had kissed her between her legs, the pleasure inside her made her writhe and buck beneath him. The pressure, the feeling, the loss of all reality grew until she nearly screamed in frustration. Then it hit her. The most amazing, wonderful vibrations took over her body. She gave in to pleasure, every nerve in her body twitching with it. The fulfillment of every promise he had made to her. He shouted her name as he pulled out of her just in time.

The shock of his withdrawal made her gasp. Lisbeth knew how hard the retreat must have been for him; she had felt bereft but also grateful. Oliver distracted her with his lips, and she soon forgot everything but him.

They kissed each other tenderly. And though no words were spoken they both knew that nothing would ever be the same again.

CHAPTER FIFTEEN

"LISBETH, YOU CAN open your eyes now. I know you are awake."

There was amusement in Oliver's tone. Had her reluctance to fully wake been so obvious?

She touched him tentatively, like he might just turn into a puff of smoke and disappear before her eyes. "You are still here." It was more a statement than a question.

He raised a brow. "You seem surprised. Did you really think I would leave you?"

"That is what men do, don't they? I mean, afterwards?"

He laughed at that. "Only the stupid ones."

His smile warmed her all the way to her toes. She reached up to capture his face so she could give him a good morning kiss. And it was a good morning, the best morning of her life.

He gathered her reassuringly in his arms. "I'm not leaving, at least, not for another hour or so," he assured her.

Oliver kissed her with the enthusiasm that she had benefitted from last night. Gentle but sure, confident but not overbearing. She felt him swell against her thigh. A feeling of great satisfaction flowed through her even as her limbs turned to melted chocolate and her heart picked up pace in anticipation of what was to come. *She* was able to make him react like that. *She* had the power to turn this strong man into a slave to her every whim. What's more, he wanted to give her the chance to discover her desire, her sensual self as a woman. She had already learned so much from him, but knew that she could have a lifetime and not learn everything there was to know about him and herself.

He made love to her less gently than last night, in no doubt now of her response. He wasn't rough but the power of his strokes brought her body into sharp relief. She matched him stroke for stroke, kiss for kiss, and caress for decadent caress until they were both shuddering and gasping each other's name.

"You were made for me," he whispered in her ear.

"Only you," she replied, holding him tightly to her.

She had no idea where these new feelings for him would lead but for now she just wanted to feel his weight on her, hear his words of encouragement, and make love to the man who had brought her back to life.

He held her for a while, the two of them safe and secure in a world all their own, but eventually, as she knew it would, reality returned.

"Lisbeth?"

"Yes?" She curled more closely to him even though his chest hair tickled her nose.

"I need feeding."

"What?" She struggled to open her eyes.

"You have quite drained me, my love. I need food and a hot cup of tea."

"Oh, yes, of course. I'll ring the bell." With that she slipped from the bed, forgetting completely she was naked as the day she was born, until she heard him groan and say, "Forget the bloody bell and get back here. Next time, I'll ring the bell myself."

Lisbeth could only smile as she looked over her shoulder to see the evidence for herself. It was a most gratifying sight. He crooked his finger at her. She smiled and dropped the bell pull. He smiled as she started walking back to the bed, slowly so he could take his fill of her nakedness. She surprised even herself at her boldness in front of him.

When she reached the bed, his eyes were dark pools of desire.

She crawled onto the mattress, but he stopped her from lying down.

"Do you like to ride, Lisbeth?"

"That's an odd question at a time like this."

"Let me rephrase. Would you like to ride me?" He took her hand and guided her until she was sitting astride him. She was in no confusion as to his meaning then.

"I've never ridden a horse like this," she said to him as her hands came down to rest on his chest.

"There is a first time for everything, my dear. Besides, I'm not sure it can be done sidesaddle. We could always try that later if you wish." With that he pulled her down for a kiss.

She guided him inside her and was surprised at the exquisite fullness she felt. With his hands on her hips, he showed her the way, and it was bliss. She rode him, slowly, then fast, and then slow again. She rode him until her body contracted in bliss. She flung her head back and let out a satisfied, "Yes!" He shuddered beneath her, and she collapsed happily and fully satisfied on his chest.

"You ride very well, Countess," he drawled.

When her stomach gurgled with hunger, they both laughed and laughed and laughed.

THEY SPENT MOST of the day in easy conversation with each other. Oliver told her stories of his days in the army, many of which she found hard to believe, and she found herself horrified that he had been in so much danger while de-coding messages. He had a knack of making most of them sound implausible and she found herself laughing more than she had in a very, very long time. His stories had not all been humorous. Oliver recounted many a dirty campaign in the field, but he did not give too much away. He'd seen men die—many had been friends—and she sensed a deep sorrow within him for those who had lost their lives.

They did not talk of Nathaniel. That she had been grateful for. She had no wish to think of him ever again. They did not discuss Oliver's brother Henry either. He was not ready, and she would not push.

Eating breakfast together was a... novel experience. Lisbeth couldn't stop blushing and Oliver kept winking at her between sips from his teacup. She tried to keep up a serious façade for the sake of the servants, but it was nearly impossible. They moved to the parlor and finally they were alone and she could relax.

Oliver was obviously enjoying himself. He looked so relaxed sitting back against the chair and idly reading the newspaper. Nathaniel had never taken any meals or tea with her. She had always been alone.

"So, my dear Lisbeth, are you going to give me my copy of your schedule?" he asked behind *The Times* he was reading.

Lisbeth gasped, surprised. She had been debating on whether to give it to him or not. She still felt its comforting pull but had tried to fight the urge to carry on as normal. In the end the schedule had won.

Still behind his paper he laughed, then bent the paper in half, top to bottom and looked over the top half. "Did you really think I wouldn't notice you leaving my bed in your bare feet?"

"I did not want to wake you. And it is my bed, thank you very much." She felt the blush return to her cheeks.

Oliver ignored her attempt to censure him. "I assume you have the whole twenty-four hours planned out, although I don't recall having your wicked way with me last night being on your precious schedule."

She blushed again.

"Nor this morning," he said with a wink. "I can't imagine what trials and tribulations you have in store for me."

"Not nearly as torturous as you deserve," Lisbeth replied, sipping her tea to hide her smile.

"In that case I must confess to being a little disappointed. I've become quite attached to your particular form of torture."

Sighing loudly for effect, she put down her cup went out into the hall and returned with his schedule in her hand. She passed it to him and resumed her seat.

He laughed as he unfolded it. "Now, let me see…"

He took his time reading it. She waited for the inevitable snide remark or blusterous comment, but he said nothing. He refolded the schedule and slid it into his coat pocket.

Still, he said nothing. He picked up his cup and took a sip. Nothing.

Lisbeth raised her eyebrow, wondering what he was doing. After a few more seconds he looked up and raised a brow too.

"I take it you don't find fault with any of our appointments, then?" Lisbeth watched him, warily.

He smiled. "Why would I?"

"You know very well why."

"I have no aversion to Hyde Park. I do not harbor allergies for grass, bees, or ducks."

"But? Last night…"

"Last night taught me to listen to my intuition and to be prepared. You have no need to fear. I will keep you safe. However, I do find it fascinating that a woman such as you would want to put herself through such a ritual in the first place. A pretty and petty procession through Hyde Park at the fashionable hour is, according to what I've heard, a painfully slow process with very little… procession about it."

"You've never ridden in the park, have you?" Lisbeth put down her cup and studied him.

"Ridden, yes, promenaded like a fool, no. Sorry to disappoint you but I was a little too busy dodging lead shot, cannon fire, and sabers, I'm afraid."

She smiled. "I promise you will not have to dodge anything more alarming than a few stares and fakery."

"And we are doing this because?"

"I need to show the *ton* that despite what happened last night at the theater, I am not going to conceal myself in my house, not anymore. I refuse to hide from scandal, no matter how mad it makes my brother-in-law."

Oliver put his paper down, stood, and walked over to her chair. He leaned down, putting his hands on the arms of her chair. Then he leaned down and kissed her. She reached up and caressed his cheek which was rough with stubble. He turned his head and kissed the palm of her hand.

"I do believe I should take my leave," he said.

Alarm flew through her like a hurricane. "Why?"

"It seems I must make myself presentable if we are to send the tongues of the *ton* to twittering."

"Oh," she said, quite lost in his eyes and much relieved. She felt her body react to him, wanting him. She squeezed her thighs together. How would she ever get used to the way he made her feel?

He stood and kissed her hand. "*Adieu*, Lisbeth, until this afternoon."

When he was gone the house seemed cold and lifeless again. She stood, took a few deep breaths, and made her way to her bedroom. She too must make herself presentable.

HYDE PARK WAS a mass of carriages of all types, as well as men on fine horses. He guided the horses onto Rotten Row and joined the long and congested line of carriages. He longed to have the park empty so he could put the horses through their paces. Instead, he had to content himself with plodding. He hated plodding.

"I don't know how you do it," Oliver murmured, looking up at the sky. It was a startling summer blue with only a few scattered clouds. He thought never to see it blue again but here it was with birds ducking and diving through its endlessness like they were dolphins in the Mediterranean Sea.

"Do what?" Lisbeth was fiddling about in her reticule while trying to balance her yellow parasol over her shoulder. It matched her afternoon dress and her bonnet which was trimmed with a ribbon of the same shade and a conservative peacock feather.

"Have you looked at the sky today? Damn me, if it isn't blue," Oliver said. What was she looking for in her reticule? He would have helped her with her search, but he was driving her phaeton. A neat little beauty that she had surprised him with when he came to pick her up for this afternoon's jaunt into Hyde Park. The black lacquer shone like onyx in the afternoon sun and thankfully did not have the Blackhurst crest emblazoned on it like everything else Blackhurst had acquired before his death. Oliver's horses had been changed over to the speedy high-perched conveyance in double-quick time.

"Bellamy, language please," Lisbeth censored, giving up her search for a spyglass or whatever it was she had been looking for.

"Beg pardon, my dear. It is just that it has been raining and gray for months and the day you decide to go to the park it is as if you commanded the weather just by writing it in your schedule."

"I hope you are not blaming the terrible weather we've had on me!"

He laughed at her suddenly sour expression. "Not unless your powers extend to making volcanoes erupt."

"Oh, if only I *could* control the weather. I would command a little cloud to sit, just so, over your head and rain on you whenever you displease me," she said with a smirk.

"Then I would be soaked from dawn until dusk."

She raised an eyebrow. "Only the daylight hours?"

Oliver loved teasing her. "Of course, because I would never displease you when we were alone in bed together."

He had not been looking forward to the tedium of this afternoon. He now knew he would never be bored in her company.

She tried for a censorious expression but there was laughter in her exquisite eyes when she looked at him.

"That is a strong statement to make considering you have only been in my bed one night. Who is to say I will be inviting you back?"

"Come, Lisbeth, are you trying to deny me the pleasure of my triumph?"

She looked at him with that burning stare that made his trousers shrink. "Your modesty is unbelievable. Perhaps last night was actually my triumph. Did you think of that?"

"Perhaps we need a do over," he suggested, wiggling his eyebrows up and down. "Just to make sure, you understand."

"Oh, I understand, quite perfectly. There is only one problem."

"Which is?"

She smiled sweetly. "It is not on my schedule, and we have the Warrington ball tonight."

"That's two problems and, really, both are worth ignoring."

"You have that smug look on your face again, Bellamy. I suspect you are making plans in that head of yours. I would advise against it lest it make your head explode and ruin your hair completely. I like it in that style—new valet?"

She hadn't removed the rod from her back completely, but she was at least a little more bendable now. In fact, she was endearingly flexible in all the ways that mattered.

"Your concern for my hair is admirable. I think I like this kind and concerned side of you."

"Well, I do not want to spoil my dress, do I? That kind of stain just does not come out."

He threw his head back and laughed. He had an overwhelming urge to turn this expensive gig around and head for the nearest stand of trees. Just so he could ravish her most thoroughly.

She was laughing, too.

They traveled slowly, stopping to acknowledge the braver passersby every now and then. Lisbeth had been biding her time, waiting for the right time to ask him something which had been playing on her mind for a while.

"Bellamy, why haven't you been collecting on your wagers?"

He looked sharply at her, his eyes like amber in the afternoon light. "What do you know of it?"

"I know you haven't collected one shilling. It was part of our agreement. I want you to collect the winnings."

"Was it Rollands? Your butler is far too sneaky." She watched as he contemplated the ribbons in his hands. "It's not as simple as you make it sound."

"It is. You are making it more complicated. I wish you would not worry so much about your pride. Pride before a fall makes for a long drop, Bellamy."

"And you an expert on pride."

What was he trying to say? "I've had to swallow my fair share."

He frowned. "So you have."

They traveled a little farther, the slow pace grating on Oliver's nerves. This all felt like a pointless exercise to him.

"I want to see it," she blurted out when they had stopped again.

He raised a brow. "I beg your pardon?"

"The list. The list of wagers. I want to see it." She held his gaze. He couldn't decide if she was the bravest woman he had ever met or the most foolish.

"You already have it."

She crossed her arms. "The proper list, Bellamy. One I can read, if you please." She held out her hand, palm up.

He took her hand and kissed it. "I think not, Countess."

Her expression was puzzled. "Why? Are they so terrible? So unimaginative you had to write them down in code?"

He shook his head in disbelief. "Unimaginative? Ha! You have no idea how depraved the *ton's* gentlemen can be." He took her hand and placed it back in her lap. "Half the wagers were committed to various betting books when the men in question were foxed. Do you really think they would put down nice, civilized things like have a picnic in the park, or stroll down Bond Street? For all your Black Raven reputation you really are naive, aren't you?"

Her beautiful mouth formed a perfect O, but she recovered quickly. He felt regret for having to be so blunt with her, but she had to realize that if she insisted on this farce, what exactly she was likely to discover. He didn't want to put her through that, if he could avoid it.

Now her lips were pressed together, and he knew he had lost his fight to protect her and instead brought out her fierce need to know everything.

"I still want to see it. I think I have a right. They are about me, after all."

He sighed and shook his head. "I don't suppose I can talk you out of this?" She shook her head. "Fine!" He pulled the phaeton over onto the grass and out of the way of the other traffic. "Here, read them for yourself," he said, handing her the list from his jacket pocket. "But don't say I didn't warn you."

She took it from him, biting her lip in indecision.

"You don't have to read it, Lisbeth. It won't do you or me any good." He jumped down and handed the reins to a young boy. "Keep them safe and there will be a coin in it for you," he said to the lad, before handing Lisbeth down. He guided her down to a bench where she dutifully sat with list in hand.

"I'll be contemplating the plight of the ducks." With that he walked off, down to the edge of the serpentine that ran through Hyde Park only a few feet away.

Lisbeth sat on the bench and watched him walk away. Her heart squeezed in her chest. She looked down at the folded list in her hand. Did she really want to know what was on it? Part of her yelled, *No!* The other half told her she must know, no matter the consequences. If nothing else, it might give her an insight into why Bellamy wouldn't collect on his wagers as per their agreement.

She unfolded the list and read the contents with shaky hands. She read down the list, noticing that some were already ruled out with a line, where he had completed them. Her hands shook and her heart raced as she continued down the list.

My God! She was such a fool. Of course, the men who had placed these wagers would want to humiliate her. They always had. Why, two years later should it be any different?

She lifted a hand to her mouth in a quick involuntary move. He had tried to warn her, but still, the shock of finding out just how degenerate men could be had her gasping. Oliver had been right. She should not have read it, but she had now, and she would have to deal with it.

She gathered her breath and stood, looking around her. The park was filled to capacity, most likely due to the unusually fine weather. The sun may be peeking through but inside her it felt like it was cold and raining. A thunderstorm was brewing in her mind ready to strike out. How dare these men write such things about her, about anyone? She wanted to slap every man in sight but then she looked at Bellamy… and knew that she was wrong. Not all men were painted with the same brush. Some men held pride and honor above all else. Bellamy had tried to stop her from reading that revolting list of insults, but she hadn't listened.

Lisbeth made her way to the stand of trees down near the water's edge where Oliver was standing. He looked good, even from the back. The tails of his coat lifted slightly on the breeze, giving her a glimpse of his magnificent backside in buck-colored breeches. He was tall and so handsome gazing out over the water, his hat sitting at a slight angle on his head.

This man had loved her last night like she never knew she could be loved. He had opened her eyes to desire and pleasure so intense she thought she would go up in flames. He had offered her more than just his body last night. She had seen it in his eyes. Even now, he had tried to protect her, save her from hurt.

She saw now that she would have to find some other way around their arrangement, but how? He would never take money directly from her and yet she knew he needed this money. Whatever fool thing his brother Henry had done, besides put his money and his faith in her late husband, Oliver should not have to pay for it. Still, if he would at least collect on those wagers he had already completed…

She was so deep in thought she hadn't realized she had made it to the river's edge. She looked at Oliver and he looked at her. Was that pain she saw in his gaze?

"Are you satisfied now, Countess? Has your curiosity been fulfilled?"

She raised her chin a notch higher. "There are some wagers on this list I am willing to do," she said.

Oliver gaped at her. "What?"

"You were right. Most of them are… repulsive, but there are a few I would consider."

Now he looked astonished. She would have laughed at him under normal circumstances, but these were not normal circumstances.

"Which ones in particular are you referring to?"

"Well, the waltz for one."

He raised a brow at her.

She raised one back. "I know what I said, but that was before."

He nodded. "All right, what others?"

"I will kiss you here, in Hyde Park and… and let you expose my ankle at the next ball.

"Really," he replied. Apparently, not at all convinced. "Even the kiss?"

"I will not enjoy it, but I will do it."

"Well no, we can't have you enjoying my kiss, can we?"

"I meant the humiliation of the wager and the circumstances surrounding it. Not the kiss itself."

He shook his head. "I feel so much better now."

She ignored his sarcastic tone. "Now, shall we do it here or in the phaeton?"

Oliver laughed because it was all so ridiculous. "Stop," he said, putting up his hand. "We are going to walk back to the horses, and then I am going to take you home."

"But the wager," she said, as he took hold of her arm and started dragging her back up to the path.

He was not going to kiss her for money. No! He wanted to kiss her, more now than ever, but he would not do it for the entertainment of others. He'd already made up his mind that he would not be doing any more wagers from that damn list. He would find some other way to pay the bank back what his brother owed against the estate, even if it took the rest of his life to do so.

"But our agreement demands that you collect on some of the wagers, Bellamy. At least collect what you are owed."

"And this will make you feel better about your idiotic arrangement? I don't care about my side of the arrangement and neither should you. It was my choice."

"Bellamy," she said as they reached the horses.

"Not a word," he replied. He paid the lad and helped her back into her seat. He took up his place beside her and turned back towards the entrance of the park. This fine day felt dark and dim to him now. He looked over at Lisbeth and saw she was biting her lip again. He hated to upset her, but he had to stand his ground on this.

THE WARRINGTON BALL was always a crush. The fact that Ashton had ordered they attend made him feel even less like attending. He wondered what his friend intended to do. He would not let him interrogate Lisbeth. Tony would be more tactful than that. He had a way of knowing when people were lying. He was very observant. Perhaps he just wanted to test her, to see how honest she was. He would find her defensive but not dishonest, of that Oliver was sure.

"Now, please, be nice to Ashton's family. I think you will find them charming."

"It is your friend Ashton's youngest sister who is having her coming out?" Lisbeth asked as the carriage jostled while turning into Grosvenor Square where the Duke of Warrington lived.

"Yes, Lady Marianne. Only but a babe last time I saw her. But then I've only seen her twice when home briefly on leave. Delightfully wicked as a child but I put that down to having four older brothers."

"Oh, the poor child," Lisbeth said. Four brothers! *She would be the most over-protected young woman… and no doubt the most loved. She was a very lucky young lady. If only her own brother had lived long enough to have protected her. Would it have made any difference?*

"Exactly. Ashton thinks she is a complete hoyden, but what did he expect? He still thinks the sun shines from her, of course."

"I admit to being a little nervous about tonight." She looked over at him and he smiled that crooked smile at her, the one that crinkled his eyes and made her want to jump into his lap and kiss him.

"Have no fear of Warrington or the rest of the family. They are no strangers to scandal or gossip for that matter. They will not treat you ill. Everyone is terrified of Warrington, you know."

"Really, why?"

"He is kind of… scarily disapproving. Part of it is on account of his height. Part is the fact that he never smiles and is not approachable in the least. He does, however, always do his duty."

"Like me? Perhaps he too is hiding a seemingly insurmountable hurt."

"Perhaps. I never thought of him like that, but of course, knowing you I can see how it could be possible. Whatever hurt he felt, it was many, many years ago." Oliver looked out the window as the carriage jerked to a stop. "Ah, we are here. Come."

He got out and handed her down, kissing the top of her hand before placing her hand on his arm. She wanted to lean her head on his shoulder and sigh in contentment. The sound of music wafting down the stairs reminded her that she had yet another ball to get through, another set of strangers to impress, another night of being the Black Raven. She wanted to shed the mask of her reputation, but she had yet to prove her innocence and only Bellamy knew the real her. She would do her best to make Oliver proud tonight. He wanted her to like his friend Ashton and his family and so she would do her best to be civil no matter how they reacted to her.

A footman dressed in the Warrington livery of green and gold met them at the door. He took their hats and coats and ushered them towards the receiving line. This was the most tedious part of any ball, waiting to be greeted by the hosts. The line moved fairly fast, made easier by Oliver's easy banter.

"Have I told you how beautiful you look tonight?"

"Three times, but who is counting?" She smiled just so he would smile back.

"I like this color on you. It brings out your eyes." He was referring to her gown of sapphire blue.

"Thank you. It is new."

"I can't wait to take it off later," he whispered in her ear, his hand on her waist.

She stifled a smile. "I would prefer you kept your hands respectful. There are others in this line you know."

"Are there?" He looked around as if seeing the other guests for the first time. "Gad, you're right, hundreds of them too."

"If you say you only have eyes for me, I may just cast up my accounts."

"Even if it were true?" This time he winked at her but did not remove his warm hand from her waist. He was impossible to chastise.

Lisbeth gasped when she got her first glimpse of the Duke of Warrington. He was tall, very tall, with dark hair that was slightly graying at the temples, and when he looked at her over the sea of heads he studied her for a few moments. His eyes were a stormy gray, hard like steel and ready to do battle if necessary. She returned his regard with an unflinching look of her own. She knew this game. The duke's eyes narrowed a moment then gave her an infinitesimal nod of his head, that she was sure was for her alone. Oliver gave her a little push, whispering, "I told you he was frightening, didn't I?"

The line progressed steadily until finally they found themselves before the dowager duchess.

"Bellamy, so glad you could make it," said the dowager. Her smile was easy, her eyes guarded, but then Bellamy had always found her a contradiction.

"I am glad to be here," he said with a smile as he bowed over the duchess's hand. "May I introduce the Countess of Blackhurst."

"Lady Blackhurst." The dowager nodded in acknowledgement. "This is my son, Warrington."

The duke bowed over Lisbeth's hand and shook Oliver's, but said nothing.

Oliver explained the others in the welcoming party to her in a whisper. "Charles, Earl of Harlow, and his wife Gabrielle. Thomas, Viscount Epping, and his wife, Anna. Lord Anthony Ashton and Lady Marianne."

Lisbeth couldn't help but stare as they made their bows and curtseys to each other. They were all so handsome. Lady Marianne was a beauty, too, but she had yet to grow into her full beauty. She would be stunning in a few years.

Lord Anthony lingered over Lisbeth's hand a little too long. She felt him assessing her as she greeted the others. He was handsome, but in a different way to the rest of his family. If anything, he most resembled his eldest brother William, except that he was fair. His summer blue eyes showed appreciation at what he saw in her but instead of revolting her it intrigued her.

"I hope you will do me the honor of a dance, Lady Blackhurst," he said, giving her an assessing look.

She understood his reservations. Bellamy was his friend. She just hoped he would give her the benefit of the doubt. "I would like that, Lord Anthony, thank you."

"I hope you will do me the honor of a dance, Lady Marianne?" Oliver asked. Marianne giggled and gave her curtsey. He took up her dance card and scrawled his name in the appropriate place. She smiled then and Lisbeth knew that yes, stunning was exactly what she would be when she had grown a little more in confidence.

Lady Marianne was her not so long ago. She too had been young, eager, and hopeful of a good match. All the while she had been overwhelmed by all the men who had fought for her attention.

Nathaniel had seemed like a god to her then. Tall, dark, and handsome with an air of power about him that Lisbeth had found intoxicating. She had been blind to his faults, if he had shown them at all, in those few short weeks he had courted her. He had been nothing but the utmost gentleman. He did not even kiss her until she had accepted his proposal. After that his attentions had waned dramatically. He had what he wanted, her dowry. Why put in any more effort than was necessary? She had told herself it was because he was a busy man and she had much to do anyway planning the wedding. She should have seen the signs, but in her innocence she had not known what to look for.

She hoped for a very different result for Lady Marianne.

THE BALL WAS progressing well and soon Lord Anthony was bowing over Lisbeth's hand. She caught Oliver giving his friend a narrowed look of warning. She tried to put them both at ease.

"Do stop frowning, Bellamy. I assure you, I shall bring Lord Anthony back to you without any broken toes."

"It is not *his* toes I am worried about."

"Do not listen to him, Lord Anthony," she said, as she took

his arm.

"I rarely do, Lady Blackhurst," he replied with a smile.

They had just completed the first set when Lord Anthony spoke. "Lady Blackhurst, I must admit that anybody who can put up with Bellamy for more than an hour has my undying admiration."

"Thank you, Lord Anthony. I agree that he can be most vexing at times, but he has charmed his way into my affection."

"Yes, it is most annoying how he does that." They parted as they turned and skipped to the other end of the line.

"I know you have questions for me," she said when they were again opposite each other.

"I do. Some you may think ungentlemanly of me to ask."

He was watching her reaction, perhaps expecting her to swoon from guilt or blurt out a confession. "Will you ask them anyway, Lord Anthony?"

He smiled. "With so many ears about it would be indelicate of me to do so. However, I am concerned."

"About whether or not I killed my husband or whether or not I would repeat such an act with your friend?"

If he was shocked by her boldness, he did not react. They moved through a few more sets before he spoke again. "I do not care about your dead husband and Bellamy can look after himself. He is no easy mark. Are you aware that Bellamy's brother invested with your husband?"

"I am aware."

"Have you told him this?"

"He has asked me what he wanted to know about his brother and the speculation. I have answered his questions."

"Have you told him about your involvement in the speculation?"

"I am afraid you will find the answer very dull indeed, for I had nothing to do with the speculation, nor do I know why my husband left the majority of his fortune to me."

His light eyes seemed to scan over her features. "You must

admit it looks unfavorable."

"I have not touched a sovereign of the money from that speculation. We can make an appointment with my banker tomorrow if you wish to see proof."

He let his eyebrow raise a little. "Why not?"

"Why not? Because it is not mine. Legally it is of course but morally I am stuck in a dilemma. Any businessman would say that the investors were foolish to trust my husband and demand no paperwork and therefore do not deserve compensation. This is also what my solicitors told me at the time. My husband's solicitors have spent many months looking for documents, anything really that would help us find out the particulars of the speculation, but it appears no one has any."

"I know. I asked them."

It was her turn to raise her brow in surprise. "Then why would you ask me?"

He smiled then with a slightly sheepish look in his eye. "You can tell much from asking the same question to many."

"So you can," she replied. *You can also form a picture of someone from how they answer those questions. I wonder what picture you have formed of me, Lord Anthony?*

The smile left his face then. "I do not want to appear rude, but Bellamy is my friend," he began.

"He is mine also," she responded.

"I do not like my friends used and ill-treated, Lady Blackhurst, so please tread carefully on his heart."

"Then we are in accord, Lord Anthony."

The dance ended and Ashton kissed her hand before escorting her back to Bellamy's side.

"Thank you, Lady Blackhurst, for a very… enlightening dance. Bellamy, I have returned her to you, all toes intact," Ashton said before taking his leave of them.

She smiled for Bellamy's benefit but wondered if she had just made a friend or an enemy of Lord Anthony Ashton.

OLIVER HAD STUNNED her earlier by putting his name against the waltz. Did this mean he was going to accept the wager?

He had done his duty by Lady Marianne and had even danced with the dowager. It felt strange without him by her side. She was so used to his eternal presence.

"Lady Blackhurst, come sit by us," called Tony's sister-in-law, Anna, Lady Epping. Lisbeth could hardly decline so she sat in a chair by the two women.

"Gabrielle is finding this evening very tiring and is anxious, but she will not leave Lady Marianne's big night," Anna explained.

"Lady Marianne is doing well, don't you think?" Gabrielle asked, patting her belly and looking towards the dance floor where Lady Marianne was dancing with a young man. Lisbeth glanced away quickly from her babe-swollen abdomen and looked towards the dance floor.

"She is doing exceptionally well," Lisbeth agreed. "She has been a great success. It will be a great relief to her mother."

"Yes, although she would be more relieved to have Ashton and Warrington married off too," said Gabrielle.

"Oh, I had not realized that Lord Warrington was not married." Her gaze went to the tall duke standing beside his mother and looking completely bored.

"Widowed," said Anna. "A long time ago now."

"Poor Harlow is starting to get worried that he may stay the heir and actually inherit," added Gabrielle.

"He does not wish to inherit?" Lisbeth asked.

"Goodness, no. Harlow is an outdoorsman. He sees how many hours Warrington puts in, sees how it consumes him, and wants to run for the hills."

Anna frowned a little. "Warrington does not seem inclined to marry again, even though his mother is very persistent in her persuasion."

Lisbeth sensed that Anna did not approve of the dowager's methods of… persuasion.

"I am sure when the right woman comes along he will fall. I hazard to say that it would take a great and consuming love to change him." Gabrielle caressed her belly and looked towards her husband who was in a group of men talking. He glanced over, as if sensing her gaze, concern etched on his face. Gabrielle shook her head when he went to leave the group and return to her.

"I take it yours was a great and consuming love match?" Lisbeth asked.

"Yes, although it did not start off that way."

"She hated him," Anna put in.

"I did not hate him. I merely disliked him with a passion," Gabrielle qualified.

"Ah, here is Bellamy come to claim his dance," Anna announced with a smile for Lisbeth. "I see something special between you two as well. Oh, it's no use trying to say otherwise. I'm very good at these sorts of things."

Lisbeth didn't get to answer and really she was relieved. For, what to say? She wasn't sure what she and Bellamy shared right now, only that she was enjoying it for what it was. She didn't want to think about tomorrow. Not yet.

CHAPTER SIXTEEN

"L ADIES," BELLAMY SAID as he approached. "Lady Blackhurst, I believe this is our dance." He offered her his hand and suddenly she felt nervous. It seemed ridiculous to be so, considering how intimate they had been together, but just the feel of his hand in hers made her heart beat erratically. The tingles started again, and she realized with a resounding thud that she was completely, utterly, and beyond redemption in love with him. But was it a great and consuming love? Part of her was jumping for joy while the other part was nervously worrying that these feelings were a very bad idea.

He led her to the dance floor and took her in his arms. It felt right to be there. He looked down at her and frowned. "Smile, Lisbeth, it is only a dance."

"I know that." But she could not summon the smile he requested. Her body was reacting to his touch as it always did. They made the first turn before he spoke again.

"I'll kiss you," he said.

"What?" She looked up at him then. She was already blushing at her own thoughts.

"I will, kiss you, right here, in front of everyone if you don't relax."

"Do not talk nonsense," she replied worried that he may make true on his threat.

"You think I won't? Care to make a wager?" He laughed then

at her expression. "No wager then." He took her into a turn, pulling her closer. He was a good dancer, sure-footed and confident. It was easy to dance with him, except for the emotions that were playing havoc with her head and the constant turning of the dance.

"You make me mad with wanting you," he said softly in her ear. She closed her eyes, letting his words wash over her. When she opened them and looked up at him, she felt her face flush red. When he looked at her the way he was now, she knew what he was thinking and she wanted it too but…

"Why would you say such a thing on a dance floor in front of hundreds of people?"

"Because," he said in a whisper. "I want you to know exactly how I feel when you are in my arms, when I look into your eyes, when I smell your perfume." He held her secure in his embrace, leading her in the steps that were so new to the world of the *ton*.

"You should not say such things. It is unfair."

"Unfair? To whom? Me and my distracting desire for you or you and your female sensibilities?"

"I refuse to answer that question," she replied, pinning him with one of her glares.

He laughed. "That only makes me want you more."

They said nothing further for a few seconds until Lisbeth tried to get back onto a safer subject. "Where did you learn to dance the waltz?"

"In Germany. Did I ever tell you that story about the—"

"Bellamy," she whispered, clutching his shoulder in alarm. The room began to swim around her making her feel dizzy, out of control.

"Focus on me," he said. "Do you feel dizzy? It happens some-times when you are not used to all the turning."

"Focusing on you makes it worse," she replied trying not to panic. He slowed down so the outside world did not spin so fast.

"Better?" he asked.

"Yes," she answered dutifully but in truth it was more than

just the dance that had made her feel faint. It was the overpowering realization that she might just love him. Did he love her? How could he? If he did, he shouldn't. She desired this man, wanted to consume him, savor him like one would the last lemon drop in the box. Oh, how she wanted to kiss him, right here, right now. It was then that she realized how little time they had left with each other. The season ended soon, and he would be free to go—and she would let him. She would have to watch him go, taking with him her heart, but she had known that from the start—that he would leave her.

"Right, that's it," he said, as he suddenly stopped dancing, took her by the hand, and led her off the dance floor. He walked slowly, smiling and nodding to the people they passed but he did not stop, and she was too tense to take notice of where he was leading her. He halted for a moment then pushed her gently into a hall. He took her hand again and dragged her along at a quicker pace.

"Where are we going?" she managed to gasp out.

He did not answer. Instead, he looked from side to side, and then chose a door on the right. He dragged her through and closed the door behind them before hauling her up against the wall and kissing her ardently. Relieved beyond words, she kissed him back, winding her arms around his neck and wrapping her legs around his waist as he lifted her.

Nothing else mattered in this moment. His lips on hers and his arms protective and strong around her made her feel safe and wanted. He rocked between her thighs, his hands now under her skirt skimming up her legs to cradle her bottom. She didn't even notice the hard wall at her back. The only sensation she felt was an irresistible need for this man. This combined with her overwhelming want to weep at the injustice of having fallen in love with a man she could not have forever. She would take everything he had to give her because she knew in the darkest parts of her soul that this may be her only chance.

He wanted her and she wanted him and it didn't make sense,

but it did. Everything about him was right and yet they both knew it wouldn't, couldn't last. Perhaps it was this that made their coupling so intense, so reckless, and so fragile. She cupped his face and kissed him with all her desperate heart.

"Lisbeth, don't cry," he said, softly reaching up to wipe away at tears that she had not even noticed. "Everything will work out. Ashton said that they all adore you. Why are you crying?"

She didn't respond, couldn't, so she just kissed him and kissed him until he too forgot everything but her. He made love to her against the wall, a completely indecent act that would have horrified her under other circumstances but with Oliver she didn't care.

She loved him.

THE THRILL OF their lovemaking still echoed through every nerve in her body and put a smile on her face. The Warringtons' garden was beautiful but Lisbeth only had eyes for the man who was leading her up the garden path. Literally. She laughed at the thought.

"I'm not going to even attempt to ask you what you are thinking," Oliver said as he returned her smile.

"Perhaps I am just happy," she replied.

"Perhaps?" He lifted a brow.

"Fine. I am happy."

He laughed and kissed her softly on the tip of her nose. "Perhaps I should have my way with you in dark rooms more often."

As she walked slowly down the meandering path she hugged Oliver's arm a little tighter and laid her head on his shoulder. A strong, dependable shoulder. A shoulder she wanted to trust. It had been so long since she had felt this way. The feeling was liberating.

"Gabrielle and Anna are lovely," Lisbeth said as they headed towards a bench in the middle of the garden. She hoped he would kiss her on that bench.

Oliver nodded. "They are indeed, and what do you think of Ashton?"

She contemplated her answer for a moment. "He is suspicious of me. He hides it well, but I see it. He wants to find fault with me. I can't blame him. He is only looking out for you."

"He is a good friend but perhaps he wants to decide for himself about you. Form his own opinion instead of what the *ton* has decreed."

She looked at him, but he was looking towards the house. "Is that what you told him to do?" she asked.

He turned towards her then and frowned at her wary expression. "No, but as you have so quickly surmised, he is naturally curious."

"From his time in the army with you?"

"A man can hone many useful skills when he needs to. It is how one stays alive."

"So, you trust him?"

He looked her square in the eye and said, "With my life."

She was startled by his answer and relieved at the same time. "Well, that is praise enough for me. However, I think he will not take me on as friend until I have somehow proven myself." Like she'd had to do constantly with everyone she had met lately, including Oliver.

"You prove yourself every day," Oliver said, taking her hand in his and pressing a small kiss to her palm. "It is only a matter of time before he adores you too."

Adores me too? "To you maybe, not to the masses that still believe me guilty of heinous crimes of murder and mayhem. I have to find Nathaniel's killer; it is the only way they will ever believe me. We have ruled out many from my list but there has to be someone who might know something."

"What if the killer is not even one of the *ton*? Maybe it was a hired thug?"

Lisbeth sighed. It seemed so easy for him to dismiss her concerns. It was not his life that had been ruined by a wrongful accusation. "Nathaniel let him in. He would not have done that unless he knew him or had invited him there in the first place. I don't have time to speculate on other theories; believe me, I've thought this through quite thoroughly. The season ends in a week or so and the *ton* will start leaving for the country. We must concentrate on the clues we have. The list grows smaller but not small enough. We need something solid."

"I could enlist Tony's help. He is prodigiously clever at searching out the truth."

Lisbeth gasped. "He knows? What have you told him, Bellamy?" Her voice was soft in the garden, but it was laced with anger.

"I haven't told him… much," Oliver confessed looking only a little contrite.

She gasped. "Oliver! You know how I feel about this. How could you?" She wanted to throttle him.

"I just bandied some names around and asked him what he thought, that's all."

"And what, pray tell, did he say?" She was finding it hard to contain her anger.

"Not a lot. He said he may have some information for us, but he wants to verify it first. He would never tell me something he was not sure of. And he does not know the reason behind my request."

"I wish you had kept him out of my business, Bellamy!" She stood up and took a step away from him. "He is not a fool; he will surely figure out what we are up to in no time. It is little wonder he was looking at me strangely, like he was trying to read my mind."

"No, that would be his normal look," Oliver replied with a smile.

She did not smile back.

He walked over to her and turned her towards him. "I did

what I thought needed to be done. We were not finding what we needed going on as we are and as you said we are running out of time. He's a professional, Lisbeth. He would never betray me."

"Maybe not you, but what about me? He has no reason to help me."

"He is helping you, because I asked him to. He knows you mean a lot to me. He understands I want to get to the truth of the matter. So do you, so I see no reason not to use all resources at our disposal. I did it for you." He touched her face, skimming his finger down her cheek and lifting her chin so he could kiss her lips. "Don't be angry with me, my love."

All anger drained away as her heart sped up and her body moved closer to him, needing his touch, his kiss, his love.

"You make it nearly impossible not to when you go ahead and do things like this," Lisbeth said, looking into his warm brown gaze. "Maybe we should return to the house now. People will wonder where we have gone." *And what we have been doing.*

Oliver offered his arm. "As you wish, my dear."

My love, he had said, but was it just a turn of phrase?

IN THE SHADOWS Dalmere watched the pair leave the quiet haven of the garden. He gritted his teeth together until his jaw hurt. His eyes burned with anger and frustration. He was right to think they were up to something more than just dallying in disused rooms at the balls and soirees they had attended this season. Although, he had doubted himself for a brief moment earlier tonight, when he had seen them go into the room off the hall, when he had heard them together. He had followed them only because he was inquisitive.

He moved out of the shadows and from behind the fragrant bush he had been hiding behind. He had been close enough to clearly hear their exchange. They'd been so focused on each other he could have stood right behind them and they would not have noticed.

Now he knew the pair was up to mischief. They were trying to find out who killed Blackhurst. He would have laughed under normal circumstances but now they were involving Ashton. This was not good news. How could *he* use Ashton to his own ends if Bellamy was now enlisting Ashton's aid? Bellamy had been useless in finding anything of use concerning the Black Raven's involvement in the speculation, but then her pretty blue eyes had easily distracted him from his job.

The Blackhurst witch was just as deceitful as he had thought her, just as deceitful as her dead husband had been. She was playing Bellamy for the fool, and now she was going to try it on Ashton like she had everyone else.

It had been up to him to put her in her place, after he had disposed of Blackhurst, to make sure her life was a misery. He should have got rid of her when he had killed Blackhurst, but the dignity of a quick death was too good for the likes of her. She was supposed to have hung, humiliated and shamed, for killing her husband, but she had not. She should have rotted in Newgate prison, got the pox, and died with her legs spread for some guard, but she hadn't. Somehow, someway she had gotten off on a technicality and he'd had to work incredibly hard to keep her reputation suitably tainted.

Oh, the rumors he had spread, the tales he had told, the lies he had made up. As fun as it had been to play Machiavelli, none of his defaming had been sufficient to get rid of her. The stupid woman didn't even have the sense to move to the Continent until the hubbub died down. He'd been as surprised as anyone that the landlord had sold her the townhouse, after her acquittal. But then again, who wanted to rent a house where someone had been killed? There were some advantages to having inherited nearly all the blunt Blackhurst had squirreled away, he supposed. Dirty, devilish money earned through deceit and lies by her bastard husband.

He knew she would want to seek out the truth, eventually. On her own she was no threat, but now with Bellamy at her side he had begun to worry. If Ashton joined their merry band of mischief, there was a real chance he could be found out. He would not let it happen. He had just started to get over his own financial hardships and it had not been without great sacrifice on his side. He had vowed his revenge on Blackhurst's bride when she had refused to return the capital from the speculation.

He ripped a flower off at the bloom and crushed the soft fragrant petals in his fist. She must die. It was the only way. He smiled then in the dim garden. Yes, killing the Black Raven was going to be so very, very satisfying. After all, he'd been the one to name her so he should be the one to snuff her out. He would enjoy seeing the life fade from her eyes. Only then would he be safe. Only then would he feel justice had finally been served.

LISBETH WAS HAPPY to be left at the refreshment table while Oliver danced with Anna. It gave her time to sort through her rolling emotions. Tonight had felt a bit like an out of control carriage ride, exciting and thrilling but also dangerous and scary. Was bringing Ashton into this a good thing?

Her eyes found Bellamy and Anna as they danced. She liked Anna a great deal. She was kind and she looked Lisbeth in the eye when she talked to her. She seemed as if she genuinely was interested in what Lisbeth might want to say. She liked the feeling and wanted more, but she had to be realistic. She may never find out who killed Nathaniel before the end of the season. Lisbeth knew better than to get her hopes up. She must be happy with having Marie and her grandmother back in her life, for now. However, she also knew she would never give up trying to clear her name with or without Bellamy.

She looked to her right and saw that Gabrielle was leaving.

She waved to Lisbeth from across the room. Lisbeth waved back and she felt oddly happy about the whole gesture. Such a normal thing to do, but not for her, and certainly not lately. It was only now she was realizing how much she had missed the normal, everyday things one did without even thinking.

Lisbeth had avoided looking at Gabrielle's baby belly all night, looking only at her face when they had talked earlier and asking her no questions about the baby. In the wake of last night's confession to Oliver she missed her son Daniel even more. A deep ache that had taken residence in her heart after his death was now throbbing and squeezing, the pain increasing whenever she even thought of him. How can she hold this grief inside her and yet be so happy and contemplating love whenever Bellamy was around? It didn't make sense, and she didn't know how to un-jumble her feelings.

It wasn't that she was jealous of Gabrielle, but she was envious of her relationship with her husband Harlow and his obvious angst for both her and the baby.

Would she ever have the chance to hold another of her own babies in her arms? To have someone who loved her and her baby? Who would worry about her swollen feet and whether or not she was tired, as Harlow did for his wife?

It was no use dreaming of things that would never happen. She would never want to bring a child into the world while her reputation as the Black Raven hung around her neck like shackles.

Finding a seat, she sat to watch the festivities around her. She watched Lady Marianne giggling with a bunch of other girls and sighed.

"Such a pretty picture, wouldn't you agree, Lady Blackhurst?"

Lord Dalmere came and sat next to her. His golden curls, his light blue eyes, and the endearing and easy smile he gave her completed the picture of a very handsome man. He was reserved and quietly spoken, his manners impeccable. Everything about him was gentlemanly. Women adored him but he took little notice of them. He was Oliver's friend and had been Henry's too, so for them she would try to push away her concerns of their first meeting. He had been nothing but nice to her; she must at least give him the courtesy of the same.

"Yes, the first season is a very big moment in a young lady's life," Lisbeth replied. "Being presented at court, making sure you remember all the rules of polite society, remembering everyone's names and titles. It can be all a bit much for some."

He looked at her and smiled. "Ah, the first blush of youth with all its perils. I remember you at your first ball, you know."

This startled her. She looked over at him. His eyes told her he was not lying. "You were at my coming out ball?"

"Indeed, I was. You were the picture of perfection. Every man was in love with you." He laughed. "Even me."

She smiled back. "Really, Lord Dalmere, you are determined to see me blush."

"Of course, you only had eyes for Blackhurst, even then. None of us stood a chance." He looked at her then, his expression one of regret. "Such a terrible thing that happened to you. I'm afraid people will believe anything, if they hear it often enough." He looked contrite. Was he apologizing for believing the rumors? It could not be.

"Thank you, Lord Dalmere. That means a lot to me."

"I do want to make it up to you. I have heard they are having a balloon ascension at Vauxhall Gardens tomorrow afternoon and later there will be fireworks. I would be honored if you and Bellamy would join me. His brother, Henry, and I had planned to watch one but unfortunately... we never got the chance." He shrugged. "It would mean a lot to *me* if you would."

She had always wanted to see a balloon ascension. "Well, I would have to talk to Bellamy first, but I am sure he would be... pleased."

"Excellent. I will send a note around in the morning with the details. Until tomorrow, have a wonderful evening, Lady Blackhurst."

With that he stood, bowed over her hand, and left her sitting with her plate in her lap and her mind in confusion. Perhaps she had misjudged Dalmere after all. Maybe he had simply been as wary of her as she had been of him. Perhaps she had let her own feelings of unease rule her judgment.

She danced a quadrille with Bellamy when he returned, managing this time to make it through the whole dance. She told him of Dalmere's invitation.

"I think that would be wonderful. He has been a good friend to me. Declining would hurt his feelings. Besides, I have never seen a balloon ascension before, have you?"

"No, I haven't. I think it will be quite spectacular."

"Then it's decided."

"Anna, I mean, Lady Forsham, said she would call on me tomorrow morning. And mid-day tomorrow is Grandmother's luncheon. She said she has sent an invitation to your aunt."

Oliver raised a brow and smiled. "There, you see? I told you that Lord Anthony and his lot were of the good sort. Well, my girl, you will be busy tomorrow. I had better take you home before your social diary fills up completely."

"I doubt that will ever happen, but Lady Forsham is very kind to think of me. Do you think your aunt will come to the luncheon?"

"I am not sure. She is getting on and she sometimes forgets where she is. I am sure her companion will advise me on whether or not she is well enough to go."

"I had not realized she was so frail. You must worry about her."

"I do. She is my last living relative. When she is gone, I will be the last."

WHEN LISBETH ARRIVED back at Blackhurst House she was met at the door of the carriage by a very dour Rollands with an umbrella. Once inside, he took her coat. Oliver saw that something was amiss.

"Do you want me to stay?"

She looked at Rollands, who gave her a subtle sign which told her this was not something she most likely wanted to share with Bellamy. She shook her head. "No. I'm very tired and we have a big day tomorrow."

He kissed her hand. "Are you sure?"

"Of course. I will see you tomorrow."

She missed his warm presence as soon as he left, but tried to focus on the matter at hand.

"What has happened here? You all look like we ran out of jam," she said as she followed Rollands into the parlor. Mrs. Rollands was standing in the parlor wringing her hands and looking very anxious.

"Whatever can be wrong?" Lisbeth asked in concern as she came up to her housekeeper.

"Hahmm. It appears that Mrs. Rollands has something she needs to tell you, your ladyship."

She looked from one to the other. "Really? Should I sit down for this?"

Mrs. Rollands nodded. Lisbeth felt even more apprehensive now. She sat.

"It is just that I wasn't sure what they were when I first saw them," Mrs. Rollands said, still wringing her hands.

"You have me all at a quandary. Please just tell me what you found," Lisbeth asked, wondering what on earth she could have found.

"A book."

Lisbeth blinked. "A book?"

"Well, two actually," Mrs. Rollands replied looking paler by the minute.

"And where did you find these books, Mrs. Rollands?"

"In the master's study. When I were cleaning up after, well, after you two made such a mess in there. I couldn't leave it like that you understand."

"I understand and I am sorry about that, Mrs. Rollands, but my husband had many books in his study."

"Not like these two," Rollands supplied.

That got her attention. "Can I see them, please?"

Mrs. Rollands turned and picked up two books. She offered them up like a sacrifice to her mistress. "I'm so sorry, your ladyship, but I didn't want to bother you unless I knew for sure if they were something worth bothering you about. When I showed Mr. Rollands, he was angry at me for keeping them to myself."

"She showed me just this evening, my lady. I am sure they are a ledger and a journal."

"Not just any ledger, I'm guessing, Rollands?" Lisbeth asked as she took the longer book from the housekeeper. She hoped they could not see how her hands were shaking.

"No, my lady. I believe it is *the ledger* from the last speculation. The names on the list are very familiar to me. Many are on the list we compiled."

The book from the speculation? Lisbeth felt the blood drain from her face. This was the evidence she had been looking for but now she had it in her hand, she felt reluctant to open it. The ledger would help ascertain who put in what amount of money, but not that she had nothing to do with it. What would everyone think if she were just to announce this evidence had only come to light right now? Would it in fact make it worse for her? She studied the book on her lap for a moment. "You are right. Many of these names are on my list."

This would mean she would know exactly who had invested with her husband. How much they invested and how much she would have to pay back. Who had the most to lose and who had the most motive to kill Nathaniel. She should be overjoyed, but instead she felt anxious and unsure. These two books changed everything. They had the potential to destroy all she had worked for or give her all she needed to finally put this horrible mess behind her. She needed time to read them, think things through.

The thought of being able to pay back all the investors should be a happy one. It wasn't that she worried over her own finances. She led a fairly simple life and gave herself a modest allowance. She paid her staff well and on time every quarter and she dined sufficiently for one who lived mostly on her own.

She ran her finger down the list. Oliver's brother was there, so were Dalmere and several other men she had met this season, thanks to Bellamy. There were a few on the list she had not known to be investors. Perhaps tomorrow, while watching the balloon ascension she could hint that she knew Dalmere was an investor and question him on it. Should she tell Dalmere or Oliver about the ledger? First, she must be sure it was for the right speculation, for her husband had been dealing in investments for many years. When she knew for sure, then she would tell him.

She turned then to the other book. The journal. What would it say? Did she want to know? She could skip the parts about her and just look for entries where he may have spoken about the speculation. She already knew he had despised her; it was no use upsetting herself further by knowing exactly how much. Lisbeth knew, despite her reasoning not to read about herself in the journal, she would read every damning word Nathaniel wrote in that infernal journal.

She should be celebrating; these two books could contain the evidence she needed to prove her innocence. She could be holding in her hands the ticket to her salvation or the name of the killer.

She looked up. Both Mr. and Mrs. Rollands were waiting for her to say something.

"Thank you for bringing these to my notice. I will read them and decide what is to be done with them."

"Are you sure you want to read them?" Rollands asked.

She knew he was trying to tell her it was all right to ignore them if she wished. How could she? They were hard and real in her hands.

"Where were they hidden?" she asked her housekeeper.

"They were sticking out from beside one of the bookshelves. I only noticed because I was putting the other books away on the shelf."

Lisbeth gave Mrs. Rollands a reassuring smile. "You did the right thing, bringing them to me. However good or bad the contents may be. You can both go to bed now."

She waited until both of them had left the room and then she opened the journal to a random page towards the back.

My preparations are nearly complete. I have made good my finances and prepare to disappear.

Lisbeth gasped. He had planned to run away and take everyone's money with him? How typical. She shouldn't have been so surprised.

I will be rich and live like a king! Those fools will never find me.

Lisbeth slammed the book shut and let it drop to the floor like it had burned her fingers. He really had planned it to the letter. What had he planned to do with her? Leave her to bear the consequences? Probably. Take her with him? No, why would he bother to do that? She was nothing but a burden to him. Then why did he leave her all the money? It still didn't make any sense. Maybe he had planned for her to be blamed for his disappearance. It was quite likely he had planned to empty his coffers and then run off to destinations unknown, leaving her with his mess. Perhaps the journal would tell her, but she felt sick to her stomach at the thought of reading it.

Lisbeth picked up the ledger and, reluctantly, the journal and went upstairs to bed. Tomorrow she would decide what to do.

CHAPTER SEVENTEEN

From the journal of Nathaniel Carslake, Earl of Blackhurst.

July, 1813…My wife is like a timid mouse. I hate her. She is so annoyingly weak. There is no fight in her. She bores me. Even when I bed her she makes not a sound. I slap her about but it is not the same as when she used to fight me…

January, 1814…I have lost my son, my heir. I am furious she has given me a weakling son. A weakling like his mother. I am glad he did not grow up to be like her. Insipid and stupid. She caterwauls from dawn 'til dusk grating on my nerves. I dragged her by the hair into our room and threw her against the wall yelling at her to shut up but she kept on crying…

July, 1814…I have tired of London. I have tired of the stupidity of my peers. I have a plan that will set me up for life. It is so cunningly clever even I am in awe of my brilliance. Those fools will never know until it is too late…

Lisbeth closed the journal and placed it on the table next to her. Tears threatened to stream down her cheeks in rivers of misery. She would not let them flow, would not give Nathaniel the satisfaction, even if he was dead. The fire was roaring in front of her but inside she was colder than a winter blizzard.

If nothing else, the journal proved that Nathaniel had planned to fleece his friends and run off to the Americas to build a new life there—without her. His last entry was two days before his murder and did not mention any suspicions regarding his wellbeing. It also proved that she had not been part of the speculation. This much, at least, was good news, but how could she show this to Oliver—to anyone? He would read it and think her a woman who had let her husband turn her into a wraith, who gave up on herself. The truth was she had. She had been that weak woman. A sad excuse, but at the same time it was the only way she knew how to survive him.

What surprised her about his scribbled, spiteful words was the anger she'd felt at herself. How could she have let it become so bad? Thankfully, she was not that same woman now. Lisbeth had lived through a trial, incarceration, and the torment of the last two years as the Black Raven and was stronger for it. Stronger than she'd ever been. If nothing else came of all of this she knew one thing—she would never let a man rule her as Nathaniel had.

However, a decision had to be made about the dreaded diary. Could she let his diary and all the vile truth it contained be read by others? She felt ill at the thought. It did not paint a pretty picture of either her or Blackhurst. Letting the diary go public just to prove she wasn't involved in Blackhurst's plans would only cause humiliation and more scandal for her family. She had just reunited with her sister and grandmother; she couldn't bear to lose them again. After all, it didn't help her prove she hadn't killed him. If anything it would strengthen the possibility. For who had more motive than she? It would end up doing more harm than good. Lisbeth decided she would keep the diary to herself, for now.

"EH?" AUNT PETUNIA looked up from the lap blanket Mrs. Grey had just put around her legs. "Virginia Marsdon, Lady Fortesque? I remember her well. She was second cousin to my first husband… or was it first cousin to my second husband? Younger than I, of course, but I could out dance her any day of the week. I was quite the dancer in my day, you know."

Oliver took his seat opposite her in the carriage. "I bet you were."

"I used to host luncheons and picnics. Oh, how people would fall over themselves to be invited to one of my picnics."

"I believe Lady Fortesque holds excellent luncheons," Mrs. Grey said.

"I thought it was a picnic," she replied, looking a little confused.

"No. It is a luncheon," Oliver assured her.

"Will they have sandwiches?" she asked.

He chuckled. "I have no idea."

She crossed her arms over her chest. "If they don't have sandwiches, I'm not going."

"I'm sure they will have sandwiches, of some sort, Aunt Petunia."

"Fine, but if there are no sandwiches I'm holding you responsible, my dear boy." She turned to her companion. "Mrs. Grey, it appears we are going on a picnic."

"Luncheon," Oliver and Mrs. Grey said at the same time.

Aunt Petunia raised a gray brow. "No need to get disagreeable about it."

This could be a very interesting day, Oliver thought.

"Is your Lady Blackbird going to be there?" Aunt Petunia asked when they had finally got underway. "I have read that she made a lovely study at the park yesterday. Not sure what it was that she was studying, especially at a park. Black birds I assume."

Oliver sat forward. "It is Lady Blackhurst, and where did you read that?"

She looked at Oliver. "Blackhurst? Henry did not like her husband. Said he was despicable and someone should put him straight."

Oliver felt the hairs on his neck stand up. His conversation with Dalmere at the Wainwright ball coming back to him. "Put him straight?" he asked his aunt. "Did he say anything else?"

"Well, let me see. It was some time ago, but I do remember he came in all agitated like he had on a badly starched shirt and it was bothering him. He was pacing up and down fit to wear out my rug. I told him to sit down or buy me a new rug."

"And?"

"And?" His aunt raised her brow in some confusion.

"What else did he say about Blackhurst?" He was dreading the answer.

"Oh, yes, Henry. He said the man deserved some lead shot. I didn't quite understand why he wanted to give him such a thing when Blackhurst was obviously rich enough to purchase his own."

Mrs. Grey looked at Oliver and then at his aunt before saying, "I don't think he meant it quite like that, my lady."

She waved her hand as if dismissing Mrs. Grey's announcement. "He wanted to run away with her and all. I told him not to be so ridiculous. One does not run off with another man's wife even if the husband was a disgusting excuse for a human being, which is what Henry said he was. He was quite adamant he was going to save the… lady."

"That would be *Lady* Blackhurst. I remember you telling me about Henry's affections for her," Oliver said, but he was feeling deflated and more than a little confused. Every indication suggested that Henry wanted to kill Blackhurst, had maybe even planned to do it. The question was, would his usually mild-mannered brother have actually pulled the trigger?

"If her name is Blackhurst why on earth is she called the Black Bird?"

"They call her the Black *Raven*, Aunt. It is just a pet name the *ton* has given her," he explained, still his mind coming to terms with his aunt's words. He knew she was not always with him in the present but her long-term memory seemed to be very much intact.

"Eh? She has a pet raven. Well, I don't think that is an appropriate pet for a young lady. She should get a dog."

He ran his hand through his hair. "Yes, Aunt."

And so the questions went on until his aunt fell asleep about five minutes later. He was thankful for the silence. He loved his aunt dearly, but he was beginning to think bringing her to the luncheon was a bad idea. What if she brought up Henry and his feelings for Lisbeth while talking to her? What if she brought up Blackhurst? How would Lisbeth react? He would make sure that Mrs. Grey paid close attention when he was not there and made sure to distract his aunt if she brought up Blackhurst or Henry.

They made their way slowly to a light airy room at the back of Lady Fortesque's house. Again he was awestruck by the amazing fresco on the ceiling of the main hall, but again, time and duty prevented him from being able to truly appreciate it. French doors opened wide, inviting one to wander in the extensive garden beyond. A few couples were taking advantage of the opportunity to explore while a little sun poked through the ever-present clouds.

Oliver helped Mrs. Grey settle his aunt before looking around for Lisbeth.

His eyes went straight to her. She stood with her sister, looking at a miniature. She was smiling down at the palm-sized painting in her hand. Marie was laughing. He could only assume it was Marie's son they were looking at.

Lisbeth was the most striking woman he had ever seen, and it amazed him how he always felt this way on seeing her. When she sensed him looking at her, she met his eyes across the room. His heart stopped at the sight of her. Her hair curled around her face in delightful ringlets. Oh, how his fingers burned to feel the silky texture of those ebony strands. Had it only been a few hours since he had been with her last? He felt drawn to her like a moth to a flame. He knew his heart was in danger but still needed the heat of the blaze. When she smiled his way, he knew he was doomed but didn't care. All he wanted to do was take her in his arms and kiss her, Lady Fortesque and her luncheon be damned.

Her gaze never left his. He watched as she said something to Marie, who looked up, smiled, and then whispered something in her sister's ear before leaving her. Lisbeth moved gracefully across the room, oblivious it seemed to the myriad of obstacles in her way, most at knee height. She navigated around the furniture with ease and Oliver was left to watch her in awe.

"Ah, now I see why you are so smitten, Bellamy," Aunt Petunia remarked.

"She is beautiful," Mrs. Grey agreed.

She is mine! He wanted to shout it out for the whole room to hear, hell, for all London to hear. Instead he said, "She is exquisite."

He took two paces forward and met her on the rug. She took his offered arm with a raised brow. "You look like you're up to something."

He grinned as he took her for a small turn around the room. "So suspicious. I just wanted a moment alone with you before I introduce my aunt."

"Oh, really?" she asked, raising a brow.

He gave her one of his half smiles, then looked at his aunt who was waving them over. "She is adorable but… she can also be a little confused. Not all the time but sometimes she… forgets things, says things without thinking."

"Bellamy." She squeezed his arm. "I'm sure everything will be fine."

With that he nodded and escorted her over to where his aunt and Mrs. Grey were sitting.

"Aunt, this is Lady Blackhurst. Lady Blackhurst, may I introduce my aunt, Lady Mortimer, and her companion, Mrs. Grey."

"I am very happy to make your acquaintance, Lady Mortimer. Mrs. Grey." Lisbeth made her curtsey.

Aunt Petunia smiled up at Lisbeth. "You don't look like a bird at all."

Lisbeth looked to Oliver before she smiled down at his aunt.

"Well, thank you.

Aunt Petunia took her hand and pulled her down closer to her. "Bellamy said there would be sandwiches but I haven't seen any."

Lisbeth nodded. "I am sure there are sandwiches. In fact, I saw some not that long ago. I shall ask a footman to fetch you some."

Oliver's aunt patted her hand and let go of her. "You are a good girl, and so pretty. Just like your mother."

Lisbeth sat on the small stool next to Lady Mortimer. She had to admit to being a little shocked. "You knew my mother?" She must have looked how she felt for the old lady gave a little chuckle.

"Oh yes. She didn't look like a black bird either or have one as a pet. You really should get a dog, you know."

Lisbeth looked up at Oliver, but he only shrugged. She looked back at Oliver's aunt. "I shall consider it. Thank you for the suggestion."

"I'll explain everything later," he whispered in her ear.

"You have your mother's eyes. Such a lovely singing voice she had. Do you sing?"

"Not very well, I'm afraid. My sister Marie inherited my mother's voice. If we are lucky, she may sing for us today."

"Well, don't fret about it. As long as you can sew a straight stitch you may get yourself a husband yet. Bellamy is free, you know."

"Aunt," Oliver said in a warning tone.

"Well, you are and you're not getting any younger. And the nursery has been barren these thirty long years. You must do your duty, my boy, and do it soon."

Thankfully, sandwiches soon arrived and his aunt was delighted to see such a variety of fillings. Thankfully, she completely forgot about barren nurseries.

Oliver steered Lisbeth away once his aunt was happily sipping punch.

"I'm so sorry about all that," he said as soon as they were alone.

"She is charming. I wish I had an aunt like her. It is obvious she adores you."

"She is dear to me, and I confess I worry over her health."

"Because then you'll be alone? You won't be, you know. You have friends who care about you."

He raised a brow. *What did she mean by that? Did that include her?* He wanted to believe that what they had between them was more than passion, more than an *arrangement.* He had avoided thinking about the end of the season, their so-called agreement about the wagers, and what it would mean when it all ended. Could he hope that she meant something else? That she cared?

She looked away, playing with an earring. When she looked back at him, he paused. The question he really wanted to ask stuck on the tip of his tongue. *Do you care for me, Lisbeth?*

Her expression was guarded, unreadable. Her Black Raven mask firmly in place, only he knew the woman underneath. Could he be mistaken in how she felt about him? He wouldn't accept that she felt nothing. He wouldn't accept that she would simply walk away from him at the end of this blasted season.

His heart dropped at the possibility he was yearning for something that could never be. He wanted to say, *what if I want more. What if I want forever?*

But he couldn't.

Instead he kissed her and wished for the season never to end.

LISBETH SPENT HER time between Oliver, his aunt, her sister, and her grandmother. All in all, it hadn't been as bad as she had thought. Her grandmother's guests were wary but polite and although there was still the occasional whisper and wary look, she was learning to ignore them.

Oliver was entertaining a group of older ladies who had gathered around his aunt. It was pleasing to see him so attentive. When she had first seen him earlier, she'd had the unladylike urge to run across the room, hurl herself into his arms, and kiss him senseless. Such a wanton she had turned out to be! Who would have guessed?

"Lisbeth," Marie whispered next to her. "You are staring at him again. He is not going to disappear if you pay attention to someone else… like me."

Lisbeth turned toward her sister. "I'm sorry, Marie."

Marie steered her over to a corner. "Now you can stare at Bellamy in a less conspicuous way." They both stared at him. Marie sighed. "He is very handsome."

"I think I love him," Lisbeth blurted out. She put her palm over her mouth. She hadn't meant to say it out loud. She looked at Marie. Her hand was over her mouth, too.

Then Marie started giggling. "Well, of course you do. Anyone can see it. He is totally smitten with you, too. He looks at you like you are the most delicious dish on the table and he a starving man. It would be sickening, if it weren't so romantic."

Lisbeth turned away from the crowded room. "Oh Lord, what am I going to do?"

"Why, marry him of course!" Marie suggested.

She clutched at her sister's hand. "I can't. I mean, he doesn't want to marry me."

"Has he told you this?" Marie looked surprised.

Lisbeth closed her eyes briefly. "No, but we have this agreement, although he… it's complicated."

"I don't think so. Have you told him how you feel?" Marie's face clearly showed her concern.

Lisbeth shook her head. "No! I couldn't."

"Why not? Men are simple creatures, Lisbeth. It is best to deal with them directly. Tell him in easy, short sentences that you love him and wish him to marry you."

Her eyes widened. "And if he says no?"

"He won't."

"I can't." Lisbeth looked back over at Oliver; he was offering his aunt more sandwiches.

"You can," Marie urged.

"I'm not sure."

"Then test him. I think he will do anything you ask him."

"I think you're wrong," she said, thinking of the wagers he refused to collect on.

"If you love him, isn't it worth taking a risk? At least then you will know for sure."

Could she take a risk on Bellamy? Could she put her heart in his hands and hope he didn't crush it into dust?

WHEN THE LUNCHEON was over Lisbeth waved off Oliver's aunt and her companion. Oliver returned to her and kissed her hand and said, "I'll hire a hack to Vauxhall. Do you think you can bear it? Dalmere will be waiting, and we do not want to miss the balloon ascension, do we?"

"A hack will be fine. It is only a short trip. I must confess I am looking forward to tonight. Afterwards, you must come home with me, for I have something important to discuss."

He frowned. "What is it?"

"I don't want to get into it now. It will be more appropriate to show you later, when we can be alone."

"Alone? I too am anxious to have you alone. Naked and alone," he whispered in her ear, the soft sound sending sparks of desire through her whole body.

She wanted nothing more than to be naked and alone with Oliver. Pretending the outside world and all its problems didn't exist was so easy when they were together. She would show him the ledger and maybe together they could decide what was the best way to handle this new situation. She had already organized for her solicitors to meet with her tomorrow. She wanted the ledger to be dealt with in a legal manner and all monies returned as soon as was possible to those who had invested.

She touched his cheek briefly as a footman hailed a passing hackney. The trip to the gardens was pleasant and they laughed and kissed the whole way there. They were to meet Dalmere at the front gates where there was already a crowd of people milling about. She felt so at ease in Bellamy's company. She longed to be with him always. It was strange. She thought she would never feel this way with a man. Nathaniel had tried to beat any sense of contentment out of her. She was happy to see that maybe, just maybe, he hadn't succeeded after all.

They alighted, paid their entrance fee, and waited for Dalmere. It was no chore as there was much to see and take in.

"Lord Bellamy! Is there a Lord Bellamy here?"

"Over here!" Oliver shouted. A young lad came scurrying up with his cap in his hand.

"Ever so sorry m'lord. I've a message for ye. I was told you were coming here. It's Lady Mortimer, she's taken ill and the doctor wants you right quick."

Just then Dalmere arrived. "Something amiss, Bellamy?"

Oliver paid the lad who ran off into the crowd. "I have to go. My aunt has taken ill." He looked pale and worried.

Lisbeth touched Oliver's sleeve in comfort. "I hope she didn't overdo things today," Lisbeth said, her tone matching his expression.

"I hope so, too." He took off his hat, ran a hand through his hair, and put his hat back on.

"I'm happy to be Lady Blackhurst's escort until you return," Dalmere offered. "You wouldn't want her to miss out on the balloon ascension, would you? There will not be another one until next season."

Lisbeth smiled. "I really don't mind, Lord Dalmere. I'm happy to return home. Bellamy, please give your aunt my well wishes and let me know how she is when you can."

"Ah, but I insist," said Dalmere. "It's a mild night. We should make the most of the weather."

Bellamy patted her hand that was still on his arm. "I'm sure my aunt is fine. She probably had one too many sandwiches. That's all. I'll return as soon as I can."

"Are you sure?" Lisbeth asked. Oliver nodded and she released his arm and turned towards the other man. "Then I would be pleased to have you escort me, Lord Dalmere." For what other course did she have without offending him?

"The pleasure will be all mine, I assure you, Lady Blackhurst." Dalmere bowed in front of her and offered her his arm.

Bellamy turned to leave but looked back. "I hate to leave you."

"I'll be fine. Go," she replied, giving him a smile of reassurance even though she did not feel it. How would he be if his aunt died? She did not want to think about it. She watched as he strode off towards the entrance and was gone.

"He is very protective of you," Dalmere said. "It's very… sweet."

Lisbeth gave a small laugh. "Yes. He is very attentive."

"I can't blame him. You are a beautiful young lady, and beautiful things should always be kept safe." He smiled and then pointed towards a large, half-filled balloon. "It looks like it will be some time before it is ready to lift off the ground. Shall we walk around and enjoy the sights?"

Lisbeth smiled. "That would be delightful." She had not been to Vauxhall in an age, before she was married if she remembered correctly.

She did need to talk to Dalmere about his part in the speculation. She could even reveal to him that she had found the ledger. She planned to go public with the matter on the morrow, anyway.

He would no doubt be very pleased to know she intended to return the investors' capital even though she legally did not have to. She had decided last night to do this so she could help those who had lost their loved ones because of Nathaniel, and to help

Bellamy. Giving him back the money his brother, Henry, had invested would mean that in some small way she could atone for the trouble she had put him through, and he could forget about the wagers and their agreement.

Lisbeth looked around her as Dalmere pointed out the sights. She did not realize how far from the entrance they had wandered until he led her to a small marquee.

"I thought we might take some refreshment before heading back to the balloon."

"Oh, that sounds very nice. Thank you."

He smiled at her before opening the flap of the tent and ushering her through. "We wouldn't want you to miss out on your just desserts, Lady Blackhurst," he said, his tone low and quiet.

Unease filled her, quickly followed by fear when she saw the look in Dalmere's eyes. "What do you mean by that?" Her heart was beating so loudly she could hear it echoing around the tented room.

"Let me show you, you Blackhurst witch!"

CHAPTER EIGHTEEN

THE SMILE SHE'D felt playing about her lips all day fell away at the sound of Dalmere's words. Stunned, Lisbeth whirled around. A shocked gasp escaped her lips at the sight that confronted her.

Dalmere stood at the entrance to the supper tent. His usually emotionless, yet angelic face was gone, instead replaced by an ugly red-blotched fury. His eyes burned dark with hatred.

For her.

Her mind seemed to be having trouble comprehending what was happening. "I beg your pardon?"

"You can beg all you like; it will not save you," Dalmere replied.

Danger emanated from him in waves. She stepped back until her legs hit a small table laden with a tea service. The cups clattered on their saucers, the sound extraordinarily loud in the silence of the tent.

He smiled at her but it was a horrid, nasty twist of his lips.

Terror gripped her. Quickly followed by anger. It surged through her body bubbling up her throat like one of the many fountains outside. "How dare you speak to me like this," she yelled at him. She would have stormed out but he'd crossed his arms over his chest daring her to try and get past him. Her body was shaking but she was not sure if the source was from her anger or her fear. Probably both. "I have done nothing to you,

Lord Dalmere, and I don't appreciate being spoken to in this matter. Now, step aside. I wish to leave."

He took a step towards her. "You won't be going anywhere because *I* don't appreciate that you and your rotten, scheming husband tried to ruin me," he said. His fierce whisper was calm and controlled. His eyes were narrowed and focused totally on her.

Taking slow, even breaths to hide her fear, she stepped to the left and back to keep some distance between them.

"I had nothing to do with the speculation," she explained.

He took a step forward.

She took another step back.

"So you say, but you happily kept all the money, didn't you? It was supposed to be returned to us, to all of us, but you just had to cut us all a little deeper."

"Dalmere, you have it all wrong." Lisbeth put her hand up to stop him coming any closer. "If you will let me explain—"

He shook his head. "There is nothing you can say that can undo what you've done."

"We found the ledger!" she blurted out in a panic. "My housekeeper found it only yesterday. I have an appointment with my solicitors tomorrow to settle the matter."

He laughed but not in amusement. She had to admit it sounded like nothing but a stalling tactic, even to her.

"How convenient. I'm afraid it is all a little too late for you. The damage has been done. You must think me very gullible. I'm not Bellamy, you know. You can't just flash your pretty eyes at me and make me believe whatever drivel you think I want to hear." He took another step, then another.

She scooted more to the left but the tent was not large. "It's true. You will have your money back. I've not spent a sovereign of it."

He scowled at her. "I watched some of my closest friends decline into madness. Some took their lives because they couldn't fathom how they could recover from what Blackhurst had done, from what you had done." He shook his head. "You give me these lies, this false hope, in order to save yourself, but it is too late."

Lisbeth was horrified by his words. She wasn't to blame. "I was fighting for my freedom, fighting to prove I didn't murder Blackhurst. I did not intentionally ignore what had happened to some of the investors in those months after Nathaniel's death.

"I took my solicitors' advice, Dalmere, nothing more. They insisted I mustn't give the investors any money without proof of contract." *Was that so wrong?*

"We trusted him," Dalmere spat. "He promised to make us all rich. He lied to us and then you got it all. Do you honestly think we would have come begging at your doorstep had we not been duped?"

Perhaps that was how Nathaniel had planned to get away with his scheme—he had traded on their trust. And they had fallen for it.

"I understand your anger at being duped, I do. Nathaniel betrayed me too." *In so many ways.*

"Am I to sympathize with you over the fact that you suddenly became one of the richest women in England? How terrible that must have been for you."

"It was," she countered, her tone now as angry and sarcastic as his. "It was no picnic being labeled a murderer, shunned by those I loved, required to endure a trial and forced into seclusion. The money never meant anything to me."

"Your speech is very pretty, my lady, but I am afraid I don't believe you. Everyone knows you were just as much a part of fooling us as Blackhurst was."

"You are wrong!" She wished she could turn back time and insist, papers or not, for her solicitors to settle some money on the investors.

She felt an old and familiar shame come over her. She knew she couldn't change the past and by the look in Dalmere's eyes, nothing she could do or say would change his mind about her either.

"I'm sorry," she said, bowing her head. There was nothing else to be said.

"Sorry! That is all you can say? Sorry!" He took two steps closer to her, his fists clenched.

At the violence of his tone, she looked up and then all about her. Saw his fists, but no escape. There were too many things crowded into this small tent. She managed to navigate around the various chairs that had been set up but found herself cornered.

"This isn't some misdemeanor like stealing a tart from the kitchen as a child. This was our lives."

"I only did what I was told was the right thing to do under the circumstances. It's not my fault there was no paperwork or that someone killed Blackhurst. If that hadn't happened, he might have been found out and would have paid for his crimes against you all. Blame Blackhurst's killer for this mess, not me."

If Lisbeth thought this would appease him or at least direct his anger away from her, she was sorely mistaken. His eyes nearly bulged with the vehemence he was controlling.

"I made sure that Blackhurst got what he deserved, and now I will make sure you do too," Dalmere snarled.

"*You* killed him?"

It was like the pieces of a puzzle coming together. Dalmere had killed Nathaniel and now he planned to kill her.

She found herself stifling a scream in her throat as he reached out for her.

OLIVER IGNORED THE smells invading his nostrils as he maneuvered himself around carriages and carts, trying find a hackney. It was a good two miles from the gardens to his aunt's house in Grosvenor Square. He needed to get her, and quickly. He should never have suggested she go to the luncheon. The exertion must have been too much for her. This was all his fault. His guilt made him feel like casting up his accounts.

"Bellamy!"

Oliver looked around but the road was too congested with carriages, horses, and pedestrians to identify who had called out.

"Bellamy! Over here," the voice called again. He recognized it as Tony. What was he doing here?

Oliver looked behind him and saw his friend, waving out of a hackney window.

Oliver skirted around a fishmonger's wares to cross the road to where Tony was holding the door open for him. He vaulted inside.

Tony clapped him on the back. "I thought you were going to Vauxhall? I was just on my way to find you. I have news—"

Oliver shook his head. "It will have to wait. I have to go to my aunt. She needs me."

"I don't understand why—"

"She is ill, and the surgeon has been called." Oliver looked at his pocket watch in distress. He could not afford the delay that Tony would no doubt bring.

He banged on the roof and instructed the driver to go to his aunt's address.

Tony stuck his head out the window and told the driver to wait.

"What the devil?"

"Oliver, I've just left your aunt. She's fine," Tony said.

"What do you mean, you've just been there?" Confusion was warring with his guilty conscience over his aunt's health. "Why would you have been at Aunt Petunia's?"

"If you will stop interrupting, I'll tell you."

When Oliver reluctantly nodded, Tony said, "I was looking for you. Lady Fortesque's butler informed me you had left the luncheon. I went to your house but you were not there. I went to Lady Blackhurst's but her butler is nothing but a closed-lipped, livery-clad stick-in-the-mud and he told me only that her ladyship was not receiving. I went to your aunt's next where she insisted I come in. I was hoping she would tell me where you were. It took a bit of getting to the point, but she did tell me some interesting information about your brother and his hatred for Blackhurst."

"My brother did not kill Blackhurst," Oliver insisted.

"I have no doubt on the matter, but he did hate him. So did many others apparently, including your friend Dalmere."

The carriage jerked and moved a little causing both men to grab for their doors to stay seated.

"Dalmere?" Oliver asked.

"Yes," Tony said, running his fingers through his hair. "We will have to make sure Lady Blackhurst stays put until we can determine for sure." Tony looked contrite for a moment. "Oliver, I have to tell you it was Dalmere who hired me to investigate her although he did use his uncle's name and not his own. It was this that sparked my suspicions about him. I know he is a friend of yours, but I have reason to believe he killed Blackhurst. Oliver, are you all right? You've gone as pale as a ghost."

Oliver already had his hand on the handle of the door. "Tony, I've just left Lisbeth with Dalmere at the gardens."

Tony swore but Oliver was already out of the hack, running, ducking, and weaving down the street. He hurdled over dogs and skidded around carts in his desperation to get back to the gardens and Lisbeth. How could he have been so blind?

He had to get to her, but all before him stretched like an endless winding road. The distance between him and the gates to the gardens felt miles and miles away. Time ticked in slow motion. What would he do if he did not get there in time? How would he live if something happened to her?

She had his heart, had for weeks.

He loved her.

He needed her.

"Lisbeth," he said in a pained voice, increasing his speed.

His chest heaved with exertion and his thighs burned, but he didn't care. *Bloody, bloody hell!* Dalmere had been under their noses the whole time. How had they not connected him with

Blackhurst? *Dalmere used his own connection with Henry to play me,* Oliver thought. It was like Dalmere had orchestrated this whole mess with Lisbeth, Tony, and the speculation. What then of the Black Raven wager and his insistence that she was not to be trusted? Had he been setting him up?

Tony had distrusted Lisbeth, too, but he knew Tony would never have run all around London looking for him unless he knew his information about Dalmere was accurate. This only made him more anxious about Lisbeth. He had to have her safe in his arms. But first he was going to kill Dalmere.

Tony caught up to him, but they exchanged no words and just kept on running. Finally, the gates of Vauxhall gardens appeared. They didn't stop to pay the entry fee but ran right past and into the crowd.

"Eh? Nobody gets through my gates wifout payin'," the gate keeper yelled as, at his direction, his thug took off in pursuit of Oliver and Tony.

Oliver pointed towards where the balloon ascension was being held, and they both headed for the crowd. *Damn!* How would they find Lisbeth in this crush? Both of them started to ask people if they had seen Lady Blackhurst. One gentleman pointed towards the path that led to the supper tents.

The thug was catching up, yelling for them to stop. "Hey, you buggers. I'm coming after you, I am. You better stop now or else I'm gunna have to thump ya."

Tony and Oliver started running again. If the thug kept following them he'd be useful as a witness when they found Dalmere.

Panic swelled when he saw how many supper tents, all identical, were lined up on both sides of the path, ready to please the crowd after the ascension. He damped it down. He used every technique he had ever learned in the army to control his emotions and do his job. He concentrated on his breathing. Find her.

"You take one side. I'll take the other," Oliver instructed.

That's when they heard her scream.

DALMERE LAUGHED AGAIN when he saw she was about to scream the tent down. "Save your breath, Lady Blackhurst. Screaming in a place like this will only give you a sore throat, and that is my job, eventually. One doesn't want to rush these things. I want to enjoy toying with you like your husband toyed with us."

Lisbeth's eyes burned with tears, but she didn't want Dalmere to see them. She looked around the tent searching for any possible escape route. The tents were pegged down tightly at the bottom with the only opening being at the front. She watched him as he took a long swallow from a flask he'd just taken out of his jacket pocket.

He took another swig while he considered her. "I had hoped to save us both from this unpleasant business, but like an irritating fly you would not leave. I thought that the trial would get you out of the way, but somehow you managed to elude execution or even transportation." He shook his head. "It was inconceivable."

He recapped the flask and returned it to his pocket. "Technicalities are the bane of our legal system it seems. Then I thought to make your life such a living misery by spreading some malicious rumors."

Lisbeth's mouth fell open. "You started all those rumors about me?"

He gave her a self-satisfied smile. She wanted to slap him, but that would mean placing herself within his reach.

"Such a cunning plan if I don't say so myself," he said. "The Black Raven idea was mine too. It took off with the ferocity of a tenement fire. I couldn't have been more pleased at the time. I have to admit I thought it would drive you over the pond, or even to the Americas, but you are one stubborn female." He studied her for a moment which made her edge a little more along the wall.

"I suppose you think Bellamy will come and save you. He won't, you know. I think he will be relieved, actually, once you are dead. With you out of the picture he can do as he originally planned and marry a rich heiress and rebuild his life. Thanks to his brother, he is quite in the suds. It is all a bit pathetic actually. He came to me that night trying to find a way to get some money. I suggested the Black Raven wager. Didn't think you'd let him in, of course, because you never had before, but look how well it worked out." He gestured around them. "He has been collecting a tidy sum, and you have been helping him."

She knew of Oliver's financial situation, but Dalmere did not know she knew. Nor did he seem to know that Oliver had not collected on any of the wagers bar the first one. He was trying to taunt her, make her think Oliver did not care for her. She knew her heart. Despite her efforts a tear slipped unbidden down her cheek. She wiped it away but not quickly enough that Dalmere did not see it.

"Ah, I see that you have feelings for him. Your eyes tell me everything. He would never have married you in any case; surely you knew that?"

She knew, had perhaps always known, but these last few weeks had been so joyous she had let her mind and her heart think otherwise.

"Tainting his family line would be just as bad as the scandal his poverty would have had on his reputation. He would not risk his family name for you," Dalmere explained. "It is all he has, after all, thanks to Blackhurst."

Lisbeth knew she should not let his words wound her, but they did, simply because she knew what he was saying was essentially true. Although, she had hoped that her reputation would simply fade away, or that the *ton* would get bored with hating her. She had been fooling herself. A woman's reputation was all she had, and Lisbeth had lost all respectability long ago.

Thanks to Bellamy she had come to be barely tolerated by the *ton*, but she knew she would never be able to remove the stain of her past.

She turned all her anger and hurt towards Dalmere in a look that should have made him burst into flames and combust right then and there.

Instead he laughed. "Oh, did you think he would? What a fool you are."

Oliver might never have married her, but he loved her. She could feel it with every beat of her heart. Whatever his feelings about her, he would never have knowingly placed her into the hands of this mad man who wanted to kill her.

Dalmere went over to the curtained entrance and pulled the curtain cord from its hook, winding it around his hands.

Lisbeth gasped. Her heart stilled in the cold knowledge that she would never see Oliver again. Never get to tell him how much she loved him.

"You don't know how long I have dreamed of killing you," Dalmere said as he advanced. "There are so many ways to kill, you see. I decided the most enjoyable way would be strangulation." He gave the rope a quick tug as if to test its sturdiness. "It's fairly quick. It's not messy and well, I think I will take much pleasure in watching the life fade from your eyes."

Lisbeth couldn't take her eyes off the rope. She was trapped like a wounded animal and panic had set in. Now she was almost panting with distress. No, this was not how she wanted her life to end.

She used all her might, and all the courage she could muster, and slapped him hard across the face. The sound of her palm connecting with his cheek echoed through the tent as she scrambled to get to the entrance.

"You stupid cow!" He lurched for her from behind and Lisbeth screamed and knocked over everything that she could get her hands on, kicking out at Dalmere with all her might.

Nathaniel had liked it when she fought him; Dalmere seemed

to like it too. There was no escape. Tears sprang in her eyes, but she forced them back; she would not die meekly.

He put the cord around her neck, and she tried to scream again. He swung her around and onto the ground. She looked straight into his eyes. She was mad to think he had an ounce of humanity in him.

Her hands came up to the rope at her neck. The pressure was uncomfortable, but she could still breathe. Dalmere was breathing hard.

He pulled the rope tighter. Lisbeth gasped against the pressure on her throat. "I should have shot you like I did Blackhurst and have done with you," he said as he put even more pressure on her throat.

Lisbeth tried to kick out but the tent was getting dim.

She gasped but no air came to relieve the heaviness in her chest. *Oliver. I love you. I'm sorry.*

Oliver flew inside the tent, grabbed Dalmere off Lisbeth, and threw him onto his back. Dalmere's expression was shocked. Oliver looked over at Lisbeth lying motionless on the ground. Dalmere distracted him by rolling back to his feet and throwing a punch that landed wide on Oliver's cheek. Oliver gave him an uppercut to the jaw that sent Dalmere sprawling again. Blood oozed from the side of Dalmere's mouth.

"You're too late, Bellamy. I've already killed her," Dalmere chuckled.

"Tony?" Oliver demanded.

Tony knelt by Lisbeth's side. "She's alive," he said.

"No!" Dalmere replied. The shock was evident on his face. He elbowed Oliver in the chest, but Oliver was focused now on one thing. Punishing Dalmere. He punched Dalmere again and again, only mildly satisfied by the sound of bones breaking.

"Stop!" Dalmere pleaded, his voice thin and pathetic now.

"I should kill you," Oliver said in a snarl. He grabbed Dalmere and brought him to his feet. "But I'll let the law do that."

Dalmere kicked out and caught Oliver in the shin. Oliver

swore and grabbed Dalmere's arm and pulled it back until he heard it pop. Dalmere howled in pain and Oliver shoved him out the tent door and onto the gravel path. The thug was standing there, looking down at Dalmere.

"Did you hear his confession?" Oliver asked the thug.

"I did," the thug replied, looking down at the pitiful sight before him.

Dalmere was still swearing and spitting blood onto the path.

"Make sure he doesn't go anywhere."

Oliver went straight back to Lisbeth's side.

Lisbeth looked up at him and started to cry. He could tell she was in pain, and he wanted to soothe her. He picked her up, kissed her on the forehead, and said, "Hush now. You're safe, Lisbeth. I have you."

She nodded and rested her head on his shoulder.

Tony appeared beside him. "I've tied Dalmere up. Tom here says there is a surgeon at the balloon ascension." He pointed to the thug.

"I could go fetch him for you," Tom offered.

"I'd be much obliged," Oliver replied.

Tom took off at a run. Tony indicated to a bench and Oliver sat down with Lisbeth in his lap. Her breaths were shallow and harsh but at least she was breathing.

"I've never been so scared in all my life. I am so sorry, Lisbeth. I should never have left you with him," he whispered into her hair.

"It's a good thing you didn't kill him," Tony said, glancing back towards the moaning Dalmere. "It will be so much the better to send him to some place resembling hell, before he actually ends up there."

Oliver could only agree but he didn't care about what was to happen to Dalmere as long as the dastard couldn't get anywhere near Lisbeth again.

The sound of carriage wheels heralded the arrival of the surgeon, who jumped out and began to examine Lisbeth immediately.

"Well?" asked Oliver impatiently, as the surgeon took his time examining Lisbeth's neck.

"She's lucky to be alive," he replied. "I won't know the extent of the damage to her vocal cords until she has had time to rest."

The surgeon then spoke to Lisbeth directly. "You must not talk under any circumstances, Lady Blackhurst, until I am satisfied you are ready. Is that clear?"

Lisbeth gave the slightest nod but winced again. Her throat felt like she had swallowed broken glass. The surgeon gave her a sympathetic smile and then ordered her to be put into the carriage. Inside, Oliver gathered her up in his arms again. The surgeon climbed in, frowned at the scene, but tapped on the ceiling to tell the driver to go. Lisbeth was glad of Oliver's warmth and did not care what the surgeon may think of them.

"How long until we know the extent of the damage?" Oliver asked the surgeon.

"A few days at least, maybe a week. She has some nasty abrasions from the rope which will take some time to heal. Her voice, if it has not been too damaged, will still be hoarse for some time. She will have some trouble swallowing. The bloodshot eyes are from the pressure. They should also heal within a few days."

"She seems to still have trouble breathing," Oliver stated.

"Yes, she will be quite shallow of breath for a while, and the wheezing is also normal. I will, however, be keeping a close eye on her for the next twenty-four hours."

"Thank you. I am glad you will be attending her."

Lisbeth listened to the conversation but of course stayed silent even though she had a million of her own questions. Oliver smoothed her hair. It felt nice. It felt right to be in his arms. She had her eyes closed but was fully aware of where she was.

There was so much she wanted to say. Needed to say. But for now, she would have to be content to be in the embrace of the man she loved. He had come to save her. Did that mean he loved her? But what did it matter if he did?

Lisbeth's eyes flickered and then opened. She saw the balloon rising high into the air through the window, saw Oliver looking down at her. Saw his concerned smile, and then felt his lips on her forehead again.

She took his hand in hers and squeezed it. He squeezed back. Her throat hurt and her head hurt. In fact, all of her hurt and she was so very, very tired. She was glad she had been able to see the balloon had gained its freedom and was even now rising higher and higher into the murky gray sky. She was glad she'd had Oliver with her when she saw it. She only wished she had the energy to lift her hand and touch his face. That she had enough breath to tell him how much she loved him.

She closed her eyes again and let the sway of the carriage and the whispered tones of Oliver and the surgeon soothe her.

"Tomorrow," Oliver whispered into her ear, "all will know of your innocence, Lisbeth. I will make sure of it." Oliver's voice had an edge of determination in it. She tried to smile but it hurt too much so she just squeezed his hand again and was happy when he gathered her closer to his chest so she could hear his heart.

CHAPTER NINETEEN

LISBETH WOKE WITH a start, images of Dalmere looming above her filled her mind, his eyes filled with hatred and murderous intent. Frantic, she swept her gaze around and saw, except for the many vases overflowing with a profusion of flowers of all sorts and colors, that her bedroom was empty.

Relief washed over her as she drew in a breath. Every attempt she made at swallowing had agony ripping through her. It felt like the silk rope of the supper tent still surrounded her throat, still constricted her breathing. Still tried to steal the life from her.

Oliver!

She wanted to scream out his name, have him rush to her, comfort her. Take her away from here. Her mouth remained silent, and her room remained empty. She pushed back the heavy covers and sat on the edge of the bed. Her bare toes dangled above the floor, her nightgown twisted and damp against her skin. She felt woozy and the room spun in a slow arc around her. Closing her eyes, she tried to calm the military tattoo drumming away in her chest.

She was fine.

She was alive.

She was in her room.

No need for such hysterics.

Lisbeth opened her eyes and looked out the window. It was dark and gloomy, as it had been every day this year. Only, this wasn't every day. This was the day she was finally free of the mantle of *murderer*.

The Black Raven had taken flight and flown away for good. She had completed her vow to reclaim her life. She should be overjoyed. So, why wasn't she?

The clock chimed in the hall and Lisbeth jumped. The sharp intake of breath hurt so much she found she had to clutch her throat to stop the pain. What time was it? For the first time in years she had no idea. She had no schedule to guide her, no pocket-watch to remind with its incessant ticking.

It was strange, daunting, but at the same time it felt good. Her schedule had been a blessing and a burden. Now she was free of it, could she manage on her own? Take her days as they came and live without the deep-seated terror Nathaniel had implanted in her all those many horrible years ago?

If Oliver was by her side, she was sure she could do anything.

She heard the sound of singing gradually becoming louder. Marie. It made her smile. Her sister was here. She wasn't alone, hadn't been abandoned. Marie came into the room with a massive flower arrangement in front of her, still trilling like a songbird. Lisbeth had never had her sister's talent for singing, not that it mattered, now. Then the thought struck her with the force of a runaway carriage. What if she never was able to talk again? What if this damage was permanent? The thought was as horrifying as it was shocking. Her fingers stroked gently over the bruised flesh of her throat. Dalmere may not have killed her, but he may still have damaged her forever.

"Oh, you're awake!" Marie exclaimed when she turned from putting down the flowers. She rushed over to Lisbeth and hugged her fiercely. "Oh, my dearest. You look very pale. Would you like some water? Or lukewarm tea?"

Lisbeth made a T with her two index fingers. Marie smiled and briefly went out into the hall. Lisbeth let one tear escape down her cheek before she wiped it away. Now was not the time to grieve for a voice she was not sure she had yet lost. When

Marie returned it was with yet another vase of flowers. Lisbeth lifted a brow at her sister in question.

"Oh, these?" Marie read the little note attached. "These are from the Warrington hothouse in Sussex. Aren't they stunning? They have the best hothouses in all of England. Flowers have been arriving all morning from all manner of people. I imagine there was many a shocked face reading the papers this day. Finally, everyone knows the truth, Lisbeth. You can finally get rid of the Black Raven for good." Marie hugged her tightly, pulled back, smiled, and then hugged her again.

"In any case, I have decided not to read those awful scandal sheets ever again and only read *LaBelle Assemblée* from now on. I won't know any of the gossip, but I shall be very well dressed." Marie twirled around and laughed. Lisbeth clapped her hands and stifled a laugh she knew would only bring her pain.

So, everyone knew. It appeared Oliver had made good on his promise to report the truth. Yet he did not know the whole truth, for she had yet to tell him of the ledger and diary. How would he react to the fact he was to get back the capital his brother had invested in the speculation? Surely, that would make him happy. Surely then they would be on even terms. But first she had to release him from whatever duty he may feel towards her. Set him free as she had been set free. It was only fair.

Marie returned with a maid and together they helped Lisbeth dress before moving into her sitting room to sit near the cheery fire with a cup of tea. Marie sat happily with her, chatting.

"My dear Fenwick's face was comical when I told him it was Dalmere all along who had killed Blackhurst. My husband is dear to me but sometimes he can be very narrow-minded. Dalmere had everyone fooled as to his character, it seemed."

Lisbeth smiled and indicated for something to write on. Marie jumped up and went to Lisbeth's writing desk in the corner and bought the small table over for her. Lisbeth took up a pencil and wrote, *Where is Bellamy?*

"At home or at his club, I suspect. Grandmother insisted he

go home and change his clothes and stop hanging around like a lost dog in need of scraps. She said he could return this afternoon when you were rested."

Grandmother is here? Lisbeth wrote. She wasn't sure why she felt a thrill run through her. Was it because her grandmother cared enough to be here, for her? Lady Fortesque was a force to be reckoned with on a normal day. Today was not a normal day. She had to admit she was somewhat relieved her grandmother thought to come over and take on the household duties leaving the nursing to Marie. Lisbeth's grandmother had never been the type to dote.

Marie laughed. "Oh yes, she is downstairs *terrorizing* your staff. Rollands is quite put out." Marie rolled her eyes.

She mustn't dismiss anyone. They are my staff. Lisbeth would not repay her loyal staff by having the wrath of her grandmother's viperous tongue upon them.

Marie patted her hand. "Of course. Don't fret. Your servants are safe. She is just ensuring the house does not fall down around your ears because the coal wasn't ordered or the menu not organized."

Well, that made sense. However, Lisbeth was not completely useless just because she could not talk. The sooner she was back in charge the better she would feel.

When is the doctor due? Lisbeth wrote next. The sooner she was given permission from the doctor to talk, the sooner her new life could begin. The thought of sharing it with Oliver sent her pulse to skittering erratically and her whole body to feeling warm. Would the mere thought of him do this to her in years to come? She had the distinct feeling it might.

"The doctor said he would be here at eleven so not long now." Marie got up and smiled down at Lisbeth. "I am so glad you are all right. I don't know what I would have done had Dalmere taken you from us. Wretched man. I hope they hang him."

Yesterday, she would have wholeheartedly agreed. Now?

There was a time when there had been a real danger she might have met the same fate. The difference being that he had committed the crime and she had not. Still, she felt uneasy about sending another person to their death. Blackhurst had done a heinous thing to the investors of the speculation, but did he deserve death? Blackhurst had treated her terribly and unjustly but as much as she had on many occasions wished him to Hades she had never considered murder.

I am glad you are here too. You are doing such a good job of looking after me.

Marie hugged her. "Well, it is the least I can do considering all that has happened between us. I should never have doubted you. I know you have forgiven me, but I still feel… miserable about the whole thing." Marie seemed surprised by her tears and turned away.

Lisbeth took her hand and showed her what she had written. *Please don't cry. I am just so happy to have you, Fenwick, little Michael, and Grandmother back in my life. That is all I need right now.*

Marie gazed at her with moist eyes. "What about Bellamy? You still love him, don't you?"

Lisbeth bent her head and scribbled frantically on the paper. *Yes, I do, but first I have to let him go. If he loves me too then maybe we have a future together.*

"What is this talk of letting him go? Of course he loves you. You must tell him and be done with it." Marie reached for the teapot. "Now, come have some more tea. We cannot have you fading away. Grandmother would kill me!"

THE DOCTOR ANNOUNCED Lisbeth was doing well, but it was better for her not to try and speak for the rest of the week. She had hoped for a better result but at least he wasn't saying she would never talk again.

She spent a good half hour trying to compose her note to

Oliver. Marie's words spun around her mind trying to find a comfortable spot. *Just tell him and be done with it?* She couldn't just blurt it out. She had so much to tell him, about the ledger, about her decision to give the investors back their capital, her need to know that he was with her because he loved her too and not because he felt some misguided duty toward her.

Her floor was soon littered with paper balls of varying sizes depending on how bad her attempt had been. Eventually she decided on firstly releasing him, then when she had done that, she would be able to gage how best to proceed with her declaration of love.

Dearest Oliver

I can never repay you for all you have done for me. Now the truth is known by all I think it only fair that I release you from our agreement.

With affection,
LC

Simple was best. Marie had said to be direct. Lisbeth thought if Oliver had any questions she would simply write the answers down for him, but she felt her note clear enough. She wanted there to be no feeling of obligation between them. She wanted him to be sure it was she he wanted. It was she he loved.

OLIVER WORE HIS best frock coat. He wanted to be well-dressed when he asked Lisbeth to marry him. When he told her his heart was hers. What had happened in the last few days had made his feelings clear. He loved her. He smiled at the thought of her face beaming with joy. At how she would fling herself into his arms and kiss him. Tears of happiness escaping her amazing blue eyes.

He whistled happily as he strolled down the road. He had decided to walk as his body was too full of nervous energy to sit in a hack. As it was, he was continually stopped by passers-by who asked if the rumors were true. He was happy to confirm they were. Dalmere was imprisoned and would appear before a court of his peers. They would not go lightly on him as the murder of Blackhurst was not an act of honor, no matter what dishonorable act Blackhurst had committed. Things may have been very different if Dalmere had simply killed Blackhurst in a duel. The fact he had tried to hide his crime behind the skirts of a woman only made him seem more cowardly.

Oliver reached Lisbeth's house and stood for a moment on the steps where it had all begun. It was here on this step he had misguidedly started on this journey with her, while waiting to win The Black Raven Wager. It was here he wanted to propose to her. It seemed fitting.

Decided, he knocked on the door. This time when it was opened Rollands almost looked pleased to see him.

"Good afternoon, Rollands. Would you be so kind as to ask your mistress to come to the door?"

The butler frowned. "The door, my lord?"

"Yes, the door. The hard wooden thing you are currently hovering in front of and have such a wonderful time slamming in unwanted guests' faces."

"It's not done—"

"Well, it's done today. Don't be difficult and ruin my surprise. I plan to propose to your mistress so be quick about it."

Rollands looked at him for a moment as if not quite believing he had heard Oliver correctly. He no doubt saw the stupid grin. A grin that had refused to leave Oliver's face since he had decided to marry Lisbeth.

Rollands gave the hint of a smile. "Very well. Would you like to step in and wait?"

"I'm fine just here."

The door closed and Oliver stifled a laugh. The door had been closed in his face the night he had met her, too. He was convinced this was the perfect place for his proclamation of undying love.

A few minutes later Lisbeth stood in the doorway, a bemused expression on her face. He bowed. She looked around but then shrugged and curtseyed. She thrust out her hand before he could open his mouth to start his very impressive speech. A speech he had worked on all morning.

"What's this?" He unfolded the papers and saw one page was her list of wagers, all in code. "I don't understand."

She motioned towards a second page.

He read it.

Frowned.

Read it again.

He felt the blood leaving his face. A strange kind of dizziness came over him and caused him to grip the rail on the steps for support. She was dismissing him? Just like that? Now Dalmere was caught and she was free of her murderous reputation, she was letting him go?

"No!" he said, shaking his head.

Lisbeth blinked. She shook her head and pointed to the last sentence again. *Now the truth is known by all I think it only fair to release you from our agreement.* She opened a small notebook and began writing.

I am setting you free, she wrote.

"Oh, well, thank you, I had not realized I was imprisoned." He knew his voice was verging on sarcastic anger but he couldn't help it.

I do not want you to choose duty to me over your own future, she wrote next.

Oliver took a step back. "In other words, you want me to leave and find a future with someone else?"

She shook her head vigorously. She began to write again.

He held up a hand to stop her from writing. "Oh, I understand," he said. "I don't blame you. After all, I have nothing to offer you. Except myself and that's not exactly a lot, is it? I'm nothing. A man in my position could not possibly tempt a woman like you."

She was still scribbling madly in her little book, but he had a sour taste in his mouth and no want to swallow yet more bitter disappointment.

Had she used him only to get what she wanted? Now she had it she no longer needed him? Suddenly, just like his bank account, he felt empty. Like his estate he was worthless.

She didn't love him.

The realization of these facts felt like a right hook to the jaw and a low punch in the gut from the famous boxer *Gentleman Jackson*. All his breath seemed to leave his body, leaving him gasping.

He was sure he felt his heart break, its pounding turning to a sluggish flip-flop in his chest, like a fish floundering on the shore. Oliver turned on his heel and numbly started to walk down the street. There was no destination. It didn't seem to really matter where he ended up. He no longer cared. The only thing he felt was a deep ache which had invaded every nerve in his body. He saw nothing but a dark abyss opening up before him. Would it be too much to hope he would fall into it and be done with this pain?

Oliver walked onto the road, heard the shouts of people all around him, horses neighing loudly above him, but he just kept walking.

LISBETH COLLAPSED IN the doorway. She was only vaguely aware Rollands had caught her before she hit the floor.

Oliver had walked away! He had misunderstood her note and refused to stay and let her explain. Once again, she cursed Dalmere for taking her voice. Looking down at her notebook, she read the frantic scribble she had attempted.

You will never be nothing to me. I love you. Don't leave me.

Tears dripped onto the page. Why had he left her so easily? Had he never loved her at all?

She put her hand on the door knowing he was somewhere on the other side. Hurting, just like her.

Marie and her grandmother were by her side, and she should have felt comforted by their presence but right now she wished to curl up in a ball and cry. Cry for all she had lost and all she may never get back.

"Is this what you told him?" her grandmother asked looking down at her notebook. "No wonder he stormed off."

Lisbeth let out a keening cry.

"We will fix this," Marie said, giving their grandmother a wide-eyed glare. Her concern and determination was evident in her tone. "We will help you write him a proper letter explaining it all and how you never meant to send him away. He will feel foolish and return, begging you to have him back."

"I will deliver it myself, my lady," Rollands said.

Lisbeth nodded, for she needed to hold on to some remnant of hope this disaster could be fixed.

"I don't understand it, my lady. Lord Bellamy told me he came here to propose to her." Lisbeth heard the words Rollands whispered to her grandmother, and tried to block them out with her hands but then all she could hear was the blood rushing in her ears, like a chant. Fool, fool, fool. She had thought she was being so noble letting him go. Although, perhaps he'd never really been hers in the first place.

Now she may never be able to explain about the ledger and the money that would soon be returned to him. Never be able to tell him how he had saved her in every way that counted.

This should have been the happiest of days but instead she wished nothing more than to do it all over. To wipe away the hurt she had caused him.

Outside, a cold wind whipped up the leaves on the trees outside her window and thunder rumbled in the distance. Rain fell in big fat drops saturating everything in its path in misery. An echo of her own desolation.

OLIVER WAS WET to the bone. If he was lucky he would die of a chill. Who said words couldn't cut as deep as a knife? He certainly felt as if all his life's blood had been drained from him, leaving him nothing but a husk of himself. Dragging himself into his brother's house, Oliver climbed the stairs to his brother's room and ordered his valet to pack every bit of clothing he owned. He then told the butler, Kinsdale, to start closing the house and have everything packed and shipped to Whitely Hall as soon as practical. Oliver planned to leave in the morning.

He undressed and crawled into bed with a bottle of his brother's finest brandy, having decided to drink it until either he passed out or the bottle was dry.

How could he have forgotten the reality of his situation? Love was blind and when it turned on you it was like having your eyeballs scorched in their sockets by a red-hot poker. He had been such a fool. She should have skewered him with that fire poker on the night they met. It would surely have been less painful than what he was experiencing now.

He should hate her, but he couldn't. He shouldn't love her, but he did. This in itself made him pathetic to the point of, well, something more pathetic than pathetic.

Tony would say he'd had a narrow escape. That he had eluded the clutches of Madame Marriage, dodged a life of the doldrums, and shimmied out of the shackles of matrimony. He would say the way to a happy life was not through a wife.

Tony would be wrong on all counts.

About halfway through the bottle of brandy, Oliver decided the time had come to at least earn the title of the Earl of Bellamy.

CHAPTER TWENTY

O LIVER SAT STARING at a cold cup of tea. In the gray and dismal light of dawn, and a near whole bottle of brandy later, things were even more complicated than they had been the night before. Rain beat against the windows to his left in relentless torrents, like fists against his skull.

All around him was the commotion of packing. It was like a constant ringing in his ear. Nothing he could do would shut out the noise.

Last night he had been committed to leaving, to rusticating in the country, to being forgotten. This morning all he could do was think about how he would never see Lisbeth again. And it bloody-well hurt.

Lisbeth's aim could not have been more accurate. Like a master archer her arrowed words had hit their mark dead center—to the deepest heart of his insecurities. Did she know how those few scribbled sentences would affect him? Emotions, wild and desperate, had taken over and his only instinct had been to go, to run, and to escape further torturous words.

He'd always had an issue with his own self-worth. From an early age he'd felt redundant, a loose end flapping in the breeze with no useful direction. Henry had become the earl, and he had become… nothing. It was the reason he had left for the army at such a young age. Oliver had found some purchase in his career as a code breaker and unofficial spy for the Crown, but even then he was just another soldier in Wellington's army.

When he returned home after Henry's death, it was to find that nothing had changed with gaining the title of Earl of Bellamy. Confronted with the financial fall in the family finances, he again floundered. He had no training to prepare him for the responsibility his new title had thrust upon him.

Lisbeth telling him she no longer needed him had been a crushing blow to his already battered ego. Of course, she no longer needed him, but he had hoped she may still have wanted him... loved him. If she had but told him she loved him, he would have done anything to prove his worth to her.

Working alongside Lisbeth had given him a distraction from the reality of his situation. Now he had no excuse but to face the music and it was so awfully out of tune it hurt his ears.

Oliver left the room for no other reason than he could no longer stay where he was with his morbid thoughts. He looked around him. He'd never liked this house. The entryway to the townhouse was like a cavernous box. Dusty echoes of his brother swirled around him like chilly drafts of memory. He would be glad to leave this house and its constant reminders of his failure to live up to Whitely family expectations.

It wouldn't take his brother's butler, Kinsdale, long to shut up the house. There was little enough to pack since Oliver had purged the house of anything he could sell only days after moving in. He had never understood why Henry had stuffed it with the bric-a-brac of wealth; it had served no purpose.

To what purpose was anything anymore when the woman who had stolen his heart had then so cruelly twisted it into dust before his very eyes? ... And in so very few words.

Oliver rubbed his forehead, but it did little to erase the tension throbbing in his temples and the slightly sick feeling in his stomach.

"My lord, I am to remind you of the letter which came for you early this morning," Kinsdale said, holding out a neat, sealed letter. "I took the liberty of keeping it with me as you seemed to have left it on your desk, which has now been packed."

Oliver looked at the letter that Kinsdale offered him. He knew who it was from. He knew why he had left it unopened on his desk. Should he take it? Burn it? Read it and let her words finish him off?

"Sir? Mr. Rollands brought it himself. At dawn. He implored me to tell you that his mistress stressed the importance of the contents."

Oliver took the letter and put it in his jacket pocket. "Thank you, Kinsdale. How long before we can depart?"

LISBETH KNEW NOT all things look brighter in the harsh light of day. Sometimes, the harsh light of day just makes things look… harsh, inhospitable, impossible, bleak.

Lisbeth had not slept well, but then she had not slept well for near on seven years. Since her wedding night. Last night she had not even attempted to sleep. Somewhere in the desperation of her mind she kept thinking Oliver would come back. He would realize he had misunderstood and throw all caution to the wind. He would come racing up the stairs to her room, throw open the doors, and tell her he loved her, that he wanted no other but her.

He had not come.

She was a fanciful, desperate fool.

There was nothing more she could do. Rollands had delivered the letter first thing this morning. She would simply have to wait and hope.

Calling cards had been arriving since yesterday but she was not up to visitors, especially from those who wished to befriend her again, now that she was *respectable*. It wasn't like she could converse with them anyway with her being silenced for at least another week.

"Lisbeth, do stop pacing in the hall. You will wear out the rug."

She turned to see her grandmother frowning at her from the doorway of the parlor. Marie had left her in the hands of her grandmother.

"Come and have some tea. The doctor said you should add some honey for your throat."

Lisbeth sighed and went into the parlor.

Lady Fortesque handed her a cup. "There is something calming in the taking of tea, don't you think?"

Lisbeth couldn't give a fig about tea. Had Oliver read her letter yet?

She looked out the window. The rain was still falling, and it was cold, but no amount of shawls or heated bricks could comfort her. She stared at her teacup. She was sure if she drank it, she would be sick.

Oliver, please read my letter.

"I think we should have a ball," her grandmother announced.

Lisbeth looked up from her cup, her eyes wide. *A ball?* She shook her head.

"It is near the end of the season, and we should celebrate your return."

My return? To what? Misery? She shook her head again. The last thing she wanted to have was a ball.

"Think about it. Have you seen the amount of calling cards piling up? The only way to address them all is to have a ball. Get it over and done with all in one go."

It did make sense. It didn't make her want to do it. Her grandmother was looking at her as if waiting for her to give in to her plans with a nod. Instead, Lisbeth took up her notebook and wrote, *I'll think on it.*

"Well, don't think on it too long. A ball doesn't happen overnight, you know. There are invitations, menus, decorations, and music to consider. It is all very time consuming. It will keep your mind off… things."

Things. Oliver. I can't stand this anymore, she thought. Lisbeth stood up and rushed out of the room with her teacup still in her hand. She was going to go and see him herself. She would stand there until he read her letter. She would stand there all day, all week, if necessary.

Gathering her spencer and a cloak she headed back downstairs.

"My lady?" Rollands asked, his eyebrows nearly hitting his hair line.

She showed him her notebook. *Call me a hack please, Rollands.*

"But, my lady, it is raining."

She glared at him and pointed at her request again.

He grabbed an umbrella. "I'll get one right away."

She waited by the door.

"You cannot mean to go out there?" her grandmother asked from behind her.

Lisbeth nodded.

"Are you mad?" she said. "You'll catch your death."

Lisbeth wrote in her book and turned it towards her grandmother who had to come closer to read it.

I have to. I love him.

Lady Fortesque searched Lisbeth's face. She must have seen the truth of Lisbeth's words in her eyes for she nodded then said, "Shall I come with you, for support?"

Lisbeth shook her head.

"I can't talk you out of this can I?" Lisbeth shook her head again. "Then good luck, my dearest." She placed a kiss on Lisbeth's forehead.

Lisbeth raced out into the weather and into the hired conveyance.

THE CARRIAGE ROCKED from side to side as it negotiated the muddy streets. Deep in his depression Oliver watched as the grand houses of his neighbors were exchanged for more commonplace abodes. He felt like he was running away. He had never felt more alone. He felt wretched.

He pulled out the letter. He had to know, for better or worse, what she had written. He broke the seal. He took a deep breath and opened his eyes. The precise handwriting was smeared in places. Had she been crying while she wrote it? He started to read.

Dear Oliver

I am so sorry about yesterday. I am sorry that I hurt you with my thoughtlessness. Please let me explain my actions.

These last few days have been so conflicted I hardly know how to start. Let me firstly say what I should have said as soon as I knew. You have no longer to worry about your brother's debt. Before you think the worst, I would never dream of paying you for your services. Mrs. Rollands found Blackhurst's diary and ledger a few days ago. I wanted to tell you after the balloon ascension but well, Dalmere happened.

In any case the result is that I can now return the capital your brother and the others put into the speculation. Although, I was again advised I was not legally obliged, I have decided to disseminate the money anyway. It was never mine to keep.

I know you will be relieved by this news.

Was this the purpose of her letter? To inform him that the guilt she felt over the speculation had finally forced her hand? It was very convenient for the ledger to turn up now. He wondered for a moment whether or not she had made up a ledger or had always had it in her possession? A red-hot rage engulfed his body. After everything they had been through it had come down to this? A payment?

He banged on the roof and told the driver to take him to Blackhurst House. He would tell her he didn't want her damn money.

But there was more. His hands shook as he turned to the next page.

Secondly, I want to explain what I meant by my first note. I wanted to release you from any duty you might have felt regarding our agreement. I was not releasing you from my affections. I could not even if I wanted to.

What? Was this meant to mollify him? Make him forget about her part in the speculation? Although she had never directly implicated herself in her husband's schemes, always protesting her innocence. And he had believed her. Did he believe her still? Confusion waltzed with anger and bowed to hope in a dance of intertwining emotions. Part of him wanted more than anything to believe. He frantically read the rest of the letter hoping there might be something to help him decide how he felt about her.

I wanted our future to be on equal footing, with no misunderstandings, but in the process only muddled everything up. I am so very sorry. I would never intentionally hurt you.

If I could use my voice I would tell you, you are my heart, my soul, my life. I cannot seem to breathe without you.

Oliver, I love you. You are not nothing to me, you are everything. Everything I have ever needed. Everything I have ever wanted. Everything that I am.

Please come back to me.

Lisbeth

He was shaking. Was he really her heart, as she was his? The anger he had felt a few minutes ago was now directed at himself. He should have known, he should have waited, and he should have taken her in his arms and kissed her and proposed to her on those damn steps as he had intended. Instead, he had let his own insecurities come between them. He cared nothing about the money. Although it was nice to know he would be able to pay the bank and use what little capital he had left to rebuild.

But it all meant nothing if he didn't have her.

Lisbeth.

The carriage jerked to a stop, and he flew from it like his

pants were on fire. He raced up the steps of Blackhurst House, slipping slightly on the wet stoop. He bashed on the door.

Rollands wore a surprised expression when he opened the door. "Lord Bellamy?"

He didn't wait to be asked in but made his way into the entryway. "Yes, yes. Where is she?"

"She's not here."

"What? Where the hell is she?"

"She was going to your townhouse," Rollands replied.

"My… my townhouse? Why?"

Rolland stepped forward. "She was convinced you had not read her letter, sir. The letter I had delivered *at dawn this morning.* She went to ensure you read it."

"I'm not at my townhouse."

"Apparently not," Rollands replied.

"I mean it is closed up. I was on my way to Whitely Hall. I had better get back to the house."

"Or you could wait here for her to return? I am sure Lady Fortesque would be more than pleased to converse with you." Rollands raised a brow.

Oliver was at the door in a second. "No, it will be faster if I go to her." He turned on his heel and raced back out into the rain.

"Back to the townhouse, John," he instructed his driver, who simply shook his head in confusion but quickly whipped up the horses.

Oliver didn't blame him; he felt like he was going mad. His heart was beating erratically, like it knew not what tempo to be in. His lungs were burning and his eyes stung. He put his fist to his mouth to stop the cry aching to tumble out, and Lord knows what would happen after that. He kept his gaze out the window and concentrated on the houses. Each number took him closer to Lisbeth.

Then he saw her, in a hack going the other way. He jumped out of the carriage heedless of the danger and the rain. Slipping and sliding over the cobbles, he made his way after the vehicle. It was going slowly due to the weather and the always-ridiculous traffic. After what felt like years, he finally reached the hack and swung open the door, leaping inside.

Lisbeth's face was at first horrified then wary as she recognized him. He must have looked fearsome invading the interior of the carriage, dripping wet and looking wild.

"I went to your house," he said.

She pulled out a notebook and began to write. *Did you get my letter?*

"Yes, I did. I'm so sorry, Lisbeth. I was a fool."

No! I was the one who did wrong by you. Please forgive me.

"There is nothing for me to forgive, for it is I who should beg your pardon for being such an arse."

Lisbeth's eyes widened again at his choice of words then softened and her lips curved. He loved her eyes, and he especially loved her lips. He wanted to kiss them more than anything.

"Do you still love me, Lisbeth? Despite my many deficiencies?"

He waited while she wrote.

I love your deficiencies. I love you. Can you love me despite my need to control everything and everyone? I may yet turn into a crazy old lady.

He laughed at that. "And I love you," he said, picking up her cold hand and pressing a kiss to her knuckles. "I happen to have a soft spot for crazy old ladies. I'm even warming to your grandmother."

She laughed but it came out sounding like a hyena. It filled him with such sadness and joy.

"Your voice, what did the doctor say?"

She scribbled away frantically again. He hated that Dalmere had done this to her, that he had not got to her in time to prevent her injury.

It will return in time but may not be the same. Can you live with a woman who may sound like a horse?

He kissed her then because he needed to show her that she didn't need to talk to show him how she felt. "I quite like horses," he replied, and kissed her again.

She kissed him back with more gusto than he expected. He found himself surrounded in Lisbeth. Her arms wound around his neck, her breasts delightfully squished against his chest, and her lips firmly on his. She straddled his hips, and his hands found their home on her backside. This was grand. This was how he had wanted to be greeted yesterday, which reminded him he still had a question he needed to ask her.

"Lisbeth, will you let me love you for the rest of our lives?"

She looked at him curiously, and then nodded.

"That is good news," he said, grinning.

She raised an eyebrow and looked around for her notebook.

"What? You want more?" He was enjoying this just a little too much. She hit him in the arm, playfully. He sighed dramatically. "Very well. Lisbeth, my darling, my love. Will you marry me?"

She leaned in close to his ear and whispered, "Yes, I will." The husky tone was there, as before, but more so. It made him hot. It made him tingle all over. It made him very, very happy.

This time when he looked at her it was to see tears streaming down her face and the most brilliant smile upon her face. She was apparently very happy too. He loved it when she smiled. Hell, he loved her when she did anything, including when she used those eyes to burn a hole through his skull when she was miffed with him.

He loved her and she loved him. The feeling was so freeing, so liberating that he would have happily shed his clothes and done a jig in the street. Thankfully for all those who may have been witness to such a scene, the urge was redirected by her insistent wiggling on his lap.

Oliver smiled and used his fist to bang on the side of the hack and called out to the driver, "A trip around Hyde Park, I think, driver."

Lisbeth nuzzled into his neck and whispered something very naughty in his ear.

"Better make that two trips!"

EPILOGUE

"You can't escape him now you have married him, you know," Lord Anthony Ashton whispered in Lisbeth's ear as they watched Oliver bow over Anna's hand as their dance ended.

"I suppose I will just have to learn to live with him then," she replied, a small smile at the edge of her lips.

The wedding had been an intimate affair. Her grandmother had hosted the ceremony at her townhouse and neither Oliver nor Lisbeth had protested. It was what both of them had wanted, just family and good friends. Both the bride and groom had been on time, and no one had been remotely surprised.

"I believe that you are both going to be very happy together. He adores you."

"Thank you, Lord Anthony. I adore him, too."

Oliver and Anna arrived back, and Oliver kissed Lisbeth's hand. "May I have this waltz, Lady Bellamy?"

Lisbeth smiled. She liked how it felt on her face. "Why yes, you may, Lord Bellamy."

Anna and Ashton both smiled at each other as the newly married couple made their way to the small dance floor.

"Finally," Oliver said. "It feels like an age since I had you in my arms."

Poor Oliver, Lisbeth thought. The last few weeks had been hard on him, but a wedding could not be arranged in haste, and her grandmother would not be overruled on the subject.

When finally they waltzed together, she felt there could be no more perfect moment to tell him the news she had been keeping.

"I presume you know about spring?" she began.

Oliver laughed as they went through a turn. "I've vaguely heard of it, why?"

"What usually happens in the spring?"

He gave her a concerned look like she might have indulged in too much champagne. "Flowers bloom? Not that spring ever came this year."

"Yes, but what else happens?" she urged.

He gave her a pained look. "Must I guess?"

She flashed her eyes in return. "Yes."

"Erm… lambs frolic?"

She smiled for encouragement.

He sighed again. "I must confess I have no idea what your point is."

"Well, it is just that there may be a certain *lamb* frolicking its way into *our* lives this spring."

She waited as his frown of confusion disappeared and understanding dawned. "No, really?" he said, but his smile betrayed the words. They made a turn, and he dipped her carefully. "Well, well, a lamb of our very own, eh? Are you sure?"

"Yes. I've known for a week or two. It is still early days, and I was concerned it may have been a false alarm."

He kissed her forehead, then her nose, and then, tenderly, her lips. "You are such a clever girl," he whispered into her ear. "Oh, how I love you, my wonderful, beautiful, darling wife."

It made her tingle all over and suddenly, she had the overwhelming impulse to look at his watch to see what time it was. She wanted him alone. She wanted to be naked in his arms. She wanted to show him how much she loved him.

"I didn't do it on my own, you know. We are both very clever to have picked each other to fall in love with."

They danced then in silence just looking into each other's eyes.

"She must have your eyes. I insist," he said in a confiding tone as he rested his forehead on hers.

"She?"

"Absolutely!"

"And what would we call her?"

He thought about this for a moment. "Petunia."

"Petunia," Lisbeth agreed. "And if it rebels and comes out a boy?"

"Henry."

Lisbeth smiled again. "Perfect." Then, "I shall be hideously fat, you know."

"And still, I will love you," he said, as if amazed by the notion. "My dear, darling Lisbeth, you have given me a happiness I thought I would never have—a family."

"I shall love you for an eternity, at least. I hope you are prepared." This seemed to please him immensely, but she knew he could not comprehend the full magnitude of how much she loved him. How much she would always be grateful for the night he took on The Black Raven Wager and demanded entrance into her life. A life which was no longer cursed by the black raven, bad luck, or death. Only happiness. She was determined to show him every day how grateful she was.

An unusual feeling came over her whole body, warming her from the inside out. She realized it was joy. A true and wonderful feeling of hope and contentment that had always felt so far out of reach filled her heart to overflowing. She felt tears prick behind her eyes.

"I hope those are tears of happiness?" he asked, a frown upon his brow. He wiped away her tears with the gentlest of touches.

She hastened to reassure him. "Yes, oh yes, they are. I could not be happier than I am right now."

Later she may tell him how she had wept with joy when the doctor had confirmed her pregnancy. How all the memories of her sweet little son had come flooding back, reminding her of how much she missed him and filling her with doubt. She knew the future for this baby; their baby would be so very different. For this child would be born from love. This child would grow up loved and cherished by both parents. She would never forget Daniel for he would always hold a special place in her heart no matter how many other children she may be blessed with.

Oliver pulled her closer, his warm brown eyes alight with love for her. "I do believe I will kiss you now, wife."

She laughed. "I do believe I will kiss you back, husband."

Finally, they had found a home for their wayward hearts, in each other.

The End.

About the Author

Cassandra believes she should have been born in the 1800s, but since she wasn't, she decided to write about the Regency period instead. She loves costume dramas, witty banter, Jane Austen and all things Regency. She lives with her husband on the sunny south coast of Sydney with their dog Buddy and cat Angus.

Social Media Links

Facebook – CassandraSamuelsAuthor
Instagram – cassandra_samuels_author
Goodreads –
goodreads.com/author/show/8958384.Cassandra_Samuels
Website – www.cassandrasamuels.com

www.ingramcontent.com/pod-product-compliance
Lightning Source LLC
Chambersburg PA
CBHW070532310726
48976CB00002BA/609